A PLUME BOOK

PIRATES OF THE LEVANT

ARTURO PÉREZ-REVERTE is the bestselling author of more than seven books, including *The Queen of the South* and *The Club Dumas*, which have sold millions of copies in many languages and fifty countries. Originally a war journalist, he now writes fiction full-time.

ALSO BY
ARTURO PÉREZ-REVERTE

PIRATES OF
THE LEVANT

Arturo Pérez-Reverte

TRANSLATED FROM THE SPANISH BY

Margaret Jull Costa

A PLUME BOOK

PLUME
Published by the Penguin Group
Penguin Group (USA) Inc., 375 Hudson Street, New York, New York 10014, U.S.A. • Penguin Group
(Canada), 90 Eglinton Avenue East, Suite 700, Toronto, Ontario, Canada M4P 2Y5 (a division of
Pearson Penguin Canada Inc.) • Penguin Books Ltd., 80 Strand, London WC2R 0RL, England •
Penguin Ireland, 25 St. Stephen's Green, Dublin 2, Ireland (a division of Penguin Books Ltd.) •
Penguin Group (Australia), 250 Camberwell Road, Camberwell, Victoria 3124, Australia (a division
of Pearson Australia Group Pty. Ltd.) • Penguin Books India Pvt. Ltd., 11 Community Centre,
Panchsheel Park, New Delhi – 110 017, India • Penguin Group (NZ), 67 Apollo Drive, Rosedale,
Auckland 0632, New Zealand (a division of Pearson New Zealand Ltd.) • Penguin Books (South
Africa) (Pty.) Ltd., 24 Sturdee Avenue, Rosebank, Johannesburg 2196, South Africa

Penguin Books Ltd., Registered Offices: 80 Strand, London WC2R 0RL, England

Published by Plume, a member of Penguin Group (USA) Inc. Previously published in a
G. P. Putnam's Sons edition.

First Plume Printing, August 2011
10   9   8   7   6   5   4   3   2   1

Originally published in Spanish as *Corsarios de Levante* by Alfaguara, Santillana Ediciones
Generales, S.L., Madrid.

Ⓟ REGISTERED TRADEMARK—MARCA REGISTRADA

The Library of Congress has catalogued the G. P. Putnam's Sons edition as follows:

Pérez-Reverte, Arturo.
   [Corsarios de Levante. English]
   Pirates of the Levant / Arturo Pérez-Reverte ; translated from the Spanish by Margaret Jull
Costa.
        p.   cm.—(Las aventuras del capitán Alatriste ; 6)
   "Originally published in Spanish as Corsarios de levante by Alfaguara, Santillana Ediciones
Generals, S.L., Madrid."
   ISBN 978-0-399-15664-9 (hc.)
   ISBN 978-0-452-29730-2 (pbk.)
   1. Pirates—Fiction.   2. Spain—History—Philip IV, 1621–1665—Fiction.   I. Costa, Margaret
Jull.   II. Title.
   PQ6666.E765C6713   2010   2010005105
   863'.64—dc22

Printed in the United States of America
Original hardcover design by Marysarah Quinn

PUBLISHER'S NOTE
This is a work of fiction. Names, characters, places, and incidents are either the product of the author's
imagination or are used fictitiously, and any resemblance to actual persons, living or dead, business
establishments, events, or locales is entirely coincidental.

To Juan Eslava Galán and Fito Cózar,

for the Naples we never knew

and the ships we never plundered

The hurly-burly movement on the galleys,

The falling into flames or into water,

The brave deaths in a hundred thousand ways,

The furies and the terrible disquiet,

The hauling down and hoisting up of flags,

The killings, then the deaths that must be paid.

—CRISTÓBAL DE VIRUÉS

PIRATES OF
THE LEVANT

1. THE BARBARY COAST

Chasing after a ship makes for a long chase, and I swear to God this one had tested our patience to the limit. Our mood was little improved by having spent an afternoon, a moonlit night, and a whole morning pursuing our prey over a buffeting sea, which, every now and then, shook the galley's fragile frame with its blows. With her two taut sails aloft, the oars stowed, and galley slaves, soldiers, and sailors all sheltering as best we could from the wind and the spray, the *Mulata*, a twenty-four-bank galley, had traveled nearly thirty leagues in pursuit of the Berber galliot that we now finally had within range, and which, as long as we didn't break a mast—the older sailors kept glancing anxiously upward—would be ours before the Angelus.

"Tickle her arse!" ordered don Manuel Urdemalas.

Our galley captain was still standing in the stern—he

had scarcely moved from the spot in the last twenty hours—and from there he saw how the first cannon shot splashed into the water beside the galliot. When they saw how close the shot had come, the gunners and the men at the prow, standing around the cannon in the central gangway, all let out a cheer. Things would have to go very badly wrong for us to lose our prey now, when it was there within our grasp and to leeward as well.

"They're shortening their sail!" shouted someone.

The galliot's only sail, a vast canvas triangle, flapped in the wind as they rapidly brailed it in, lowering the mast. Swaying about on the swell, the galliot showed us first its stern and then its port side, and that was when we got our first proper look at it—it was a long, slender half-galley with thirteen banks, and, we reckoned, a hundred or so men on board. It resembled one of those light, swift craft described by Cervantes:

> *The thief who hopes to strike*
> *And never yet be caught*
> *Should move as fast as lightning—*
> *A hit, then home to port.*

The galliot had been nothing but a sail to windward, but had revealed itself to be a corsair when it brazenly approached the merchant convoy, along with three other Spanish galleys, that the *Mulata* was escorting between

Cartagena and Oran. We had gone after her under full sail, and she had then become just a fugitive white triangle and a stern that, little by little, and with the help of a south-westerly wind, grew gradually larger as we closed on her.

"The dogs are finally going to surrender," said one soldier.

Captain Alatriste was by my side, watching. With the mast lowered and the sail furled, the crew was bringing out the oars.

"No," he murmured. "They're going to fight."

I turned toward him. He was screwing up his eyes against the dazzle of the sun on water and sails, and beneath the broad brim of his old hat, those eyes appeared still paler and greener. He was unshaven and his skin, like that of everyone else, was grimy and greasy from days at sea and sleepless nights. He was intently following the activities on the galliot: some men were running along the deck toward the prow, the oarsmen were turning the vessel, with those on one side rowing in one direction and those on the other in the opposite direction.

"It looks like they want to try their luck," he added calmly.

He pointed at the pennant fluttering at the top of our mainmast, indicating the direction of the wind. During the chase, this had swung around from northwest to north-northeast, and there it was staying—for the moment. Only then did I properly understand. The corsairs, realizing that flight was impossible and having no desire to surrender, were using the oars to position themselves to face into the wind. Galleys and galliots alike had but one large cannon at the prow and short-range *pedreros*—stone-throwers—along the sides. The crew of the galliot were less well armed than we, and there were fewer of them, but, if they were prepared to play their last card, one lucky shot could unmast us or injure some of our men on deck. And they could maneuver themselves with their oars despite the adverse wind.

"Lower both masts! Shirts off! Row!"

It was clear from the orders he gave, sharp as pistol shots, that Captain Urdemalas had also understood. The two masts were quickly lowered and the sails furled as the galley master took up his position in the central gangway, whip in hand. "Come on! Come on!" he urged, forcing the galley slaves, bare-chested now, to take their places, four men per bank on either side and forty-eight oars, while that son of a whore lashed their backs until they bled.

"Soldiers, to your posts!"

The drum beat loudly while the soldiers, muttering the oaths and complaints and blasphemies typical of the Spanish infantry—at the same time mumbling prayers, kissing medallions and scapulars, and crossing themselves five hundred times—padded the sides of the galley with mattresses and blankets to provide some protection from enemy fire, then equipped themselves with the tools of the trade—harquebuses, muskets, and *pedreros*—and took up their places in the prow and in the corridors that ran along either side of the galley, above the oars with which the slaves were already keeping a good rhythm. Meanwhile, the galley master and under–galley master were using their whistles to mark time while they gaily continued flogging slaves' backs. From prow to stern, the match-cords of harquebuses were starting to smoke. I still lacked the strength needed to use a harquebus or a heavy musket onboard ship because we Spaniards took aim by holding the sight to one eye, and if your hands weren't strong enough to cope with the rolling motion of the galley, the recoil could dislocate your shoulder or knock out your teeth. So I took up my pike and my sword—a short, broad one because a long sword was too cumbersome on the deck of a ship—tied a kerchief tightly around my head, and, thus armed to the teeth, I followed Captain Alatriste. As an experienced, trustworthy soldier, my master—well, he wasn't my master anymore, but old habits die hard—took up his position in the bulwarks, the very position, ironically enough, that good don Miguel de Cervantes was given on the *Marquesa* during the battle of Lepanto. Once we had taken our places, the captain glanced at me distractedly and, smiling only with his eyes, smoothed his mustache.

"Your fifth naval battle," he said.

Then he blew on the lit match-cord of his harquebus. His tone of voice was suitably cool, but I knew that he was as worried about me as he had been on the four previous occasions, even though I had just turned seventeen, or perhaps because of that. When it came to boarding an enemy ship, not even God recognized his own.

"Don't board the galley unless I do, all right?"

I opened my mouth to protest, but, at that moment, there was a loud report at the prow, and the first cannon shot from the enemy galley sent splinters as sharp as knives flying down the deck.

It was a long road that had led the captain and me to the deck of that galley, which, on that noontide at the end of May in sixteen hundred and twenty-seven—the dates are there among my yellowing service records—was about to join battle with a corsair galliot just a few miles to the south of the island of Alboran, off the Barbary Coast. Captain Alatriste's head had been only inches away from the executioner's block following a dispute with Philip IV over a shared mistress. However, after the disastrous affair of the cavalier in the yellow doublet, when our young Catholic monarch only just survived a plot dreamed up by the Inquisitor Fray Emilio Bocanegra, the Captain had managed to preserve both life and reputation thanks to his

sword—and with more modest thanks to mine and that
of the actor Rafael de Cózar—when he saved the royal skin
during a sham hunting party in El Escorial. Kings, however, are both ungrateful and forgetful, and the incident
brought us no reward at all. Moreover, the fact that the
Captain had crossed swords and words with the Count of
Guadalmedina, the royal confidant, over the king's dal-
liance with the actress María de Castro—the first time
leaving him with a cut to his cheek and the second with
some painful bruises—the count's affection for my master, dating from Flanders and from Italy, had turned to
rancor. And so the El Escorial affair brought us only
enough to balance our accounts. In short, having done our
work, we left without a *maravedí* in our purses, but feeling relieved not to have ended up in prison or six feet under
in an unmarked grave. The catchpoles led by the lieutenant
of constables Martín Saldaña—who was recovering from
a serious wound inflicted by my master—kept well away
from us, and Captain Alatriste was finally able to walk the
streets without always having to look over his shoulder.
This was not the case with the others involved, upon whom
the royal fury fell, albeit with the discretion demanded
by the circumstances. Fray Emilio Bocanegra was sent to
a hospital for the mentally infirm—as a man of the cloth
he merited a certain degree of consideration—while con-
spirators of lesser rank were quietly strangled in prison. Of

Gualterio Malatesta, the Italian hired killer and personal enemy of the captain and me, we had no certain news. There was talk of terrible torture followed by execution in a dark dungeon, but no one would swear to this. As for the royal secretary, Luis de Alquézar, whose complicity could not be proved, his high position at court and influential friends in the Council of Aragon, saved his neck, but not his position. A brusque royal order dispatched him to New Spain. And as you, dear reader, will know, the fate of that dubious character was far from being a matter of indifference to me, for with him went the love of my life, his niece, Angélica de Alquézar.

I intend to speak of this in more detail later on, so I will say no more for the present, except that this last adventure of ours had convinced Captain Alatriste of the need to assure my future by putting me beyond the reach of Fortune's caprices—were such a thing possible. Opportunity came by the hand of don Francisco de Quevedo, who, since my brush with the Inquisition, had become my unofficial godfather. His prestige at court continued to grow, and he was persuaded that, with help—in the form of the queen's fondness for him, together with the Count-Duke Olivares' continuing benevolence and a little good luck—when I reached the age of eighteen, I would be able to enter the corps of the royal couriers, an excellent first step to a career at court. The only problem was that if I was ever to be promoted to the rank of officer, I would need either a suitably impressive family background or a convincing record of accomplishments, and some military experience would carry the necessary weight. However, although I certainly had more experience of war than the average tavern braggart—I had, after all, spent two hard years in Flanders and fought at the siege of Breda—my youth, which had obliged me to enlist not as a soldier, but as a page, meant that I had no service record. I would, therefore, have to acquire one by spending some time as a proper soldier. The remedy was provided by our friend Captain Alonso de Contreras, who was returning to Naples after some time as a guest of Lope de Vega's. The veteran soldier invited us to go with him, arguing that the Spanish infantry—who were based there and where many of his and my master's old comrades were stationed—would be a perfect way of acquiring those two years of military experience. It would also provide me with an opportunity to enjoy the delights of the city of Vesuvius itself, as well as giving us a chance to amass some money from the incursions the Spanish galleys made into the Greek islands and along the African coast. "So follow your calling," Contreras advised, "give to Mars what you gave to Venus, and perform deeds of such derring-do that they will astound the incredulous! To your good health, young sir!"

The truth is that Captain Alatriste did not mind leaving

Madrid at all. He had no money, he had finished with María de Castro, and Caridad la Lebrijana had been mentioning the word "matrimony" far too often. After giving the matter much thought, as he usually did, and silently downing many pitchers of wine, he came to a decision, and in the summer of sixteen hundred and twenty-six, we set off for Barcelona, paused briefly in Genoa, then continued south to Naples, where we joined the Spanish infantry. The rest of that year, until Saint Demetrius' day, which signaled the close of the season for galleys, we pursued corsairs and enemy ships off the Barbary Coast, in the Adriatic, and the Morea. Then, during the customary winter truce, we spent part of our booty on the innumerable temptations of Naples, visited Rome so that I could admire that astonishing city, Christianity's majestic seat, and reembarked in May in the freshly careened galleys made ready for the new campaign. Our first voyage—escorting a shipment of money from Italy to Spain—had taken us to the Balearics and to Valencia, and this most recent one— protecting merchant ships carrying supplies from Cartagena to Oran—would bring us back to Naples. The rest—the galliot, the chase when we left the convoy, the battle off the African coast—I have more or less described. I will add only that I was no longer a callow youth, but a prudent seventeen-year-old, who, alongside Captain Alatriste and the other men on board the *Mulata*, did battle with those Turkish corsairs (we called anyone who sailed the sea "Turkish," be they Ottoman, Moor, Morisco, or whatever). Just what that new Íñigo Balboa had become you will find out in this new adventure in which I propose to describe how Captain Alatriste and I fought shoulder to shoulder, no longer as master and page, but as equals and comrades. I will tell of skirmishes and pirates, of blithe youth and boarding ships, of killing and pillaging. I will also explain precisely what it was that made Spain's name respected, feared, and hated throughout the Levant. Ah, but how long ago that seems, now that even my scars are old and my hair gray! I will show that the Devil has no color, no nation, and no flag. I will show, too, that all it took then to create a Hell on both sea and land was a Spaniard and a sword.

"Stop the killing!" ordered the captain of the *Mulata*. "Those people are worth money!"

Don Manuel Urdemalas was a man who liked to keep a tight hold on his purse strings and disliked any unnecessary waste. And so we obeyed, very slowly and reluctantly. In my case, Captain Alatriste had to grab my arm just as I was about to slit the throat of one of the Turks who was trying to clamber on board after having jumped into the water during the fighting. The fact is that our blood was still up,

and we had not yet killed enough to sate our desires. As the
two galleys closed in on each other, the Turks—later, we
learned that they had a good gunner with them, a Portuguese renegade—had had time to aim and fire their cannons at us, killing two of our men. That's why we had
hurled ourselves on them, prepared to give no quarter—all
of us shouting "Row, row! Ram them! Ram them!"—with
pikes and half-pikes and harquebuses at the ready. Meanwhile, amid lashes from the galley master's whip, blasts on
the whistle, and the clank of chains, the forced men rowed
for all they were worth, and our galley struck the galliot,
holing its prow. The helmsman, who evidently knew his
job, had steered us into exactly the right position, and,
within seconds, our three cannons, loaded with nails and
tinplate, had cleared half the deck. Then, after a volley of
harquebus fire and stones, the first of the boarding parties,
with cries of "Forward for Santiago and Spain!" scrambled
along the ram and onto the galliot's foredeck, killing everyone they encountered. Those Turks who did not fling themselves into the water died right there, among the benches
slippery with blood, or else retreated to the stern. To be fair,
they fought with great courage until our second boarding
party reached the bulkhead, where the last of the crew
were still fighting. In that second party were Captain Alatriste and myself, he (once he had emptied his harquebus)
armed with sword and shield and I wearing a leather corse-

let and wielding a pike that, halfway through, I swapped for a sharp spear wrenched from the hands of a dying Turk. And thus, always keeping a watchful eye on each other, attacking and advancing prudently and slowly from bench to bench, leaving not a soul alive behind us just in case, not even those lying on the deck pleading for clemency, we finally reached our comrades in the stern, where we continued to press home our advantage until the badly wounded Turkish captain and those survivors who had not jumped into the sea threw down their weapons and begged for mercy. Such mercy, however, was a long time in coming, for what ensued was neither more nor less than a bloodbath, and it took a repeated command from our captain for us men to cease our labors, exasperated as we were by the pirates' resistance—for along with those killed by their one cannon shot, the battle had cost us nine dead and twelve wounded, not counting galley slaves. Even the many Turks in the water were, as I said, shot at like ducks, despite their pleas, or lanced or beaten to death with oars when they tried to climb on board.

"Leave it," said Diego Alatriste.

I turned, still breathless from my exertions in battle. He had cleaned his sword on a piece of cloth picked up from the deck—a Moorish turban—and was putting the sword back in its sheath as he watched the unfortunates drowning or swimming, afraid to come too close. The sea was fairly calm, and many of them were managing to stay afloat, although not the wounded, who were floundering, groaning, and gasping for air, water bubbling in their lungs as they died among the red-tinged waves.

"That blood isn't yours, is it?"

I looked at my arms and felt my corselet and my thighs. Not a scratch, I discovered to my joy.

"Everything in its place," I said, smiling wearily. "Like you."

We observed the landscape after the battle: the two ships still locked together, the disemboweled bodies sprawled among the benches, the prisoners and the dying, the drenched men trying to climb on board under threat of attack by pike and harquebus, and our comrades brazenly plundering the galliot. The easterly breeze dried the Turkish blood on our hands and faces.

"Right, let's see if there are any spoils to be had," sighed Alatriste.

"Spoils" was what we called booty from a ship, but there was almost nothing. The galley, chartered in the pirate port of Saleh, had not yet taken any booty when we saw it approaching the convoy; and so even though we lifted every plank on the deck and smashed down all the bulkheads, we found only food and weapons, nothing of value, not even a gold coin to pay the king his wretched quint. I had to make do with a fine cloth tunic—and I almost came to blows over that with another soldier who claimed to have seen it first. Captain Alatriste found a large damascene knife, with a good blade skillfully worked, that he filched from the belt of one of the wounded. Then he returned to the *Mulata*, while I continued foraging on the Turkish galley and looking over the prisoners. Once the galley master had, as was the custom, taken the sails from the captured vessel, the only valuable items were the surviving Turks. Fortunately, there were no Christians at the oars; instead, the corsairs themselves rowed or fought depending on the circumstances; and when Captain Urdemalas very sensibly ordered the killing to stop, there were still some sixty men alive—those who had surrendered, the wounded, and the remaining survivors in the sea. That, on a rough calculation, meant eighty or a hundred *escudos* each, depending on where the slaves were sold. When you subtracted the king's quint and what was due to the captain and the other officers, and when it was shared out among the fifty sailors and seventy soldiers on board—the almost two hundred galley slaves, of course, got nothing—it certainly wouldn't make us rich, but it was better than nothing. That's why the captain had shouted out, reminding us that the more Turks we left alive, the greater the profit. Each time we killed one of the men trying to scramble back on board, more than a thousand *reales* went to the bottom of the sea with him.

"We have to hang the galliot captain," said Captain Urdemalas.

He said this in a low voice, so as to be heard by only a few, namely Ensign Muelas, the galley master, Sergeant Albaladejo, the pilot, and two trusted soldiers or corporals, one of whom was Diego Alatriste. They were gathered together in the stern of the *Mulata*, next to the lantern, looking down at the galliot that was still skewered by the ram of our boat, oars shattered and water pouring in through the sides. They all agreed that there was no point in taking it in tow, for at any moment it might sink to the bottom like a stone.

"He's a Spanish renegade," said Urdemalas, scratching his beard. "A Mallorquin called Boix or, to give him his in-fidel name, Yusuf Bocha."

"He's wounded," said the galley master.

"All the more reason to string him up before he dies of his own accord."

Urdemalas glanced at the sun, which was close to the horizon now. There was about another hour of daylight, thought Alatriste. By then, the prisoners should all be chained up on board the *Mulata* and the galley heading off to some friendly port where they could be sold. The prisoners were currently being questioned to find out which language they spoke and where they came from so that they could be divided up into renegades, Moriscos, Turks, and Moors. Every pirate galley was a Babel full of surprises. It was not uncommon to find renegades of Christian origin, as was the case here, even Englishmen and Dutchmen. That is why no one disputed the need to hang the corsairs' leader.

"Prepare the noose now and be quick about it."

This, as Captain Alatriste knew, was inevitable. A gallows death was obligatory for any renegade in charge of a vessel that had put up resistance and caused deaths on a Spanish galley, especially if that renegade was himself a Spaniard.

"You can't just hang *him*," said Ensign Muelas. "There are some Moriscos among them too: the pilot and at least four others. There were more as well—mostly Morisco rebels—but they're all either dead or dying."

"And what about the other captives?"

"Paid oarsmen, Moors the lot of them, and people from Saleh. There are two light-skinned men as well, and they're checking their foreskins now to see whether they're roundheads or Christians."

"Well, you know what to do. If they're roundheads, they go straight to the rowing benches, and then we hand them over to the Inquisition. If not, we'll hang them too. How many of our men did they kill?"

"Nine, not including those who won't make it through till morning. And not counting the galley slaves."

Urdemalas made an angry, impatient gesture.

"God's teeth!"

He was a blunt-spoken old sea dog, and his weather-beaten skin and gray beard bore witness to his thirty years spent sailing the Mediterranean Sea. He knew exactly how to treat those men who set sail from the Barbary Coast at night in order to reach the Spanish coast by dawn, where they frequently sacked and plundered villages before returning home to sleep peacefully in their own beds.

"The rope for all six of them. That'll keep the Devil busy."

A soldier approached with a message for Ensign Muelas, and the latter turned to Urdemalas.

"Apparently, both of the light-skinned men are round-heads, Captain. One is a French renegade and the other from Livorno."

"Right, set them to the oars."

This explained why the Turkish galliot had fought so long and so hard: its crew knew what the consequences would be. Most of the Moriscos on board had preferred to die fighting rather than surrender; and that, as Ensign Muelas remarked dispassionately, was sure proof that they had been born in Spain, even if they were now corsair dogs.

After all, it was common knowledge that no Spanish soldier would respect the life of a renegade compatriot turned corsair captain, nor the lives of any of their Morisco crew, unless, that is, the latter gave in without a struggle, in which case, they would later be handed over to the Inquisition. The Moriscos—baptized Moors whose Christian faith was suspect—had been expelled from Spain eighteen years before, after much trouble and treachery and many bloody uprisings, suspicions, and false conversions. Cast out upon the road, they were often ill-treated, murdered, stripped of their possessions, and saw their wives and daughters raped, and when they reached the North African coast, even their brother Moors failed to welcome them. When they at last settled in the pirate ports of Tunis, Algiers, and, especially, Saleh—the nearest to the Andalusian coast— they became Spain's bitterest and most hated enemies, as well as the cruelest when making raids on the Spanish coastal villages, which, with their knowledge of the terrain, they attacked ruthlessly and with the understandable rancor of someone settling old scores. As Lope de Vega put it in his play *The Good Guard*:

And Moors from Algiers—pirates—
Who lurk in coves and bays
From which they later slip
And sail their hidden frigates.

"But don't make a fuss about hanging them," advised Urdemalas. "We don't want any trouble from the captives. Wait until they're all safely chained up."

"We'll lose money by hanging them, Captain," protested the galley master, who could see more thousands of *reales* going to waste on the yardarm. The galley master was even more miserly than the captain; he had an evil face and a worse soul, and earned a little extra money, which he shared with the overseer on board, from bribes and secret payments exacted from the galley slaves.

"I piss on your money, sir," Urdemalas declared, giving the galley master a withering look, "and everything you buy with it."

Long accustomed to the captain's odd ways, the galley master merely shrugged and stalked off down the gangway, asking the under–galley master and the overseer to find some ropes. The bodies of the slaves killed during the battle—four Moors, a Dutchman, and three Spaniards who had been condemned to row in the galleys—were being unchained and tossed overboard so that their places could be taken by the captured corsairs. Another half-dozen or so badly wounded galley slaves were sprawled, groaning and still in their chains, on the gore-soaked benches, waiting to be seen by the barber, who served as both bloodletter and surgeon and whose treatment for any wound, however terrible, consisted of applying vinegar and salt to it.

Diego Alatriste's eyes met those of Captain Urdemalas.

"Two of the Moriscos are very young," he said.

This was true. I had noticed them when the galliot's captain was wounded: two boys crouched among the benches at the stern, trying to keep out of the way of all that whirling steel. The captain himself had placed them there, to save them from having their throats cut.

Urdemalas pulled a rather surly face.

"How young?"

"Young enough."

"Born in Spain?"

"I have no idea."

"Circumcised?"

"I suppose so."

Urdemalas muttered a few well-turned oaths and regarded the captain thoughtfully. Then he turned to Sergeant Albaladejo.

"See to it, Sergeant. If they've got hair on their tackle, they've got enough neck to be hanged, and if not, set them to rowing."

Albaladejo walked reluctantly down the gangway toward the galliot. Pulling down the boys' breeches to see if they were man enough for the rope or fodder for the galleys was not exactly his favorite occupation, but it went with the job. For his part, Urdemalas was still studying Diego Alatriste. He looked at Alatriste again, inquisitively this time, as if wondering whether Alatriste's concerns about the boys were based on something more than just common sense. Even if they were mere boys, born in Spain or elsewhere—the last Moriscos, from Valle de Ricote in the province of Murcia, had left in about sixteen hundred and fourteen—as far as Urdemalas and the vast majority of Spaniards were concerned, there was no room for compassion. Only two months before, on the Almería coast, the corsairs had carried off and enslaved seventy-four men, women, and children from one village, having first plundered it and crucified the mayor and eleven others whose names they had on a list. A woman who had managed to escape was later able to confirm that several of the attackers were Moriscos and former villagers.

Everyone had some account to settle on that turbulent Mediterranean frontier, which was a melting pot of races, languages, and ancient hatreds. In the case of the Moriscos, who knew every bay, water hole, and path in a country to which they were returning to take their revenge, they enjoyed an advantage that Miguel de Cervantes—who knew a lot about corsairs, as both soldier and captive—described in his play *Life in Algiers*:

Because I've known this land from birth
And all its entrances and exits,
I know how best to fight upon its earth.

"You were there, weren't you?" Urdemalas asked. "In sixteen hundred and nine, when the Moriscos were expelled from Valencia."

Alatriste nodded. There were few secrets on board a small ship. Urdemalas and he had friends in common, and Alatriste, although not an officer, received extra pay for taking on the duties of corporal. The sailor and the veteran soldier respected each other, but kept their distance.

"They say," Urdemalas went on, "that you helped to crush the rebels, the ones who took to the hills."

"I did," replied Alatriste.

That was one way of putting it up, he thought. The searches carried out among the steep, rocky hills, sweating beneath the sun. The ambushes, the sudden attacks, the reprisals, the killings. There had been cruelty on both sides, and the poor people caught in the middle, both Christians and Moriscos, had, as usual, paid the highest price, with rapes and murders going unpunished. And then there were those long lines of unfortunates trudging the roads, forced to leave their homes and sell off cheap what they couldn't take with them, harassed and plundered by peasants and soldiers alike—many soldiers even deserted in order to steal from them— those roads that led to the ships and to exile. As Gaspar Aguilar wrote:

Strip them of their house and all their wealth,
Ye powers that rule the world;
For alms, leave them their lives and petty health.

"By my life," said Captain Urdemalas with a cynical smile, "you don't seem very proud of service done for God and king."

Alatriste gave him a hard look, then slowly smoothed his mustache.

"Are you referring to the service performed today, Captain, or to that performed in sixteen hundred and nine?"

He spoke very clearly and coldly, almost softly. Urdemalas glanced uneasily at Ensign Muelas, the pilot, and the other corporal.

"I have no criticism whatever of your performance today," he replied in quite a different tone, studying Alatriste's face as if he were counting the scars. "With ten men like you, I could take Algiers in a night. It's just that . . ."

Deaf to this praise, Alatriste continued smoothing his mustache.

"It's just what?"

"Well," Urdemalas said with a shrug. "There are no secrets here. People say you were unhappy about what happened in Valencia and that you took your sword and your services elsewhere."

"And do you have an opinion on the matter, Captain?"

Urdemalas' eyes followed the movement made by Alatriste's left hand, for it was no longer smoothing his mustache, but was by his side, just inches away from the scratched and battered hilt of his sword. Urdemalas was a determined man, as everyone knew, but every man has his reputation, and Diego Alatriste's reputation had preceded him onto the *Mulata*. Mere words, one might say, but, having seen how he had fought that day, even the lowliest cabin boy was convinced. And Urdemalas knew this better than anyone.

"No, no opinion at all, I assure you," he said. "Everyone's different after all, but you can't stop people from talking."

He maintained the same firm, frank tone of voice, and Alatriste considered the matter carefully. There was not, he concluded, anything to object to in either tone or content. The captain of the galley was a wise man. And prudent too.

"Well, if that's what they say," Alatriste said at last, "they're quite right."

Ensign Muelas thought it best to try and change tack a little.

"I'm from Vejer myself," he said. "And I remember how the Turks used to attack us with the help of the Moriscos who lived there and told them when they could most easily take us unaware. A neighbor's son went out to herd the goats or went off fishing with his father and woke up in a souk in Barbary. He's probably like one of these renegades here, or up to who knows what... with his arse perhaps. Not to speak of what they do to the women."

The pilot and the other corporal nodded grimly. They knew about those villages built high up, away from the shore, as a precaution against the Barbary pirates who scoured the sea and patrolled the coast; they knew how afraid the villagers were of the pirates' boldness and of their embittered Morisco neighbors; they knew about the bloody rebellions by Moriscos who refused to accept baptism and the authority of the king, about their complicity with Barbary, and the secret petitions made to France, to the Lutherans, and to the Great Turk to join them in a general uprising. After the failure to disperse them after the wars of Granada and the Alpujarras, and Philip III's ineffectual policy of conversion, three hundred thousand Moriscos—an enormous number in a population of only nine million—had settled on the vulnerable Levant and Andalusian coasts; almost none were true Christians, and they remained rebellious, ungovernable, and proud—like the Spaniards they also were—dreaming of their lost liberty and independence, and unwilling to become part of that Catholic nation, forged a century ago and intent on waging hard and simultaneous war on all fronts, against the greed and envy of France and England, against the

Protestant heresy, and against the immense power of the Turks. This was why, until their final expulsion, the last Muslims left in the peninsula had been a dagger permanently pointing at the side of a Spain that was, at the time, master of half the world and at war with the other half.

"You could never feel at ease," Muelas went on. "From Valencia to Gibraltar, the old Christians were caught between the Moriscos in the mountains and the pirates at sea. Those supposed Christian converts, so suspiciously reluctant to eat pork, would send signals at night, then help their friends to disembark and plunder the villages . . ."

Diego Alatriste shook his head. He knew that this wasn't the whole truth.

"There were honest people too," he said, "new Christians who genuinely believed and were faithful subjects of the king. I knew a few such in Flanders—as soldiers. And they were helpful and hardworking too. There were no gentlemen, villains, friars, or beggars among them. In that respect, it's true they didn't seem like Spaniards."

Everyone stared at him in silence. Then the ensign bit off a bit of fingernail and spat it over the side of the boat.

"That wasn't the point. We had to put a stop to all that anxiety, to all those infamous acts. And with God's help, we did, and it's over now."

Alatriste thought to himself that it certainly wasn't over yet. That silent civil war between Spaniards was still continued by other means elsewhere. A few Moriscos, very few, had managed to secretly return later on, helped by their neighbors, as had happened in Campo de Calatrava. As for the others, they took their anger and the nostalgia for their lost homeland to the corsair towns of Barbary; and the power of the Turks and of North Africa had only been strengthened by those exiled *mudéjares*—unconverted Muslims—from Granada and Andalusia, and by the *tagarinos*—Muslims who passed as Spaniards—from Aragon, Catalonia, and Valencia, who were skilled in many trades, particularly in those that proved useful to the corsair enterprise. They were often to be found as harquebusiers— there were a dozen of them on the captured galliot— bringing with them their knowledge of the coasts and the villages they attacked, they built ships, made firearms and powder arms, and knew better than anyone how to sell the slaves they captured, as well as becoming the skillful captains, pilots, and crews of galleys and fustas. Their hatred and their courage, their skill as marksmen, and their determination to give no quarter in battle meant that they were as good as the best Turkish soldiers and better than those crews composed solely of Moors. This is why they were the fiercest of corsairs, the most pitiless of slave traders, and the greatest of Spain's enemies in the Mediterranean.

"You have to admit they're brave, though," commented the pilot. "The bastards fought like tigers."

Alatriste was gazing down at the water surrounding the galley and the galliot, strewn with the debris of combat. Almost all the dead had gone under by now. Only a few, due to the air trapped in their clothes or their lungs, floated tranquilly on the surface, just like the many old ghosts that floated in his memory. Not even he would have denied the need for that expulsion. They were harsh times. Neither Spain or Europe or the world was in a placatory mood, but he had been troubled by the manner of the expulsion: the bureaucratic coldness and the military brutality crowned, in the end, by an appalling lack of humanity—"they should be prevented from taking so much money with them, for some are quite happy to leave," wrote don Pedro de Toledo, chief of the Spanish galleys, to the king. And so, in sixteen hundred and ten, when he was twenty-eight, the soldier Diego Alatriste, a veteran of the old Cartagena regiment—brought from Flanders with the aim of crushing the Morisco rebels—had asked to be released from his old unit and had enlisted in Naples to fight the Turks in the eastern Mediterranean. If he was going to have to slit the throats of infidels, he argued, he would prefer to do so to infidels who were, at least, capable of defending themselves. And twenty years on, here he was—one of life's little ironies—doing exactly the same thing.

"In sixteen hundred and ten and sixteen hundred and eleven, I was in charge of transporting them like animals from Denia to the beaches of Oran," said Captain Urdemalas. "The dogs."

He placed special emphasis on the word "dogs," and fixed Diego Alatriste with a hard stare, as if trying to peer inside his mind.

"Dogs," said Alatriste thoughtfully.

He remembered the lines of rebels chained together, being taken to the mercury mines in Almadén, from which none returned. And the old Morisco in a small Valencian village, the only one who had not been expelled because of his great age and infirmity, and how he had been stoned to death by the village boys without a single neighbor, not even the parish priest, doing anything to stop them.

"Dogs," he concluded, "come in all shapes and sizes."

He was smiling bitterly, abstractedly, his green eyes fixed on those of Urdemalas. And from the expression on the latter's face, he knew that he liked neither the look nor the smile. But he knew, too—for he could weigh men up at a glance—that Urdemalas would be very careful not to give voice to his feelings. After all, no one could be said to have shown a lack of respect for anyone else. Then again, not everything happened on board ship, where military discipline ruled out any open dispute. Life was full of ports with dark, silent alleyways, moonless nights, discreet places where a galley captain, with only his sword to rely on, might easily find himself with a foot of steel between chest and back before he could say "Amen." Which is why, when Diego Alatriste seasoned both look and smile with a pinch of insolence, Captain Urdemalas, after observing for a moment how Alatriste's hand was again resting, with apparent nonchalance, near the hilt of his sword, transferred his gaze to the sea.

2. SEND A HUNDRED
LANCERS TO ORAN

When the galliot finally sank, I looked back at the lifeless bodies of its captain, pilot, and of the three Moriscos silhouetted against the fading evening light where they hung from the lateen yard, their feet almost touching the sea and almost swallowed up by its shadow. Among them was one of the young men, on whose private parts, alas, Sergeant Albaladejo had found some incriminating hair. The other boy, fortunately still hairless, had been put to row, as had some of the other captives, those who were not in chains in the hold. As for the Morisco pilot, who turned out to be a Valencian, he swore in good Castilian and with the noose already around his neck, that despite being expelled from Spain as a boy, he was a true convert and had always lived a Christian life, and was as indifferent to the sect of the Prophet as that Christian who said in Oran:

I don't deny our Lord nor yet accept Mohammed,
And if I seem to be a Moor in voice and dress,
I do so simply for the riches I'll possess.

And he had only been circumcised, he claimed, to silence wicked tongues when he was living in Algiers and Saleh. Captain Urdemalas replied that he was very pleased to hear this, for since he had clearly been and still was a good Christian, he would very soon die as precisely that, and, since there was no chaplain on board, he would need only a credo and an Our Father, plus anything else he chose to add, to be ready for the next life. For that reason, he would be perfectly happy to grant him a little time before hanging him by the neck. The Morisco pilot took this very badly and blasphemed against God and the Holy Virgin, less in Castilian this time and more in the lingua franca of Barbary laced with the dialect of the Valencian Muslims. And he only paused in these insults to spit a well-aimed gob of saliva that landed on Captain Urdemalas' boot. The captain then ordered that the ceremony be brief, and there would no bloody credos either, he said. The pilot, hands tied behind his back, was hoisted straight up onto the yard, kicking furiously and without having had a chance to consign his soul to God. As for the other wounded corsairs, regardless of whether they were Moriscos or not, they had been thrown unceremoniously, hands bound, into the sea. There was only one man left standing, and he, despite having been stabbed in the neck, could not be hanged. His wound was half a span long, although no vein had been cut and he wasn't bleeding very much, and viewed from one side, the poor devil looked as fresh as a daisy, albeit somewhat pale. The overseer was of the opinion that if they hanged him, the wound in his neck would tear, which would make for a very ugly scene. The captain agreed after taking a look at him, and so the man ended up being tossed into the sea along with his comrades.

When I went in search of Captain Alatriste, almost feeling my way in the dark, a gentle northeast wind was blowing, the moon had not yet come up, and the sky was thick with stars. The deck was packed with soldiers and sailors resting after the battle, having first eaten some salt fish and drunk a little wine to restore their strength, and I won't say that they stank, although they did, because I myself was part of the stink and was, I'm sure, contributing more than my fair share of odors and emanations. The galley men, their oars stowed and having left the ship to the care of that favorable wind, had received some hardtack and a little oil and vinegar, which they ate lying down between their benches, talking quietly, occasionally singing softly to pass the time or complaining about their cuts and bruises. The lines from a song came softly to me, accompanied by the clink of chains and the slapping of hands on the leather that covered the benches:

I'll have it known
Through all the lands
That Christian galleys,
Short of feet,
Are always short of hands.

It was a night like many others. The *Mulata* was drifting slowly through the darkness, heading south on a calm sea and with her sails full, billowing and swaying above the deck like two great pale stains that alternately concealed and revealed the starry sky. I found Captain Alatriste at the prow of the ship, next to where the ropes and cables were kept. He was standing utterly still, leaning against the netting over the side of the ship and gazing at the dark sea and sky, where, toward the west, there was still a trace of reddish light. We talked a little about the events of the day, and I asked him if it was true, as the men were saying, that we were heading for Melilla and not Oran.

"Our captain doesn't want to remain at sea too long with so many captives on board," he replied. "Melilla is closer, which is why he prefers to go and sell them there. We can then continue on our way, less heavily laden."

"And richer too," I added, smiling. I had made my calculations, as had everyone else, and the day should bring us at least two hundred *escudos*.

The captain shifted his position slightly. It was growing

cool in the darkness, and I realized he was fastening his buffcoat.

"Don't get your hopes up," he said at last. "In Melilla, slaves don't fetch such a good price, but because we're alone, near the coast and forty leagues from Oran, Urdemalas is anxious to avoid any unfortunate encounters."

I was pleased, nonetheless, for I had never visited Melilla. Captain Alatriste was quick to undeceive me, though, telling me that the town was little more than a small fortress built on a rock within sight of Mount Gurugu: a few fortified houses always ready for battle and surrounded, as were all the Spanish enclaves on the African coast, by hostile *alarbes. Alarbe* or *alárabe*—if I may enlighten the idle reader—was the name we gave to the bellicose, untrustworthy country Moors, to distinguish them from the city Moors, whom we referred to simply as Moors, in order to differentiate them, in turn—although they were, in fact, Berbers—from the Turks of Turkey, of whom there was never any shortage, for they were always shuttling back and forth between there and Constantinople. That was where the Great Turk lived, and Moors and Berbers or whatever you called them, paid fealty to him in one way or another and, depending on the times, did so more or less faithfully. And that is why, to simplify matters, we called them all Turks—"I wonder if the Turks will come this year," we would say—regardless of whether they were actually from Turkey or not and regardless, too, of whether a Turkish fusta or galliot was from Saleh, Tunis, or Anatolia. To this we must add the intense trading that went on between all nations and those populous corsair cities, where, as well as the local Moorish inhabitants, there were innumerable Christian slaves- -Cervantes, Jerónimo de Pasamonte, and others experienced this firsthand, and I leave them to describe it in their own words—as well as Moriscos, Jews, renegades, sailors, and traders from all shores and all nations. You can imagine, then, what a complicated world that interior sea was, bordering Spain to the south and east, a sea that belonged to no one and to everyone, an ambiguous, shifting, dangerous place where diverse races mixed and mingled, making alliances or doing battle, depending on how the dice rolled. It must be said, though, that while France, England, Holland, and Venice negotiated with the Turk, and even made alliances with him against other Christian nations—especially against Spain when it suited them, which it nearly always did—we, for all our many errors and contradictions, always held firm to the one true religion, never retracting so much as a syllable. And being both arrogant and powerful, we poured swords, money, and blood—until there were no more—into a struggle, which, for a century and a half, kept at bay the Lutherans and the Calvinists in Europe and the Mohammedans in the Mediterranean.

There, where pants the rebel Belgian,
And where the Berber, sweating, stands,
Working, the one, with his bare hands,
The other wielding his bare sword,
To fashion for locks a master key,
Locks that long have had a ward,
Our fleets its shape, its shape our sea.

I hope don Francisco de Quevedo will forgive me for mentioning his enemy, Luis de Góngora, who wrote these Gongoristic lines in sixteen hundred and ten in praise of the taking of Larache, which was followed, four years later, by the seizure of La Mamora. Both were Barbary towns which, like all such towns, we took from the Moors by dint of great effort, clung on to at the cost of great suffering, and, to our great shame and misfortune, finally lost, as we lost everything else, due to our own idleness. In this, as in most things, we would have done better to do as others did and pay more attention to profit than to reputation by opening ourselves up to the horizons we had discovered and broadened, instead of becoming entangled in the sinister soutanes of royal confessors, in the privileges of blood, in our dislike of hard work, in matters of the cross and the sword, meanwhile leaving our intelligence, nation, and soul to rot. But no one gave us the choice. In the end, much to history's surprise, a handful of Spaniards proved able to make the world pay very dearly, by fighting until not one of us was left standing. You will say that this is poor consolation, and you may be right, but we were simply doing our job and paid no heed to governments, philosophies, or theologies. We were, after all, merely soldiers.

We watched the last red light fade from the dark horizon. Now the only thing that distinguished sea and sky was the starry vault beneath which our galley sailed, driven by the east wind, with no moon or any other light, guided only by the knowledge of the pilot who kept one eye on the North Star and the other on the binnacle, in which the ship's compass was lit by a tenuous candle glow. Behind us, near the mainmast, we heard someone ask Captain Urdemalas if they could light the poop deck lantern, to which the reply came that if anyone lit a light, however small, he would personally dash his brains out.

"As for rich soldiers," Captain Alatriste said after a while, as if he had been turning over my words in his mind, "I never met one yet who was rich for very long. It all goes on cards, wine, and whores. As you very well know."

There was a significant pause, brief enough for it not to sound like a reproach, but long enough for it to be just that. And I knew exactly what he was referring to. We had been together for five years, but had spent only some seven months in Naples and on the galleys, during which time he'd had ample opportunity to notice certain changes in my person. Not only physical ones—for I was as tall as he was now, slim but elegant, with good legs, strong arms, and not a bad face—but other deeper and more complex changes. I was aware that ever since I was a child, the captain had wanted me to have a future away from the army, and he had, for this reason, always tried to encourage me—with the help of his friends don Francisco de Quevedo and Father Pérez—to read good books and translations from the Latin and the Greek. The pen, he used to say, reaches farther than the sword, and someone learned in books and the law and with a good position at court will always have more of a future than a professional killer. My natural inclination, however, proved impossible to change, and although, thanks to his efforts, I did acquire a taste for literature—after all, here I am, all these years later, writing our history—my destiny was shaped by the character I inherited from my father, who died in Flanders, and by having lived at Captain Alatriste's side since I was thirteen, sharing his dangerous life and adventures. I wanted to be a soldier, and I was, and I applied myself to the task with the resolute passion and energy of my youth.

"There are no whores on board, and the wine's scarce and very rough," I replied, rather wounded by his comment. "So you have no reason to reprimand me. As for cards, I don't intend giving to a louse the money I risked my life to earn."

I was not using the word "louse" lightly either. Captain Urdemalas, sick of the quarrels over cards and dice, had banned both, threatening any transgressors with being shackled. But the horse knows more than its rider, and so soldiers and sailors invented a new game. They chalked various circles on a piece of board and placed in the very center one of the many lice that were eating us alive—"having visitors," we called it—and then we bet on which direction the creature would go.

"When we go back to Naples," I said in conclusion, "then we'll see."

I kept looking at him out of the corner of my eye, expecting some riposte, but he remained a dark, silent shape by my side, rocked, as I was, by the swaying of the boat. The truth was that, however vigilantly, however hard he tried to protect me, Captain Alatriste could not keep me from the less savory aspects of military life—the usual risks of the profession apart—just as, in the years since my poor mother had entrusted me to him, I had found myself embroiled in certain of his own murky enterprises, with grave risk to liberty and life. Now I was a grown man, or about to be, and the captain's sage advice, when he proffered it—he was, as you know, a man who preferred sword thrusts to words—did not always find the expected response, for

I believed myself to be a man of the world who knew everything about everything. And so, because he was experienced, discreet, and wise, and because he loved me, he avoided sermonizing and tried instead to stay close by in case I needed him. And he only imposed his authority—and dear God, he could certainly do that when he needed to—in extreme situations.

As for wine, women, and gambling, I admit that he did have good reason to be angry with me. My wage of four *escudos* a month, along with the money from previous booties—two Turkish karamuzals captured in the Mayna channel, a profitable raid on the coast of Tunis, a ship seized off Cape Passero, and a galley off the island of Santa Maura—had been spent, every last penny of it, in the same soldierly fashion as my comrades', and exactly as the captain had done in his youth, as he himself would sullenly admit. In my case, though, my lack of experience and a taste for the new meant that I hurled myself into it with great gusto. For a spirited Spanish lad like me, Naples, which contained all things, was paradise: good inns, excellent taverns, beautiful women, in short, everything that could help relieve a soldier of his pay. And, as chance would have it, my fellow page from Flanders, Jaime Correas, was there to assist and encourage me. Having served in Italy for some time, he was no stranger to any of the vices. I will have occasion to speak of him later on, and so I will say only that in his company, and beneath the frowning gaze of Captain Alatriste, I had spent a good part of the winter months, when the galleys were out of action, embroiled in various escapades involving gaming houses, taverns, and—rather less assiduously on my part—the occasional bawdy house. Not that my former master was the kind of man who could die unconfessed and stand fearlessly face to face with Christ—far from it—but the truth is that gambling, which has bled many a soldier's purse dry, had never tempted him. On the other hand, if he did occasionally frequent certain ladies practiced in the art of love—he didn't need to go to whores, for he always grazed in rich pastures—they were few in number and very reliable. As for Bacchus, the captain certainly worshipped at *his* table and had the devil of a thirst. But although he often drank too much, especially when he was angry or melancholy—and then he was especially dangerous, because wine dulled neither his senses nor his quick reactions—he always did so alone and without witnesses. I think that, rather than as a pleasure or a vice, he downed whole tumblerfuls in order to quell the inner torments and demons known only to him and God.

At first light, we cast anchor outside Melilla, the Spanish fortress town captured from the Moors one hundred and thirty years before. And so as to remain safely out of sight of Moorish eyes, we anchored not in the lagoon, but in the narrow inlet of Galápagos cove, in the shelter of Melilla's soaring walls and towers. The town's imposing appearance was just that, mere appearance, as I was able to see for myself while the galley captain was haggling over a price for the slaves, when I set off to wander through the close-packed, treeless streets and along the city walls and saw how neglected it all was. Eight centuries of struggle against Islam died on that wretched frontier. Not a single *maravedí* from the gold and silver brought from the Indies ever reached those shores. What did not end up in the hands of Genoan bankers was stolen by the Dutch and English—Devil take 'em—in the western seas. Flanders and the Indies were the apples of royal eyes, and our old African enterprise, once so dear to the Catholic kings and to the great emperor Charles V, was scorned by Philip IV and by his favorite, the Count-Duke of Olivares. Indeed, many satirical verses were written on the subject:

It surely matters not a toss
If far Melilla's deemed a loss,
And do not let yourself be vexed
Should it turn out Ceuta's next.
Bring on the flags of Barbary!
No more for us the rosary,

Once the Gospel city of Oran
Bends the knee to the Koran.
What does it matter—not a jot—
If those brave Arabs take the lot?

It was a miracle, really, that these North African fortress towns survived at all, and they did so more by virtue of their reputation than anything else. For although they served to deprive the corsairs of a few ports and important bases, the corsairs still had Algiers, Tunis, Saleh, Tripoli, and Bizerta. Our soldiers were housed in cramped quarters within fortifications whose casemates and bulwarks were crumbling for lack of money; many soldiers were old and infirm with no one to relieve them, and they lived there with their families, ill-clothed and ill-fed, without so much as a scrap of land to cultivate, and with barely enough money, and sometimes none at all, to struggle and fight and resist the surrounding enemy. Any aid from the peninsula was at least a day's journey away, and such aid was far from certain, for it depended on what the conditions at sea were like and on how quickly help could be organized in Spain. And so Melilla, like our other African possessions—including Tangiers and Ceuta, which, being Portuguese, were also therefore Spanish—found themselves relying for their survival on the courage of the garrison and on diplomacy with the neighboring Moors, from whom they obtained, voluntarily or by force, the necessary supplies. As I said, I gleaned much of this simply from visiting the city and its massive water cisterns, on which life there was totally dependent. I visited the hospital, the church, the Santa Ana tunnel, and the square, *intra muros*, where the Moors from the surrounding area came to sell meat, fish, and vegetables. This was a very lively area during the day, but at nightfall, before the city gates were closed, all the Arabs left, apart, that is, from a trusted few who were allowed to stay as long as they agreed to be locked up in the House of the Moors, over which a constable stood guard. This, however, I did not see, because that same night, in order to escape the notice of the Arabs on the coast, the *Mulata* weighed anchor and left Melilla secretly, powered only by her oars; then, taking advantage of the wind blowing from the shore, we set sail in an easterly direction, and dawn found us off the Chafarinas Islands and halfway to Oran, where, on the following afternoon, we spotted the Needle Rock and anchored there without incident or mishap.

Oran was quite different, although still far from being a paradise. The town was in the same state of abandonment as Spain's other fortress towns in Africa, with poor lines of supply and even worse communications, and its improvised defenses were neglected and inadequate. In the case of Oran, though, it wasn't, as Melilla was, just an arid fortified promontory, but a real town with a river, abundant water, and surrounded by gardens and orchards. It also had a proper garrison, which, though far from ideal—at the time Oran was home to about one thousand three hundred soldiers and their families, as well as five hundred inhabitants plying various trades—was nevertheless capable of putting up a reasonable defense and, if necessary, of attacking too. So although, in general, these fortress towns had been pretty much abandoned to their fate, Oran was certainly not in the worst shape. The proof of this was the presence of the supply convoy anchored in the bay of Cap Falcon, the town's harbor, between Mazalquivir's formidable fort and Mona Point beneath the castle of San Gregorio; there we finally rejoined the convoy we had left behind in order to give chase to the corsairs. We anchored close to land, next to the tower, and were borne to shore in feluccas, where we walked the rest of the way into the town— half a league from the beach—which was built on top of a cliff and therefore had no good port of its own, which is where Mazalquivir came in. From that high vantage point, it looked out over the river, which ran between the town and the fort of Rozalcazar and offered splendid views of the gardens, orchards, woods, and windmills.

As I say, we were pleased to be back on land and with

money in our pockets, and although Oran was no Naples—
far from it—there were plenty of distractions. There were
taverns run by former soldiers—a recent truce with the
Moors meant that the market was well supplied—and
everyone was pleased to see the wheat, cloth, and gunpowder we had brought from Spain. There were even a
few decent brothels, for, in garrison towns like Oran, even
the bishops and theologians of our Holy Mother Church—
after much debate and having resigned themselves to the
inevitable—had concluded that a few sprightly doxies, as
well as salving the soldier's itch, safeguarded the virtue of
maidens and married ladies and reduced the number of
rapes and the incidence of forays into Moorish territory in
search of women. Indeed, as soon as we disembarked, soldiers and sailors alike were planning a visit to one of those
brothels as a first duty or toll payable on entering the town.
However, no sooner had Captain Alatriste and I passed
through the Canastel gate—the closer to the harbor of
Oran's two gates—than we had a most pleasant, extraordinary, and unlooked-for encounter, which just goes to show
how life, with all its twists and turns, can still surprise us.

"Well, I'll be hanged," said a familiar voice.

And there, as small and wiry as ever, was Sebastián Copons in person, hands on hips and sword at his waist, standing in the shade, chatting to some soldiers, in his role as
corporal in charge of the guard at the gate.

. . .

"And so that's what happened," he said, draining his mug.

The three of us were sitting at a table outside a small, grubby tavern, beneath a much-patched bit of sailcloth that served as an awning. True to his old self, Copons wasted few words in summarizing the last two years, which was how long it had been since we said our farewells in an Andalusian inn, after the massacre on board the *Niklaas-bergen* and that business with the king's gold, when, with the help of a few comrades, we made short work of Flemings and hired killers alike at Barra de Sanlúcar. Since then, he told us, a run of bad luck had put paid to his plans to leave the army and set himself up in Huesca with a little bit of land, a house, and a wife. The first unfortunate episode took place in Seville and the second involved a death in Zaragoza. This latter incident attracted constables, lawyers, judges, scribes, and all the other parasites that lie in wait among the paperwork like bedbugs in the seams of sheets. Relieved of all his money and with belly and pockets equally empty, he had been forced back to the barracks to earn his living. His attempts to get himself sent to the Indies all failed—it wasn't soldiers they needed now, but functionaries, priests, and artisans; then, just as he was about to enlist for Flanders or Italy, a tavern brawl, in which two catchpoles were beaten up and one constable slashed across the face, brought him up against the law again. This time, he had no money with which to blind Justice, and so the Judge—who, like him, was from Huesca—offered him a choice between spending four years behind bars or one year as a soldier in Oran for fifty *reales* a month. And there he was, one year and five months later.

"Why don't you leave?" I asked innocently.

Copons and Captain Alatriste exchanged looks, as if to say he may look like a grown man, but he's still very green about the gills, and then filled their mugs again with wine. It was a pretty rough vintage—God knows where it came from—but it was wine, we were in Africa, and it was as hot as hell. More to the point, it had been a long time since we three had shared a jug of wine, and we had been through a lot together—the Ruyter Mill, Breda, Terheyden, Seville, Sanlúcar . . .

"I can't because the Sergeant Major won't let me."

"Why's that?"

"Because, he says, the Marquis of Velada, the town's governor, won't let *him*."

And between sips of wine, he explained what life was like in Oran: the people, ill-fed and worse-paid, just rotted away between those walls, with no hope of promotion or any glory other than that of growing old there alone, or with their family, if they had one, until they were deemed too feeble to work; any complaints or petitions went unanswered. Even a veteran with forty years' service was not allowed to return to Spain because that would leave posts unfilled, and any new soldiers posted to Barbary simply deserted before they even disembarked. You just had to go for a stroll through the city to see how many ragged, vulnerable people there were; and if you did manage to buy something—food or clothes—this would be followed by weeks of hunger and dearth, because the pay never came, not even a half or a third of it, even though the troops in Oran were the worst paid in all of Spain. Some secretary in the Treasury had evidently decided—and been backed up in that decision by our master the king—that as long as there was sufficient water to be had, fertile fields, and friendly Moors on hand, the troops should have no problem making ends meet. Soldiers were only offered help in situations of dire emergency. Copons himself, after seventeen months' duty there, had not seen one *maravedí* of the one hundred or so *escudos* that were owed to him as an old soldier skilled with harquebus and musket. The only thing they could do to help themselves was to go on the occasional cavalcade.

"Cavalcade?" I asked.

Copons winked and said nothing more. It fell to Captain Alatriste to explain.

"You know, raids, incursions, the kind of thing our grandfathers did, when they'd ride out into the countryside and attack the camps of hostile Moors. They used to call them *almogavarías*."

"Because that's what Oran has had to stoop to, as if she was some old procuress," added Copons.

I looked at him, confused.

"I don't understand."

"You will, you will."

He poured more wine. He was as thin, sinewy, and strong as ever, but he looked older and wearier and, what was even stranger, he had grown talkative. Like Captain Alatriste, he was normally slow to speak and quick to draw his sword. However, it seemed that, in Oran, his silent nature had accumulated far too many thoughts and feelings, so that the warmth of our friendship and that unexpected encounter had suddenly made them flow forth. In the heat, he had unfastened his grimy leather doublet—he wore no undershirt, for he had no money for such things. Above his left ear, he bore the scar earned at the Ruyter Mill, still visible through his short hair, which had grown grayer, and he had some white hairs too now on his ill-shaven chin.

"Tell him about the hostile Moors," said Captain Alatriste.

And he did. The Arabs who lived nearby could be divided into three classes: peaceful Moors, hostile Moors, and what were known as *mogataces*. The peaceful Moors made truces with the Spaniards, sold them food, and so on. They paid taxes, or *garrama* as it was known here, and that made them "friends" until they stopped paying. Then they became hostile Moors.

"Sounds dangerous," I commented.

"It is. They're the ones who'll slit our throats and cut off our privates if they catch us, although we'd do the same to them, of course."

"And how do you tell them apart?"

The captain shook his head.

"You can't always."

"Sometimes that works to our detriment," said Copons, "and sometimes to theirs."

I considered the grim implications of this answer. Then I asked who the *mogataces* were. The captain explained that they were Arabs who fought on our side as soldiers of Spain, but without changing their religion.

"Can they be trusted?"

Copons pulled a face.

"Some of them can."

"I don't think I could ever trust a Moor."

They looked at me mockingly. I must have seemed extraordinarily naive to them.

"You'd be surprised. There are Moors and there are Moors."

We ordered another jug of wine, which was brought

to us by a man with ugly bare feet and an even uglier face, as black as pitch. I watched thoughtfully as Copons filled my mug.

"And how do you know if one of them can be trusted?"

"A question of experience," said Copons, tapping the side of his nose. "And of instinct. But let me tell you, I've seen no end of Christians in my time roaring drunk, but never a Moor. They don't gamble either, unlike us, even though the deck of cards is as old as Mohammed."

"Yes, but they don't keep their word," I objected.

"That depends on who they are and who they give their word to. When the Count of Alcaudete's men were nearly torn to pieces, his *mogataces* stood firm and fought to the bitter end. That's why I say there are Moors and there are Moors."

While we were dispatching the latest jug of wine—the jug had been much baptized—Copons continued to enlighten us about life in Oran. The lack of men was a grave problem, he went on, because no soldier wanted to come to these African outposts unless forced to: once a soldier arrived, he risked being stuck there forever. That's why the garrisons were never filled; that year alone, they were four hundred men short, and the soldiers who did come were the dregs of Spain, ill-natured and unwilling, either unruly men fit only for the galleys or else raw recruits who had been cruelly deceived, like the contingent that arrived last autumn: forty-two men who had enlisted for Italy, or so at least they were told. However, once embarked in Cartagena, they were taken straight to Oran and there was nothing they could do about it; in fact, three were hanged for mutiny, and the others assigned to the local regiment, where they were stuck now with no hope of ever leaving. It was no coincidence, after all, that the Spanish phrase to describe a particularly unpromising enterprise was to say that it was about as likely to happen as sending a hundred lancers to Oran.

"And that's how it is with the people here—they're desperate, ragged, and hungry." Copons lowered his voice. "It's hardly to be wondered at that the weakest-willed, or those who simply can't take anymore, desert as soon as they can. Diego, do you remember Yndurain, the Basque? The one who defended that old hamlet, in Fleurus, along with Utrera, Barrena, and the others, until the only ones left were him and a bugler?"

The captain nodded and asked what had become of him. Copons stared into his mug, turned to one side in order to spit under the table, and then looked at him again.

"He was here for five years and hadn't been paid for the last three. Two months or so ago, he had words with a sergeant. He stabbed the sergeant with his knife and jumped over the wall at night, along with another comrade who was on guard duty. They say that, after much difficulty, they finally arrived in Mostaganem, where they promptly joined the Moors, but who can say ..."

He and the captain exchanged knowing looks, and I saw my former master take another sip of wine and shrug. A resigned shrug for himself, for his friend, and for the others, all of them, and for poor, unhappy Spain. At that moment, I recalled some lines from a play I had seen a couple of years before in Madrid. They had shocked me then, but now I understood them:

> *I, a soldier, on bended knee*
> *Surrender my embattled blade;*
> *I can no longer stand to be*
> *Both brave and badly paid.*

"Can you imagine," the captain suddenly said to Copons, "Yndurain salaaming to Mecca?"

And he gave a kind of half-smile. Copons gave an identical smile, only briefer. They were skeptical smiles, entirely lacking in humor, proper to old soldiers with no illusions.

"And yet," replied Copons, "when the drum rolls, we never lack for swords."

This was very true, as time would continue to prove. However abandoned, neglected, and poverty-stricken these

North African garrison towns were, there was rarely a shortage of men available to defend them when the need arose. And this was done without payment, without help, and without glory, out of desperation, pride, and concern for reputation. And so as not to end up as slaves. I know of what I speak, as you, dear reader, will learn from this story. There has always been a certain kind of man for whom, at the final moment, paying dearly for his life has always brought some degree of consolation. Among Spaniards, this was an old, familiar story, and so it went until, one by one, those towns, forgotten by God and by the king, fell into the hands of Turks or Moors. This had already happened in Algiers in the previous century, when Barbarossa attacked El Peñón, whose one hundred and fifty Spanish soldiers were blocking the entrance to the harbor. And what happened? Spain abandoned to their fate those who waited in vain for help to come—"The emperor," according to his chronicler Father Prudencio de Sandoval, "had more important matters to deal with at the time." The soldiers fought like the men they were, and, after sixteen days of artillery fire that demolished the redoubt stone by stone, the Turks took only fifty battered and wounded prisoners. Barbarossa, enraged at such fierce resistance, had one of those prisoners, Captain Martín de Vargas, beaten to death with sticks. As for Larache, a few years after the events I am describing, it was attacked by twenty thousand enemy troops, who were repelled by a mere one hundred and fifty Spanish soldiers and fifty ex-soldiers who all fought like demons—the loss and recovery of the so-called Tower of the Jew was particularly fiercely fought—to defend six thousand feet of city wall. Oran, too, had withstood various assaults with great honor; indeed, one provided the inspiration for don Miguel de Cervantes' play *The Brave Spaniard*. We also owe to Cervantes—not for nothing was he a veteran of the Battle of Lepanto—two sonnets written in memory of the thousands of soldiers who died fighting alone and abandoned by their king—still a very Spanish custom. The poems, which he included in *Don Quixote*, recall the defenders of the fort of La Goleta, opposite Tunis, who were killed after resisting twenty-two attacks by the Turks and killing twenty-five thousand of the enemy, so that, of the few Spaniards who survived, not one was captured unscathed. "Life failed before valor did," says one of those sonnets, and the second begins:

> *From this battered, sterile land*
> *From these clods of earth brought low*
> *Three thousand soldiers' holy souls*
> *Rose, still living, to a better home.*
> *Having first, in vain, spent all*
> *The strength and effort of their arms,*

Until, at last, so few, so weary,
To the enemy's blade they gave their life.

As I said, all that sacrifice was futile. After Lepanto, which had marked the extreme point of the collision between the two great Mediterranean powers, the Turk had turned his interest more to Persia and eastern Europe and our kings had turned theirs to Flanders and the Atlantic enterprise. Philip IV showed no interest either, discouraged by his minister, the Count-Duke of Olivares, who disliked ports and galleys (not that he ever visited such places; the stench, he said, would give him a headache) and despised sailors, for he considered sailing the seas a low and vulgar occupation, fit only for Dutchmen, unless, that is, it brought back from the Indies the gold he needed for his wars. And so, what with kings and their favorites and one thing and another, and once the days of the great corsair fleets and the stalemate of the various empires' games of naval chess were over, the Mediterranean became a kind of blurred frontier in the hands of the minor pirates of the countries along its shores; piracy, while it changed the course of many lives and many fortunes, did nothing to quicken the pulse of history. Also, more than a century had passed since the conclusion of the Christian Reconquest, a period of nearly eight hundred years during which we Spaniards forged our identity, and the subsequent policy of carrying the fight into Islamic territory, once backed by Cardinal Cisneros and the old Duke of Medina Sidonia, had now been abandoned. So Africa, in fact, held very little interest for a Spain that was at daggers drawn with just about everyone. The garrison towns in Barbary were more symbols and outposts than anything else. They were maintained only in order to keep the corsairs at bay, as well as France, Holland, and England, who, watching for the arrival of our galleons in Cádiz, did their utmost to establish themselves there with their pirates, as they had in the Caribbean, where they were always snapping at our ankles. That is why we would not leave the way free for them, although they were already well supplied with consuls and merchants in the corsair republics. And although we will return to the subject, I will just say that, years later, Tangiers belonged to the king of England over a period of two decades—thanks to the Portuguese rebellion—and that during the siege of La Mámora in sixteen hundred and twenty-eight, a year after the events I am describing, the men digging the trenches and directing the siegeworks were English sappers. Well, bastards of a feather will flock together.

We went out for a stroll. Copons guided us through the narrow, whitewashed streets of tightly packed houses, which, apart from the flat roofs, reminded me a little of Toledo, with their solid stone quoins and few windows, the latter being set low and protected by blinds or shutters. The damp sea air caused the plaster and rendering to flake, leaving dark ugly patches. Add to this the swarms of flies, the clothes hung out to dry, the ragged children playing in courtyards, the occasional crippled soldier sitting on a stone bench or on the steps outside his house, eyeing us suspiciously, and you will have a fairly faithful picture of how Oran appeared to me. Yet there was also something inescapably military about the place because the town was really a vast barracks inhabited by soldiers and their families. But, as I discovered, it covered quite a large area and was arranged on different levels, with no shortage of ordinary tradesmen's shops, as well as bakers, butchers, and taverns. The large, grand, well-proportioned casbah, which housed the governor and the military headquarters, dated from the days of the Moors—some said from Roman times—and had a magnificent parade ground. The town also had a prison, a military hospital, a Jewish quarter—to my surprise, there were still Jews living there—and various monasteries: Franciscan, Mercedarian, and Dominican; and in the eastern section of the medina, there were several ancient mosques converted into churches, the main one of which had been transformed by Cardinal Cisneros, at the time of the Conquest, into the church of Our Lady

Victorious. And everywhere, in the streets, in the cramped squares, beneath canvas awnings, and in doorways, one saw people standing stock still—women glimpsed behind shutters, and men, many of them veteran soldiers, maimed and scarred and clothed in rags, their crutches leaning against the wall beside them—all staring into space. I thought of that former comrade Yndurain, whom I had never known, leaping over the wall at dead of night, having knifed a sergeant, prepared to go over to the Moors rather than stay there, and a shudder ran through me.

"So what do you make of Oran?" Copons asked me.

"It's as if it were sleeping," I replied. "All these still, staring people."

Copons nodded and wiped the sweat from his face with his hand.

"People only wake up when the Moors attack or when we organize a cavalcade," he said. "Having a scimitar at your throat or pelf in your pocket works wonders." At this point, he turned to Captain Alatriste and said, "Speaking of pelf, you've arrived at just the right time. Something's afoot."

There was a flicker of interest in the captain's pale eyes, which, beneath the broad brim of his hat, reflected the dazzling light in the street. We had just reached the arch of the Tlemcen gate, on the opposite side of the town from the harbor, where a few reluctant stonemasons—Moorish

slaves and Spanish convicts I noticed—were trying to patch
up the crumbling wall. Copons greeted the sentinels sitting
in the shade, and then we strolled out of the town, from
where we could see the village of Ifre—inhabited by
friendly Moors—situated about two harquebus shots from
the town wall. That whole section of wall was in a parlous
state, with bushy plants growing in between the stones and
many of the stones fallen on the ground. The sentry box
was dilapidated and roofless, and the wooden drawbridge
over the narrow moat—almost entirely clogged with rubble and filth—was so rotten that it creaked beneath our
feet. It was, I thought, a miracle that the town could resist
any attack at all.

"A cavalcade?" asked Captain Alatriste.

Copons gave him a knowing look. "Possibly."

"Where?"

"They don't say, but I suspect it will be over there." He
indicated the Tlemcen road that ran south through the
nearby fields. "There are a few Arabs there who are none too
happy about paying their taxes. There are livestock and people, so there'll be some decent booty to be had."

"Hostile Moors?"

"They can be if it serves our purpose."

I was watching Copons and listening intently. This business of cavalcades intrigued me, and so I asked for more
details.

"Remember those raids we used to go on in Flanders?" he said. "Well, it's the same here: you leave at night, march quickly and in silence, and then you strike. We never go farther than eight leagues from Oran, just in case."

"And you take harquebuses?"

Copons shook his head.

"As few as possible. The whole thing is very much hand-to-hand so as not to waste gunpowder. If the village is near, we take people and livestock. If it's farther off, we just take people and jewelry. Then we march back as fast as we can, see what we've got, sell it, and share out the booty."

"And is there plenty of it?"

"That depends. With slaves we can earn maybe forty *escudos* or more. A healthy female of childbearing age, a strong black or a young Moor mean thirty *reales* each in the common pot. If they're suckling babes and in good health, ten . . . We did really well out of the last cavalcade. I made eighty *escudos* clear, that's double my year's wages."

"Which is why the king doesn't pay you."

"As if he damn well would."

We were strolling now near the fertile, leafy banks of the river, along which there were mills and a few waterwheels. An old Moor and a little boy, both wearing threadbare djellabas, passed us on their way into town, carrying baskets full of vegetables on their backs. I admired the pleasant view—the green terraced fields dotted with trees between the river and the town's walls, the town with its casbah perched halfway up the hill, and, downriver, the sea, spreading out like a blue fan in the distance.

"Without the cavalcades and what these fields produce," added Copons, "we wouldn't be able to survive. Until you arrived, we'd spent four months with just a bushel of wheat per month and sixteen *reales* for any soldier with a family. You've seen the state of the people here, almost naked because their clothes are literally falling to pieces. It's the old Flanders trick, eh, Diego? You want your pay? Well, you see that castle full of Dutchmen over there? You go and attack it, and then we'll pay you. Moors or heretics, it's all one to the king."

"Do they take the royal quint off you here, as well?" I asked.

"Of course," said Copons. There was the king's quint, and the governor's "jewel," as it was known. He got the pick of the bunch: the best slaves or even a village chief's entire family. Then it was the turn of the officers, and the soldiers were last in line, according to how much they earned. Even people who hadn't gone on the cavalcade had a right to a share. Not forgetting the church.

"You mean even the monks dip their fingers in?"

"You bet they do, to supplement their alms. The caval-

cades benefit everyone, including tradesmen and merchants, because the Arabs come into town later to buy back
their loved ones with money and merchandise. The whole
city becomes one great bazaar."

We stopped beside a lean-to made of planks and roofed
with palm leaves, which provided shelter at night for the
guards at the bridge connecting the town and the fields
with the castle of Rozalcazar on the other side of the
Ouahran River, and with the castle of San Felipe farther
inland. Of those two castles, Copons told us, the former
had almost completely collapsed and the latter had not yet
been fully fortified. For, although Oran was famous for its
fortresses, they were, in fact, little more than show, the
town itself having only an old wall with hardly any moat
to speak of, no ditches, no stockade, no covered entrance,
no parapets, and no redoubts. And so the town's only real
fortifications were the living, breathing bodies of those
who, most reluctantly, had to protect it. As some poet or
other had said: our only gunpowder our swords and our
only walls the balls of Spain.

"Could *we* go?" I asked.

Copons glanced at me, then at Captain Alatriste, before looking back again at me. "And where exactly do you
want to go?" he asked with an indifferent air. I adopted a
bold, soldierly demeanor and held his eyes without a
flicker.

"Where else?" I replied coolly. "With you, on the cavalcade."

The two veterans again exchanged glances, and Copons rubbed his chin.

"What do you think, Diego?"

My former master studied me thoughtfully, then shrugged: "A bit of extra money always comes in handy, I suppose."

Copons agreed. The problem, he said, was that, in these cases, the whole garrison usually wanted to take part in these outings and so get a bigger share of the profits.

"Although sometimes," he added, "when there are galley crews in town, they do take reinforcements. In fact, you may be in luck, because there's a lot of fever about at the moment—brought on by drinking bad water, because there's no shortage of water here, but it's very brackish—and a number of people are either ill or in the hospital. I'll speak to Sergeant Major Biscarrués. He's a Flanders veteran too and a countryman of mine. But keep mum. Not a word to anyone."

He wasn't addressing the captain when he said this, but me. I returned his gaze rather knowingly at first and then loftily and reproachfully. Copons stood thinking for a while, then turned to Captain Alatriste.

"The little lad's grown up," he murmured. "Damn him."

Then he looked me up and down. His eyes lingered on

my thumbs looped through my belt, next to my dagger and sword.

I heard the captain beside me sigh. He did so with a touch of irony, I think, and a touch of weariness too.

"You don't know the half of it, Sebastián."

3. THE CAVALCADE TO WADI BERRUCH

In the distance, a dog howled. Lying facedown among the undergrowth, Diego Alatriste jerked awake. He had been resting his head on his folded arms, but, woken by his old soldier's instinct, he looked up and opened his eyes. He had not slept for long, only a matter of moments, but, like any experienced soldier, he took advantage of every occasion to rest. In his line of work, you never knew when you might have another chance to sleep or eat or drink. Or empty your bladder. All around him, kneeling on the slope dotted with silent, motionless shapes, soldiers were making the most of their last opportunity to do just that, rather than have their guts sliced open with bladder still full. Alatriste unfastened his breeches and did the same. A man fights best on an empty bladder and an empty belly, that's what his first sergeant in Flanders used to tell him. His name was don Francisco del Arco, and he had died at Alatriste's side in the dunes of Nieuwpoort, by which time, he'd been promoted to captain. Alatriste had served under him toward the end of the last century, when he was only fifteen, in the war against the Estates General and France, during the night attack on Amiens and the sacking of the city. Now that really had been a profitable cavalcade, although the worst came later, when they spent nearly six months besieged by the French.

While he relieved himself, he gazed up at the sky. He could see the occasional laggardly star, but the gray light of dawn was growing in the east, behind the bare hills still casting their shadow over the tents and walnut trees—it wasn't bright enough yet to tell a white thread from a black—in the large dried-up riverbed that the guides called Wadi Berruch, five leagues from Oran. When he had finished, Alatriste lay down again, having first checked his belt and his weapons and fastened his buffcoat. The latter would weigh on him later, in the heat of the day, when the African sun was at its height, but, for the moment, in the dawn chill, he was glad of it. And as soon as the attack began, he would be gladder still of that old buffalo hide. A knife thrust was a knife thrust whether it came from a Moor, a Turk, or a Lutheran. He recalled the various places where he had received such blows—eyebrow, forehead, hand, legs, hip, back, et cetera; he got as far as nine—if he included the harquebus shot and ten if counted the burn to his arm—he didn't have room on his body for many more.

"Damned dog," someone nearby whispered.

The dog howled again and, shortly afterward, was joined by another. This was bad news, thought Alatriste, if they had scented the presence of marauders and were alerting the people sleeping in the encampment. By then, he reckoned, the group on the opposite side of the riverbed would already be in position, keeping their horses well back in case their neighing spoiled the surprise. Two hundred men on that side and the same number on this—including fifty *mogataces*—more than enough to take on the three hundred or so Arabs—women, children, and the old included—who were camped there with their animals, asleep and unaware of what awaited them.

He had been given the background to the story the previous evening in Oran, when the order had come to get ready, and he had found out more details during the six-hour march through the night, with men and horses tramping hard, guided by *mogataz* scouts. They had marched, first in ranks and then in single file, down the Tlemcen road, along the riverbank, and then, once past the lake, the house of the local marabout, the well, and the fields, had headed west, skirting the hills before dividing into two groups to wait in silent ambush for dawn to break.

According to what he had been told, the people in the encampment belonged to the tribe of Beni Gurriaran, who were considered by the Spanish garrison to be peaceful Moors. The agreement was that the garrison would protect them against other hostile Berber tribes in exchange for agreed quantities of wheat, barley, and livestock to be handed over every year on predetermined dates. However, last year, the wheat and barley harvest had been late and rather sparse—a third of it was still owed to the garrison—and now the Moors were trying to avoid handing over the livestock due in the spring. They still had not done so, and rumor had it that the people of Beni Gurriaran were preparing to move somewhere far from Wadi Berruch, beyond the reach of the Spanish.

"So we're going to catch them napping," Sergeant Major Biscarrués had said, "before they can say knife."

Sergeant Major Biscarrués was from Aragon; he had seen long service as a soldier and had the confidence of the governor of Oran. He was a typical denizen of those North African towns: as hard as nails, his tanned skin parched and lined by the sun and the dust and by the hardships of a life spent fighting, first in Flanders and latterly in Africa—with the sea at his back, the king in far-off Spain, God preoccupied with other matters, and the Moors only a sword's length away. He commanded a troop of soldiers whose one hope was to win some booty, and he carried out his job with due rigor, for these men of his were dangerous people, potential deserters, fodder for the gallows and the galleys, and as ready to mutiny as they were to kill each other. He was, in short, a cruel but approachable bastard, and no more venal than most. That, at least, was how Sebastián Copons described Biscarrués before we met him on the evening of the first day. That meeting took place in a small barracks in the casbah, where we found him bent over a map spread out on the table, each of the map's four corners weighted down, respectively, by a jug of wine, a candlestick, a dagger, and a small pistol. He was accompanied by two other men: a tall Moor with a white cloak over his shoulders, and a thin, dark individual dressed in Spanish fashion, clean-shaven and with a prominent nose.

"With your permission, Sergeant Major, may I introduce my friend Diego Alatriste, a fellow Flanders veteran now deployed on the galleys in Naples. Diego, this is don Lorenzo Biscarrués. The other two men are Mustafa Chauni, the chief of our *mogataces*, and Aron Cansino, our interpreter."

"Flanders, eh?" The sergeant major eyed Alatriste curiously. "Amiens? Ostend?"

"Both."

"A lot of rain has fallen since then. At least it has in Flanders, on those damned heretics, but there hasn't been a drop here for months."

They chatted for a while, mentioning the names of comrades they had in common, both alive and dead; then Copons explained the situation and obtained the sergeant major's permission for us to join the cavalcade, while Alatriste studied both him and the other two men. The *mogataz* was an Ulad Galeb whose tribe had served Spain for three generations, and in appearance he was typical of such men: gray-bearded and swarthy; he wore slippers, a curved dagger at his waist, and his head was entirely shaved apart from the small tuft that some Moors left so that, if their head was cut off in battle, an enemy would not have to stick his fingers in the decapitated head's mouth or eyes in order to carry it off as a trophy. He led the *harka* of one hundred and fifty warriors chosen from among his tribe or family—which, in those parts, amounted to the same thing—who lived with their wives and children in the village of Ifre and nearby encampments; as long as those men were assured of pay and booty, they were prepared to fight under the Saint Andrew's cross with a courage and loyalty one would like to have seen in many subjects of the Catholic king. As for the other man, it came as no surprise to Alatriste that a Jew should act as interpreter in the town, for although the Jews had been expelled from Spain, their presence was tolerated in the Spanish enclaves in North Africa for reasons to do with commerce, money, and their mastery of the Arabic language. As he found out later, among the twenty or so families living in the Jewish quarter, the Cansinos had been trusted interpreters since the middle of the last century, and even though they observed Mosaic law—Oran was alone in having a synagogue—they had always shown absolute competence as well as loyalty to the king. For this reason, the various governors of the town had honored and rewarded them, passing the profession from father to son. They combined their linguistic skills with a little espionage, for all the Israelite communities in Barbary were in regular communication. The other reason the Oran Jews were tolerated was their vital importance as merchants and traders, despite the heavy taxes imposed on them because of their religion, for, when times were hard, they were the ones who lent the governor money or wheat or whatever he might need. In addition, there was their role in the slave trade: on the one hand, they mediated in the ransoming of captives and, on the other, they owned most of the Turks and Moors sold in Oran. After all, regardless of whether they worshipped Mary, Mohammed, or Moses, as far as everyone—Jew, Moor, or Spaniard—was concerned, a silver coin was a silver coin, and business was business. As don Francisco de Quevedo would have said, Sir Money was a powerful gentleman. And the man was a fool who would bother going to light a candle at anyone else's altar.

The dog barked again in the distance, and Alatriste

touched the well-primed pistol at his waist. In a way, he thought, he wouldn't mind if the dog kept on barking so that the Moors in the encampment, or at least some of them, were awake and with scimitar in hand when Sergeant Major Biscarrués gave the order to attack. Slitting the throats of sleeping men in order to steal their livestock, women, and children was quicker and easier than slitting their throats while they were awake, but it would take a vast amount of wine to wash the blood from his memory.

"At the ready."

In a whisper that grew gradually louder, the order passed down the line. When it reached me, I, too, passed it on, and heard the words move off among the crouching shadows until it vanished like an echo fading into the infinite. I ran my tongue over my cracked lips and then clenched my teeth to stop them chattering in the cold while I tied on my espadrilles. Then, removing the rags in which I had wrapped both my sword and the blade of my half-pike to avoid making any inopportune noise, I looked around. I couldn't see Captain Alatriste in the dawn light, in which various shapes were already silhouetted against the horizon, but I knew he was lying down with the others close by. I could see Sebastián Copons, a dark, motionless figure, smelling of sweat, greased leather, and steel burnished with oil. There were similar figures in groups or scattered around, among the lentiscus bushes, the prickly pears, and the thistles that in Barbary are called *arracafes*.

"We attack in two credos' time," came the new order.

Some, either out of devotion or simply to calculate the time, started mumbling the creed out loud. I heard them all around me, in the half-darkness, in different accents and intonations: Basque, Valencian, Asturian, Andalusian, Castilian; Spaniards who only came together either to pray or to kill. *Credo in unum Deum, patrem omnipotentem, factorem caeli et terrae* . . . Those pious murmurings as a prelude to bloody battle always struck me as odd; all those male voices whispering holy words, asking God to let them survive the fight, to capture gold and slaves aplenty, to be granted a safe return to Oran and to Spain, laden with booty and with no enemies nigh, for as they all knew very well—Copons and the captain had both emphasized this point—the most dangerous thing in the world was fighting Moors on their own ground and then withdrawing and finding oneself pursued down those dried-up riverbeds and through that arid landscape, beneath the implacable sun, with no water or else paying in blood for each drop, or being wounded and falling into the hands of Arabs, who had all the time in the world to kill you. Perhaps that was why the murmur was spreading among those crouching shadows: *Deum de Deo, lumen de lumine, Deum verum de*

Deo vero . . . After a while, I found myself mechanically murmuring the same words without even thinking, like someone singing along to a particularly catchy old ballad. Then, when I realized what I was doing, I prayed with real devotion: *Et expecto resurrectionem mortuorum et vitam venturi saeculi, amen.* At the time, I was still young enough to believe in such things and a few other things besides.

"Forward for Santiago . . . for Santiago and Spain!"

The words were spoken in a howl, punctuated by a few sharp blasts on the bugle, while the men scrambled to their feet and ran through the undergrowth, holding high the king's standard and flag. I stood up too and ran forward, aware of shots being fired on the far side of the encampment, where the darkness—a black strip beneath a sky gradually growing red among the blue-gray—was dotted with the flashes of harquebus fire.

"Forward for Spain! Attack! Attack!"

It was awkward running along the sandy bed of the river, and my legs seemed as heavy as lead when I reached the other side, where a hawthorn hedge protected the livestock. I tripped over a motionless body fallen on the ground and ran a few steps farther only to scratch myself on the spiny branches. God's teeth! There was the sound of harquebus fire on our side too now, while the silhouettes of my comrades, which were no longer black but gray enough for me to be able to recognize them, rushed like a torrent through the tents, where I caught sudden glimpses of lit fires or terrified figures who either fought or fled. To the shouting of Spaniards and *mogataces*, reinforced by the thundering hooves of our cavalry charging in from the other side, was added that of dozens of women and children wrenched from sleep and who were now emerging from their tents, clinging to one another or running to their menfolk, also barely awake, but who, in trying to protect them, fought desperately and died. I saw Sebastián Copons and others hurl themselves among these people, cutting and slashing, and I followed suit, wielding my half-pike and losing it at my first encounter, when I plunged it into the half-naked body of a bearded Arab who emerged from a tent bearing a scimitar. He fell at my feet without uttering a sound, but I didn't have time to recover my pike, because another young Moor, even younger than me, came out of the same tent in his nightshirt and started lashing out at me with a dagger so fiercely that if he had hit home, Christ and the Devil would have been well served, and the people of Oñate would have had one fellow countryman less. I staggered backward, meanwhile drawing my sword—an excellent galley sword, broad and short and bearing the mark of Toledo on its blade. Fighting back with more aplomb now, I managed to slice off half his nose with my first blow and the fingers of his hand with my second. He was already on the ground when I delivered a third and final blow, slitting his throat with a backward slash. Then I peered cautiously inside the tent and saw a huddle of women and children in one corner, screaming and shouting in their own language. I let the curtain fall, turned, and went off about my own business.

It was nearly over. Diego Alatriste kicked away the Moor he had just killed, removed his sword from the man's body, and looked around. The Arabs were barely resisting now, and most of the attackers were more concerned with plundering what they could—almost as if they were Englishmen. He could still hear harquebus fire in the encampment, but the screams of rage, despair, and death had given way to the groans of the wounded, the moans of prisoners, and the buzz of flies swarming crazily above the pools of blood. The soldiers and *mogataces* were rounding up and dragging from their tents—as if they were mere livestock—women, children, the old, and any men who had thrown down their arms, while others were collecting any objects of value and rounding up the real livestock. The women—their children clinging to their skirts or clutched to their bosom—were screaming and striking their own faces at the sight of the corpses of fathers, husbands, brothers, and children; some, overwhelmed by pain and rage, were trying to scratch the soldiers, who were

obliged to beat them off. The men were clustered together
in a separate group; bewildered, bruised, wounded, and
terrified, they squatted in the dust, guarded by swords,
pikes, and harquebuses. Others—grown men and older
people trying somehow to preserve their dignity—were
shoved unceremoniously aside or slapped around the face
by the victorious soldiers. The order, as usual, was not to kill
anyone who could bring in some money, but this was the
soldiers' way of avenging the deaths of the half-dozen or
so comrades who had lost their lives in the assault. This dis-
pleased Alatriste, who was of the view that while one could
kill a man, one should not humiliate him, still less in front
of friends and family. That century, however, like most
centuries, was not particularly abundant in scruples. Embarrassed, he looked across at the outskirts of the encampment. Among the hills, the soldiers on horseback were
pursuing any Moors who had managed to escape and hide
among the reedbeds and fig trees and were leading back
those they caught, hands tied to the tails of the horses.

Some of the plundered tents were burning now, with all
the furniture, pots, silver, carpets, and clothes piled up outside, while Sergeant Major Biscarrués, who came and went,
keeping an eye on everything, shouted to his men to look
lively and get the booty together so that they could leave.
Diego Alatriste saw him squint up at the newly risen sun
and then glance anxiously about him. It wasn't hard for

Alatriste, a fellow soldier, to guess his thoughts. A column of tired Spaniards, taking with them a hundred or so livestock and more than two hundred captives—this, he calculated, was what they had gleaned from the cavalcade—would be extremely vulnerable to attacks by hostile Moors if they were not safe inside the walls of Oran by sunset.

Alatriste's throat was as dry as the sand and stone he walked on. "'Od's teeth," he thought, "I can't even spit out the dust and blood that are making my tongue stick to my palate." He looked about him and met the gaze, at once friendly and fierce, of a red-bearded *mogataz* who was earnestly beheading a dead Arab. Closer to him, an old Moorish woman was kneeling down tending a badly wounded man, whose head rested in her lap. She had a very wrinkled face, with blue tattoos on forehead and hands, and when Alatriste stopped in front of her, sword still in his hand, she looked up at him with inexpressive eyes.

"*Ma,*" he said. Water. "*Ma.*"

She didn't respond until he touched her shoulder with the point of his sword. Then she gestured indifferently toward a large tent made of goatskins and, once again ignoring everything else going on around her, continued to tend the wounded Moor who lay moaning on the ground. Alatriste headed for the tent, drew back the curtain, and went in.

As soon as he did so, he realized that he was going to have problems.

I spotted Captain Alatriste in the distance, among all the plundering and the comings and goings of soldiers and prisoners, and I was glad to see that he was safe. I tried to call to him, but he didn't hear me; and so I headed in his direction, avoiding the tents that were beginning to burn, the heaps of clothing, the wounded and the dead strewn everywhere. I saw him go inside a large, black tent, and I saw, too, that someone went in after him. I couldn't quite see who it was, but he looked like one of our Moors, a *mogataz*. Then a corporal stopped me and ordered me to keep watch over a group of Arabs while they were being tied up. This delayed me briefly, but, when I had finished, I continued on toward the tent. I lifted the curtain, crouched down to go inside, and was astonished by what I saw: in one corner, on an untidy pile of mats and rugs, lay a young Moorish woman, half naked, whom the captain was helping to get dressed. She had a bruise on her tear-stained face and was wailing like an animal in torment. At her feet lay a child of only a few months, waving its arms about, and next to her was one of our soldiers, a Spaniard, his belt unbuckled, his breeches around his knees, and his head blown open. Another Spaniard, fully clothed but with his throat slit from ear to ear, lay faceup near the entrance, with blood gushing from the wound. In the few moments in which I was still able to think clearly, it occurred to me that the very same blood was staining the blade of the curved dagger that a surly, bearded *mogataz* pressed to my throat as soon as I entered. All of these things—well, put yourself in my place, dear reader—drew from me an exclamation of surprise that made the captain turn around.

"It's all right. He's like a son to me," he said quickly. "He won't talk."

The *mogataz*'s breath, which I could feel on my face, suddenly stopped for a moment, while he studied me closely with his bright, dark eyes edged with dense eyelashes worthy of a woman. That, however, was the only delicate thing about his tanned, weather-beaten face; and his pointed reddish beard only accentuated the fierce expression that froze my blood. He must have been about thirty or so, and he was of average build, but with powerful shoulders and arms. Apart from the usual lock of hair at the back, his head was shaven, and he wore a long scarf looped about his neck, silver earrings in each ear, and, on his left cheekbone, a strange blue tattoo in the form of a cross. He duly removed the dagger from my throat and wiped it on his gray-striped burnoose before putting it back in the leather scabbard at his waist.

What happened?" I asked the captain.

He got slowly to his feet. The woman, filled with fear and shame, covered herself with a gray-brown veil. The *mogataz* said a few words to her in her own language—something like *"barra barra"*—and she, picking up her crying child and wrapping it in the same veil, walked lightly past us, head bowed, and left the tent.

"What happened," said the captain calmly, "is that these two valiants and I had a disagreement over the meaning of the word 'booty.'"

He crouched down to pick up the pistol he had just fired and stuck it in his belt. Then he looked at the *mogataz*, who was still standing in the entrance to the tent, and something like a smile appeared on his lips.

"Things weren't going too well for me and were rapidly getting worse when this Moor appeared and took my part."

He had joined us now and was studying the *mogataz* very intently, from top to toe, and he seemed to like what he saw.

"Speak Spanish?" he asked.

"I do," the Moor replied in good Castilian.

The captain looked at the dagger in the man's belt.

"That's a good knife you have there."

"I think so."

"And an even better hand."

"*Uah*. So they say."

They regarded each other for a few moments in silence.

"What's your name?"

"Aixa Ben Gurriat."

If I was expecting more words, more explanations, I was disappointed. A half-smile similar to the captain's appeared on the Moor's bearded face.

"Let's go," the captain said, taking one last look at the corpses. "But first, we'd better set fire to the tent. That way we avoid any awkward explanations."

This proved to be an unnecessary precaution. No one missed the two ruffians—we learned later that they were a pair of friendless, low-life no-goods—and their names were simply added to the list of men lost. As for the return journey, it proved hard and dangerous, but triumphant too. The road from Tlemcen to Oran, beneath a vertical sun that reduced our shadows to a dark line at our feet, was filled by a long column of soldiers, captives, plunder, and livestock, with the beasts—sheep, goats, cows, and the occasional camel—in the vanguard, in the care of *mogataces* and Moors from Ifre. Before leaving Wadi Berruch, however, we had experienced a moment of great tension, when the interpreter, Cansino, after interrogating the prisoners, fell silent, turning this way and that. Then he reluctantly informed Sergeant Major Biscarrués that we had attacked the wrong place, that the *mogataz* guides had made a mistake—or had deliberately misled us—and directed us to an encampment inhabited by peaceful Moors who always paid their dues promptly. We had killed thirty-six of them, and I assure you I have never seen anyone get as angry as the sergeant major did then. He turned bright scarlet, the veins in his neck and forehead bulged as if they were about to burst, and he swore that he would have every guide hanged, along with their forefathers, their whorish mothers, and their porcine progenitors. The fit of rage was quickly over, though. After all, there was nothing to be done, and so, ever the practical soldier, prepared for whatever life might throw at him, Biscarrués finally calmed down. Regardless of whether they were peaceful or hostile, he concluded, they would still fetch a good price in Oran. They were certainly hostile Moors now, and there was no more to be said.

"What's done is done," he said, settling the matter. "We'll be more careful next time. So not a word, eh, and if anyone's tongue runs away with him, by Christ, I'll tear it out myself."

And so, after tending the wounded and having something to eat—bread baked in the ashes, a few dates, and some curdled milk we'd found at the encampment—we marched with a lighter step, harquebuses at the ready, and keeping a watchful eye open, hoping to find ourselves safe back in town before nightfall. And on we went, with the

livestock in the vanguard, followed by most of the troops
and the baggage, and then, in the middle, well guarded, the
captives, of whom there were two hundred and forty-eight
men and women and those children of an age to walk. Another select squad of soldiers, armed with pikes and harquebuses brought up the rear, while the cavalry either
rode on ahead or protected our flanks, just in case any hostile Moors should try to block our retreat or deprive us of
water. There were, in fact, a few minor fights and skirmishes, and before we reached a place known as the her-
mit's well, where there were plenty of palm trees and
carobs, the Arabs, a good number of whom were hard on
our heels on the lookout for stragglers or some other opportunity, made a serious attempt to keep us from the
water: a hundred or so bold horsemen, shouting and hurling the usual obscenities, attacked our rear guard, whoop-
ing and screaming. However, when our harquebusiers
prepared their weapons and sprayed them with lead, the
horsemen turned tail, leaving some of their men dying on
the field, and that was that. We were in high spirits over
our victory and over the booty, and were eager to reach
Oran and claim our share. The lines from a well-known
song came spontaneously to my young lips:

Such was the custom of the age,
That a fiercely gallant knife or sword,

Which put to death a slew of Moors
Would also glorify Our Lord.

Nevertheless, two incidents overshadowed any pleasure I felt during the retreat from Wadi Berruch. One involved a newborn baby who, though dying in his mother's arms, was still not spared the rigors of the march. When he saw this, the chaplain, Father Tomás Rebollo, who had accompanied the cavalcade as part of his duties, summoned the sergeant major and said that since the child was dying, the mother had therefore lost all her maternal rights, which meant that he could legitimately baptize the child against her will. Given that there was no council of theologians on hand to pronounce on the matter, Biscarrués, who had other things on his mind, told the priest to do as he thought best, and the priest, ignoring the mother's protests, snatched the child from her and baptized it there and then, with a few drops of water, oil, and salt. The child died shortly afterward, and the chaplain congratulated himself, saying that, on such a day—when so many enemies of God, members of the pernicious sect of Mohammed, had been condemned to Hell—an angel had been sent up to Heaven to learn more of its secret judgments and to confound its enemies, et cetera, et cetera. Later, we learned that the Marchioness of Velada, the governor's wife—a very pious woman who gave alms, said her rosary and took Communion daily—praised Father Tomás' decision and ordered that the mother be sent for so that she could console her and convince her that she would one day be reunited with her son, thus converting the mother to the one true faith. This proved impossible. On the same night that we arrived back in Oran, the woman hanged herself out of despair and shame.

The other lingering memory is that of a little Moorish boy of about six or seven who kept pace with the mules on which were tied the heads of the dead Arabs. At the time, the governor of Oran offered a reward —or, rather, said he would—for every Moor killed in an act of war, and, as I said, the raid on Wadi Berruch was deemed to be just that. And so, to provide the necessary proof, we were carrying the heads of thirty-six adult Moors, who, once counted, would add a few *maravedís* to our share of the booty. Anyway, the boy was walking alongside a mule on which a dozen heads were slung in bunches on either side of the saddle. Well, if the life of any clear-thinking man is full of ghosts that come to him in the dark and keep him from sleeping—and by God, my life has more than its share— what stays with me is the image of that grubby, barefoot, runny-nosed child, his tears carving dirty trails down his dusty cheeks, walking next to the mule, and returning again and again, however often the guards drove him off, to brush away the flies from his father's severed head.

The House of La Salka was both a brothel and a smoke room, and that is where we set up our quarters the following day, as soon as the sale of booty was over. The whole of Oran had been celebrating since the night before, when, with the last light of day, once we had left the livestock in the pens at Las Piletas, near the river, we made our triumphal entry through the Tlemcen gate, marching in squadrons with the captives going before us, flanked by soldiers bearing arms. We marched along the torchlit road, heading straight for the main church, where the slaves, hands bound, were paraded past the Holy Sacrament that the priest had brought to the door, accompanied by clergy, cross, and holy water. And once the Te Deum had been sung, in recognition of our victory, every owl went off to his own olive tree until the following day, when the real celebrations began, for the sale of slaves proved highly lucrative, bringing in the goodly sum of forty-nine thousand six hundred ducats. Once the governor's share had been deducted, as well as the king's quint, which, in Oran, was used to buy supplies and munitions, and once what was owed to the officers, the Church, the veterans' hospital, and the *mogataces* had been paid out, and the remainder distributed among the troops, the captain and I found ourselves richer by five hundred and sixty *reales* each, which meant that we had the agreeable weight of seventy fine pieces of eight in our respective purses. Sebastián Copons, given his rank and position, earned somewhat more. And so, as soon as we had collected our money from the house of a relative of the interpreter Aron Cansino—we almost had to get our knives out at one point because he wanted to fob us off with coins that had not been weighed or that were worn too smooth at the edges—we decided, naturally enough, to spend a little of it. And there the three of us were, in the house of La Salka, enjoying ourselves to the hilt.

The owner of the brothel was a middle-aged Moorish woman, baptized a Christian, the widow of a soldier, and an old acquaintance of Sebastián Copons, who assured us that, within reasonable limits, she was a thoroughly trustworthy person. The whorehouse was near the Marina gate, in the terraced houses behind the old tower. From the roof there was a pleasant view over the countryside, with the castle of San Gregorio to the left, dominating the bay full of galleys and other ships below, and in the background, like a grayish wedge between the port and the blue immensity of the Mediterranean, stood the fort of Mazalquivir, with its gigantic cross before it. At the time I am describing, the sun was already setting over the sea, and its warm rays fell on Captain Alatriste, Copons, and myself as

we sat on soft leather cushions in one corner of the roof terrace, our every wish granted, well supplied as we were with
drink and food and the other things one finds in such
places. We were accompanied by three of La Salka's girls
with whom, shortly before, we had shared rather more
than mere words, although stopping short at the final
trench; for the captain and Copons, very sensibly, had managed to persuade me that it was one thing to take pleasure
in female company and quite another to loose one's bow, so
to speak, and risk catching the French disease or any of the
many other illnesses with which such public women—
extremely public in the case of Oran— could ruin the health
and life of the unwary. They were decent enough doxies;
there were two not unattractive Christians from Andalusia
who had come to earn their living in Oran where they had
ended up after suffering far worse vicissitudes, having
come from the bordellos of the Sahara, which, in their profession, were the deadest of dead ends; the third was a
renegade Moor, too dark for Spanish tastes, but a handsome creature nonetheless and skilled in arts not written
about in books. At the clink of our fresh new silver coins,
La Salka had brought them to us, telling us how clean and
sensual they were, these graduates in the art of making
the beast with two backs, although, as I say, we ourselves
did not indulge in the latter. Even so, I would give my oath
as a good Basque that La Salka was not exaggerating as

regards the woman who fell to me—the Moor, because I was the youngest.

But we did not only eat and drink, for as well as encountering some unusual spices, rather too strong for my taste, it was also the first time I had smoked the Moorish weed, prepared with great dexterity by one of the women, who mixed it with tobacco in long wooden pipes with metal bowls. I had never been keen on the stuff, not even in the form of the snuff that don Francisco de Quevedo so enjoyed, but I was a novice in Barbary and eager to try anything new. And so, although the captain declined the experience and Copons took only a couple of puffs, I smoked a whole pipeful and sat there, flaccid and smiling, my head spinning and my words slurred, feeling as if my body were floating above the town and the sea. This did not prevent me from taking part in the conversation, which, despite the generally joyful situation and the money we had on us, was not, at that moment, a cheerful one. We knew by then that our galley was due to weigh anchor in two days' time, and Copons, who would have liked to come to Naples with us or, indeed, anywhere, would have to stay in Oran, because the powers that be would still not grant him license to leave.

"So," he said somberly, "it looks like I'll be left to rot here until kingdom come."

Having said that, he downed a whole pitcher of Málaga

wine—which, although a little sour, was strong and flavorful—and sighed. I was gazing distractedly at the three doxies, who, seeing us deep in conversation, had left us alone and were standing, chatting, at the far end of the terrace and waving to any passing soldiers. La Salka knew how freely money flowed after a cavalcade and she had her corsairs well trained not to miss any opportunity to drum up trade.

"Perhaps there is a way," said Captain Alatriste.

We both looked at him with interest, especially the usually impassive Copons, who had an expectant gleam in his eyes. He knew his former comrade never spoke lightly.

"Do you mean a way of getting Sebastián out of Oran?" I asked.

"Yes."

Copons placed one hand on the captain's arm, exactly on the spot where the captain had inflicted a burn on himself years before in Seville, when he was interrogating that Genoan Garaffa.

"God's teeth, Diego, I'm not going to desert. I never have, and I'm not going to start now."

The captain smoothed his mustache and smiled at his friend. It was a rare smile in him, affectionate and frank.

"No, I'm talking about you leaving here honorably, with your license neatly rolled up inside a nice tin tube. As is only proper."

Copons seemed bewildered. "But I've told you already that Sergeant Major Biscarrués won't grant me license to leave. No one gets out of Oran, you know that. Or only those who are passing through."

Alatriste glanced over at the three women and lowered his voice.

"How much money have you got?"

Copons frowned, wondering what on earth that had to do with anything. Then he understood and shook his head.

"Don't even consider it," he said. "Even with what I earned from the cavalcade, I wouldn't have enough."

"How much?" insisted the captain.

"Not counting what I'm going to spend here, about eighty *escudos*. Perhaps a few *maravedís* more. But like I say . . ."

"Just suppose you struck lucky, what's the first thing you would do in Naples?"

Copons laughed. "What a question! In Italy and without a penny in my pocket? I'd enlist again, of course. With the two of you, if I could."

They sat looking at each other for a while in silence. I was gradually descending from the clouds and was watching them closely. The mere idea that Copons might come with us to Naples made me want to shout for joy.

"Diego . . ."

Despite the doubtful tone in which Copons uttered the captain's name, the same hopeful gleam was still there in his eyes. The captain took another sip of wine, thought for a moment longer and nodded.

"Your eighty *escudos*, plus my remaining sixty or so from the cavalcade, make ..."

He was counting on his fingers on the brass tray that served as a table; then he turned to look at me. The captain may have been fast with a sword, but that speed did not extend to arithmetic. I made a great effort to drive away the last vaporous clouds from my mind. I rubbed my forehead.

"One hundred and forty," I said.

"That's nothing," said Copons. "Biscarrués would demand five times that amount for me to buy myself out."

"We have five times that amount, at least I think we do. Let's see ... One hundred and forty, plus my two hundred from the galliot we sold in Melilla."

"You have that much money?" asked an astonished Copons.

"Yes, the strokesman—a Gypsy from Perchel, condemned to ten years on the galley and more feared than the galley master himself—he keeps it safe for me at half a *reale*'s interest per week. What does that come to, Íñigo?"

"Three hundred and forty," I said.

"Right, add in your sixty *escudos*."

"What?"

"Add them in," he said, and his pale eyes pierced me like daggers. "What does that make?"

"Four hundred."

"That's not enough. Add in your two hundred from the galliot."

I opened my mouth to protest, but from the look the captain gave me, I realized it was useless. The last threads of cottony cloud vanished at once. Farewell, savings, I said to myself, my head suddenly clear. It had been wonderful to feel rich—while it lasted.

"Six hundred *escudos* exactly," I said, resigned now.

Captain Alatriste turned to Copons, his face radiant.

"With the back pay that's owed to you—which, when it arrives, will go straight into your sergeant major's pocket—that's more than enough."

Copons swallowed hard, looking from me to the captain and back again, as if the words had got stuck in his throat. I couldn't help, once again, remembering him in different situations: on the front line at the battle of the Ruyter mill, deep in the mud of the Breda trenches, smeared with gunpowder and blood at the Terheyden redoubt, sword in hand in a Sevillean garden, or scrambling aboard the *Niklaasbergen* at Barra de Sanlúcar. Always the same: small, silent, wiry, hard.

"God's teeth," he said.

4. THE MOGATAZ

Having donned hats and buckled on swords, we left the whorehouse as evening was coming on and the first shadows were beginning to fill the most secluded corners of Oran's steep streets. It was a very pleasant temperature at that hour, perfect for a stroll. The town's inhabitants were sitting on chairs or stools at the doors of their houses and a few shops were still open, lit inside by oil lamps and tallow candles. The streets were full of soldiers from the galleys as well as from the barracks, all still celebrating their good fortune on the cavalcade. We stopped again to wet our whistles—the wine this time was a decent claret—and stood leaning against a wall opposite a small makeshift tavern installed in the porch of a house and attended by an old cripple. While we were there, a party of five captives, led by a constable, came down the street. They were all chained together, three men and two women, and had obviously been among those sold that morning. They were being led home under guard by their new master, who was dressed all in black, wearing a ruff and a sword, and who had the look of some functionary grown rich by stealing the wages of the men who had risked their lives capturing those people. All the slaves, including the two women, had been branded on the face with an "S" that identified them as slaves, and they walked along, heads bowed, resigned to their fate. Branding them was quite unnecessary, and some considered it old-fashioned and cruel, but the law still allowed slave owners to mark them like that so that they could be identified should they attempt to run away. I saw that the captain had looked away in disgust, and I imagined the mark—made not with red-hot iron, but with cold steel—that I would make on the master of those poor unfortunates if ever I had the chance. I hoped that when he traveled back to Spain, he would be captured by some Berber pirates, end up in the prisons of Algiers, and be soundly beaten. Although, I thought bitterly, people like him had more than enough money to buy their freedom. Only poor soldiers and humble folk—and thousands were captured at sea or on the Spanish coast—would rot there in Tunis, Bizerta, Tripoli, or Constantinople, with no one to pay their ransom.

It was while absorbed in these thoughts that I noticed

someone walk past and then stop a little farther on to observe us. I realized that he was the *mogataz* who had helped Captain Alatriste in Wadi Berruch. He was wearing the same clothes: a gray-striped burnoose and the classic Arab *rexa* worn loosely draped about his neck so that his shaven head—apart from the warrior's lock of hair at the back— was bare. The long dagger that had, for a moment, been pressed against my throat—it still made my skin prickle to think of its blade—was tucked in his sash, inside its leather sheath. I turned to point him out to Captain Alatriste, but realized that he had already spotted him, although he said not a word. They observed each other in silence at a distance of six or seven paces, the *mogataz* standing quite still in the street, among the passing crowds, calmly holding the captain's gaze, as if he were waiting for something. Finally, the captain touched the brim of his hat and bowed slightly. This, in a soldier and a man like him, was more than mere courtesy, especially when directed at a Moor, even if he was a *mogataz* and, therefore, a friend of Spain. Nevertheless, the Moor accepted this greeting as his natural due and responded with an affirmative nod, and then, with equal aplomb, seemed about to continue on his way. However, I thought I saw him stop again farther on, at the far end of the street, in the shadow of a low archway.

"Let's go and see Fermín Malacalza," said Copons to the captain. "He'll be pleased to see you."

This Malacalza fellow, whom I did not know, was a former comrade of the captain and Copons and now an old soldier in the Oran barracks, but who had shared dangers and miseries with them in Flanders when he was a corporal, risen from the ranks, in the squadron in which Alatriste, Copons, and my father, Lope Balboa, had all fought. Copons explained that Malacalza, old before his time, in ill health and invalided out of the army, had stayed on in Oran, where he had family. As poor as everyone else there, he survived thanks to the help of a few fellow soldiers, among them Copons, who, whenever he happened to have a little money in his purse, would drop by and visit him with a few *maravedís*. And this was the case now, with the added satisfaction that Malacalza, as a former soldier in the regiment, albeit retired, was still eligible to receive a small portion of the general booty won in Wadi Berruch. Copons had been charged with delivering it to him, although I suspect he had added a few coins from his own pocket.

"The Moor is following us," I said to the captain.

We were near Malacalza's house, walking down a wretched, narrow little street in the upper part of the city, where the men were sitting at the doors of their houses and the children were playing among the grime and the rubble. And it was true, the *mogataz*, who had stayed close by after he passed us outside the tavern, was some twenty paces behind, never coming too near, but making no attempt to hide either. When he noticed this, the captain glanced over his shoulder and, after observing the Moor for a moment, said:

"The street's free to anyone."

It was odd, I thought, that a Moor should be out after sunset. In Oran, as in Melilla, they were very strict about that, hoping to avoid any unpleasant surprises; and when the town gates were closed, all Moors, apart from a privileged few, left, and those who had come in during the day to sell vegetables, meat, and fruit went back to Ifre or to their respective encampments. Any others stayed in the guarded area known as the *morería*, near the casbah, where they remained safely until the following day. This man, though, appeared to move about freely, which made me think that he was known and in possession of the necessary safe-conducts. This only aroused my curiosity the more, but I stopped thinking about him as soon as we reached the house of Fermín Malacalza, whom, I could not forget, had been a comrade of my father's. Had my father survived the harquebus shot that killed him beneath the walls of Jülich, he would perhaps have met the same sad fate as the man who faced me now: a scrawny, grayhaired remnant, consumed by poverty; fifty years old, but looking more like seventy—seventeen of those years spent in Oran—lame in one leg and with his skin the color of grubby parchment, lined and scarred. His eyes were the only part of his face that had retained their vigor—for even his old soldier's mustache was the matte gray of ashes—and those eyes glittered with pleasure when he looked up from his chair at the door of his house and saw before him Captain Alatriste's smile.

"By Beelzebub, the whore that bore him, and all the Lutheran devils in Hell!"

He insisted that we come in and tell him what brought us there and so that we could meet his family. The small, dark house, lit by a guttering oil lamp, smelled of mold and rancid stew. A soldier's sword, with a broad guard and large quillons, hung on the wall. Two chickens were pecking at the crumbs of bread on the floor, and beside the water jug, a cat was greedily devouring a mouse. After many years in Barbary, and having lost all hope of ever leaving there as a soldier, Malacalza had ended up marrying a Moorish woman he bought after a cavalcade. He had forced her to be baptized a Christian, and she had since given him five children, who, barefoot and ragged, were making a tremendous row, running in and out of the house.

"Hey!" he called to his wife. "Bring us some wine!"

We protested, because we were already a little tipsy after our sojourn at La Salka's house and in the tavern in the street, but Malacalza would not take no for an answer.

"We may lack for everything here," he said, hobbling

about the one room, unrolling a rough mat, and bringing more stools up to the table, "but we never lack for a glass of wine for two old comrades to moisten their gullets."

"Or, rather, three," he said, when he learned that I was the son of Lope Balboa. His wife came in shortly afterward, a dark, stocky woman, still young, but worn out by childbirth and hard work. Her hair was caught back in a plait, and she was dressed like a Spanish woman apart from her slippers, her silver bangles, and the blue tattoos on the backs of her hands. We doffed our hats and sat down at the rickety pine table, where she poured wine into a motley selection of chipped mugs before withdrawing to one corner of the kitchen without saying a word.

"A fine woman," said the captain politely.

Malacalza nodded brusquely.

"She's clean and she's honest," he said simply. "A bit quick-tempered, but obedient. Moorish women make good wives as long as you keep your eye on them. A lot of Spanish women could learn a thing or two from them, instead of putting on airs."

"Indeed," said the captain gravely.

A skinny child of three or four with dark, curly hair approached shyly and clung to his father, who kissed him tenderly and sat him on his lap. The other four, the oldest of whom could not have been more than twelve, watched us from the door. They were barefoot and had dirty knees.

Copons put some coins down on the table, and Malacalza looked at them, without touching them. Then he glanced up at Captain Alatriste and winked.

"As you see, Diego," he said, picking up his mug of wine and raising it to his lips, indicating the room with a sweeping gesture of his other hand. "A veteran of the king's army. Thirty-five years of service, four wounds, rheumatism in my bones," he slapped his injured thigh, "and one lame leg. Not a bad record really, given that I started in Flanders before either you or I or Sebastián here, or poor Lope, may he rest in peace," and he raised his glass to me in homage, "were even of shaving age."

He spoke without great bitterness and in the resigned tones proper to the profession, like someone merely stating what every mother's son knows. The captain leaned toward him across the table.

"Why don't you go back to Spain? You're free to do so."

"Go back? To what?" Malacalza was stroking his son's curly black locks. "To show off my bad leg at the door of a church and beg for alms along with all the others?"

"You could go back to your village. You're from Navarra, aren't you? From the Baztán valley, isn't that right?"

"Yes, from Alzate. But what would I do there? If anyone remembers me, which I doubt, can't you just imagine the neighbors pointing at me and saying: there's another one who swore he'd come back rich and a gentleman, but, look at him, a poor cripple, living off the charity of nuns.

At least here, there's always the odd cavalcade, and there's always help too, however little, for a veteran with a family. Besides, there's my wife." He stroked his son's face and indicated the other children standing in the doorway. "Not to mention these little rascals. I couldn't take my family there, with the Holy Office's informers whispering behind my back and the Inquisitors after me. So I prefer to stay here, where things are clearer. Do you understand?"

"I do."

"Then there are my comrades, people like you, Sebastián, people you can talk to. I can always walk down to the harbor and see the galleys or to the gates and watch the soldiers coming and going. Sometimes I visit the barracks, and the men, the ones who still know me, buy me a drink. I still attend the parades and the campaign masses and the salutes to the flag, like I did when I was on active service. All of that helps to soothe any nostalgia I might have."

He looked at Copons, urging him to agree with him. Copons, however, gave only a curt nod and said nothing. Malacalza poured him some more wine and smiled, one of those smiles that requires a certain degree of courage.

"Besides," he went on, "you're never really retired here, not like in Spain. We're a kind of reserve, you see. Sometimes the Moors attack and besiege the town, and the help we need doesn't always arrive. Then they call on every man available to defend the walls and the bulwarks, even us invalids."

He paused for a moment and smoothed his gray mustache, half closing his eyes as if evoking pleasant memories. Then he looked sadly up at the sword hanging on the wall.

"For a few days," he said, "it's just like it used to be. There's even the possibility that the Moors will press home their victory and that a fellow might die like the man he is... or was."

His voice had changed. Had it not been for the child in his arms and those standing in the doorway, he would not, one felt, have minded meeting such a death that very night.

"Not a bad way to go," agreed the captain.

Malacalza slowly turned to look at him, as if returning from somewhere far away.

"I'm an old man now, Diego. I know exactly what to expect from Spain and her people. Here, at least, they know who I am. Having been a soldier still means something in Oran, but over there, they don't give a fig for our service records, full of names they've forgotten, if, indeed, they ever knew them: the del Caballo redoubt, the Durango fort... What does it matter to a scribe, a judge, a royal functionary, a shopkeeper, or a friar, whether, in the dunes at Nieuwpoort, we withdrew calmly, flags held high, without breaking ranks, or ran like rabbits..."

He stopped speaking for a moment to pour out the little wine that remained in the jug.

"Look at Sebastián. He's sitting there as silent as ever, but he agrees with me. See, he's nodding."

He placed his right hand on the table, next to the jar, and

studied it hard. It was thin and bony, with the same scars on knuckles and wrist that Copons and the captain bore.

"Ah, reputation," he murmured.

There was a long silence. Then Malacalza raised his mug to his lips and chuckled to himself.

"Anyway, here I am, a veteran soldier in the king of Spain's army."

He looked again at the coins on the table.

"The wine's finished," he said, suddenly somber. "And I'm sure you have other things to do."

We got to our feet, picking up our hats, not knowing what to say. Malacalza remained seated.

"Before you go," he said, "I'd just like to list those places on our service records that no one else cares about: Calais . . . Amiens . . . Bomel . . . Nieuwpoort . . . Ostend . . . Oldensel . . . Linghen . . . Jülich . . . Oran. Amen."

As he said each name, he picked up the few coins one by one, his eyes vacant. Then he seemed to recover himself, weighing the coins in his hand before putting them in his purse. Kissing the child on his lap and depositing him on the floor, he got to his feet, holding his mug of wine in one hand and resting his weight on his bad leg.

"To the king, may God keep him safe."

And I thought it odd that there was not a hint of irony in his words.

"To the king," echoed Captain Alatriste. "And despite the king or whoever else is in charge."

Then all four of us turned toward the old sword hanging on the wall and drank a toast.

It was dark by the time we left Malacalza's house. We walked down the street, which was lit only by the light coming from the open doors of the houses—inside we could just make out the dark shapes of the people sitting there—and by the candles burning in the wall niches of various saints. Just then, a silhouette emerged from the shadows, getting up from the ground where it had been crouched and waiting. This time, the captain did not simply give the figure a backward glance; he removed the buffcoat he had draped over his shoulders so as to leave sword and dagger unencumbered. And thus, with me and Copons following behind, he went straight up to the dark silhouette and asked straight out:

"What do you want?"

The other man, who had been standing perfectly still, moved a little into the light. He did so deliberately, as if he wanted us to be able to see him more clearly and dissipate any fears we might have.

"I don't know," he said.

He delivered this disconcerting answer in a Castilian as good as the captain's, Sebastián's, or mine.

"Well, you're taking a chance, following us like that."

"Oh, I don't think so."

He said this very confidently and impassively, looking at the captain without even blinking.

"Why is that?"

"I saved your life, my friend."

I shot a sideways glance at the captain, to see if such familiarity had angered him. I knew he was perfectly capable of killing someone who addressed him in what he judged to be an inappropriate fashion. To my surprise, though, I saw that he held the *mogataz*'s gaze and didn't seem in the least put out. He put his hand in his pocket, and at that point, the Moor took a step back as if he had received an insult.

"Is that what your life is worth? *Zienaashin?* Money?"

He was clearly an educated Moor, someone with a story to tell, and no ordinary Arab. We could see his face clearly now, his silver earrings glittering in the light of a candle. His skin was not particularly dark and his beard had a reddish tone to it. On his left cheek was that tattooed cross with diamond-shaped points. He was wearing a bracelet, also in silver, on the wrist of one hand, which he was holding open, palm up, as if to show that he was concealing nothing in it and that he was keeping it well away from the dagger at his waist.

"Then go on your way, and we'll go on ours."

We continued downhill until we reached the corner. I

turned at that point to see if the man was still following us. I tugged at Captain Alatriste's buffcoat and he looked back too. Copons made as if to unsheathe his dagger, but the captain grabbed his arm. Then he went over to the Moor again, taking his time, as if pondering what he was going to say to him.

"Listen, Moor . . ."

"My name is Aixa Ben Gurriat."

"I know what your name is. You told me at Wadi Berruch."

They stood motionless, studying each other in the gloom, with Copons and me a short distance away, observing them. The Moor was still making a point of keeping his hands well away from his dagger. I had one hand resting on the hilt of my sword, ready, at the slightest suspicious move on his part, to pin him to the wall. The captain, however, seemed not to share my unease. Instead, he stuck his thumbs in his belt, looked to either side, glanced briefly back at us, then leaned against the wall, next to the Moor.

"Why did you go into that tent?" he asked at last.

The other man took a while to respond.

"I heard a shot. I had seen you fighting earlier on, and you seemed to be a good *imyahad*, a good fighter, a very good fighter."

"I don't usually get involved in other people's business."

"Nor do I, but I went into the tent and I saw that you were defending a Moorish woman."

"Whether she was a Moor or not makes no difference. The men were a pretty unsavory pair, and arrogant and insolent to boot. The woman was the least of it."

The *mogataz* clicked his tongue.

"*Tidt.* True, but you could have looked the other way, or even joined in the fun."

"So could you. Killing a Spaniard was a sure way of getting a noose around your neck—if anyone ever found out."

"But they didn't. Fate."

They fell silent again, but continued to look at each other, as if they were privately calculating which of them had incurred the greater debt, the Moor because the captain had defended a woman of his own race, or the captain because the Moor had saved his life. Meanwhile, Copons and I were exchanging glances, equally astonished by both the situation and the conversation.

"*Saad,*" murmured the captain, in the dog Arabic spoken in ports.

He said the word thoughtfully, as if repeating the last thing the *mogataz* had said. The latter smiled faintly and nodded.

"In my language we say *elkhadar,*" he said. "Fate and destiny are the same thing."

"Where are you from?"

The *mogataz* made a vague gesture.

"From around . . . from the mountains."

"Far away?"

"*Uah*. From very far away and from very high up."

"Is there something I can do for you?" asked the captain.

The other man shrugged. He appeared to be considering the question.

"I'm an *azuago*," he said at last, as if that explained everything. "From the tribe of the Beni Barrani."

"Well, you speak excellent Castilian."

"My mother was born a *zarumia*, a Christian. She was from Cádiz. She was captured as a child and they sold her on the beach of Arzeo, an abandoned town by the sea, seven leagues to the east, on the road to Mostaganem. My grandfather bought her for my father."

"That's an odd tattoo you have on your face. Odd for a Moor, I mean."

"It's an old story. We *azuagos* are descended from Christians, from the time when the Goths were still here, and for us it's a matter of *isbah*, of honor. That's why my grandfather wanted a Spanish wife for my father."

"And is that why you fight with us against other Moors?"

The *mogataz* shrugged stoically. "*Elkhadar*. Fate."

Having said that, he fell silent for a moment and stroked his beard. Then I thought I saw him smile again, his gaze abstracted.

"Beni Barrani means 'son of a foreigner,' you see. We're a tribe of men who have no homeland."

. . .

And that is how, after the cavalcade of Wadi Berruch in the year sixteen hundred and twenty-seven, Captain Alatriste and I met the mercenary Aixa Ben Gurriat, known among the Spaniards in Oran as the Moor Gurriato, a remarkable individual, and this is not the last time his name will be mentioned. For, hard though it is to believe, that night was the start of a seven-year friendship, the seven years that separated that day in Oran and a bloody day in September sixteen hundred and thirty-four, when the Moor Gurriato, the captain, and myself, along with many other comrades, fought shoulder to shoulder on that wretched hill at Nördlingen. After sharing many journeys, dangers, and adventures, and while the Idiáquez regiment, impassive as a rock, withstood fifteen charges by the Swedes in six hours without giving an inch, the Moor Gurriato would die before our eyes, like a good Spanish infantryman, defending a religion and a country not his own, always assuming he ever had either. He fell, at last, like so many, for an ungrateful, stingy Spain that gave him nothing in return, but which, for reasons known only to himself, Aixa Ben Gurriat, from the tribe of the *azuago* Beni Barrani, had resolved to serve to the death with the unshakable loyalty of a faithful murderous wolf. And he did so in a most unusual way, by choosing Captain Alatriste as his comrade.

.   .   .

Two days later, when the *Mulata* left the Barbary Coast behind and set off north-northwest, in the direction of Cartagena, Diego Alatriste had plenty of opportunity to observe the Moor Gurriato, because the latter was rowing in the fifth bench on the starboard side, next to the stroke. He did not have to wear chains, being what was called a *buena boya*, a word taken from the Italian *buonavoglia* and applied to volunteer crew members, who were usually either the dregs of the ports or desperate men on the run, willing to serve for a wage—the Turks called them *morlacos*, or jackals—and who sought refuge on a galley much as, on land, others might in a church. This is how they had managed to get the Moor on board, since he was determined to accompany Diego Alatriste and try his fortune with him. Once the captain had sorted out the problem of Sebastián Copons' license—Sergeant Major Biscarrués had been satisfied with five hundred ducats, plus Copons' back pay—he still had some *escudos* in his pocket, which meant that it would not have been hard to grease a few palms to simplify matters. This, however, proved unnecessary. The Moor had his own money—although where he had gotten it from he did not say—and after unrolling a kerchief that he wore beneath his sash, he took out a few silver coins which, despite being minted in Algiers, Fez, and Tlemcen, convinced the galley master and the overseer to take him on board, once the usual formalities had been gone through, namely a swift act of baptism, dredged up from somewhere or other, and to which no one objected, even though it was as false as a Judas kiss. That was enough for his name—Gurriato de Orán, they called him—to be written in the galley master's book, with a wage of eleven *reales* a month. It was thus established that, from then on, the *mogataz*, despite being a new convert and a galley man, was a good Catholic and a faithful volunteer in the king of Spain's army, a situation to which Gurriato accommodated himself as best he could. Ever shrewd and prudent, he had immediately adapted his appearance to suit his new circumstances by shaving off his warrior lock—leaving his head as smooth as that of any galley slave—and replacing *rexa*, sandals, caftan, and baggy trousers with breeches, shirt, cap, and a red doublet. All that remained of his former outfit was his dagger, stuck, as usual, in his sash, and the gray-striped burnoose, in which he slept or which he wrapped about himself in bad weather or when, like now, a favorable wind meant that he did not have to row. As for the tattoo on his face and his silver earrings, he was not the only one to wear such adornments.

"He's a strange one," commented Sebastián Copons.

He was sitting in the shade of the trinquet sail, overjoyed to have left Oran behind him. At his back, the mast supporting the lateen yard and its vast canvas sail creaked in the easterly wind and with the movement of the ship.

"No stranger than you or me," replied Alatriste.

He had spent all day observing the *mogataz*, trying to get the measure of the man. Seen from there, he seemed little different from the forced men, slaves, and convicts, who had no choice but to row with shackles on ankles or manacles on wrists. There were few who rowed out of necessity or choice, barely half a dozen among the two hundred rowers on the *Mulata*. To these one had to add the forced volunteers; this contradiction in terms could be explained by the very Spanish fact that—as with the soldiers in Oran and Melilla—the lack of manpower on the king's galleys meant that some galley slaves who had completed their sentences were not allowed to leave, but were kept on and paid the same wage as a free man. In theory, they would only continue to do so until others came to take their places, but since this rarely happened quickly, there were cases of former galley slaves who, having completed sentences of two, five, and even eight or ten years on the galley—few survived ten years, which was virtually a death sentence—found themselves obliged to stay on for a few months or years more.

"Look," said Copons. "He doesn't even budge when the other Muslims pray, just as if he really wasn't one of them."

Given the favorable wind, the oars were stowed and there was no need to row, and so both forced men and volunteers were idle. The former were lying down on their benches, or else doing their business over the side of the boat or in the latrines in the prow, or delicing each other, darning their clothes, or performing various tasks for sailors or soldiers. Certain trusted slaves, freed from their shackles, were allowed to come and go on the galley, washing clothes in seawater, or helping the cook prepare the beans for the stew that was steaming on the stove to port of the central gangway, between the mainmast and the supports for the awning. Two dozen or so of the slaves— Turks and Moors—were reciting one of their five daily prayers at their benches, facing east, kneeling, standing up, and then prostrating themselves. *La illah illallah, Mohammed rasul Allah* they chorused: There is no God but Allah, and Mohammed is His prophet. The soldiers and sailors in the corridors, embrasures, and gangway did nothing to prevent this. Equally, the Muslim galley slaves took no offense when a sail appeared on the horizon or the wind changed and orders were given to take up their oars, and the galley master's whip interrupted their prayers and returned them to their rowing and the rhythmic clink of chains. Everyone on the galley knew the rules of the game.

"He isn't one of them," said Alatriste. "I think, as he says, he really doesn't belong anywhere."

"And what about that story he told us about how his tribe used to be Christians?"

"It's possible. You've seen the cross on his face. And last night he was telling me something about a bronze bell that they kept hidden in a cave. The Moors don't have bells. And it's true that in the time of the Goths, when the Saracens arrived, there were people who refused to convert and took refuge in the mountains. It may be that over the centuries, the religion was lost, but things like that remained. Traditions, memories... And he does have a gingerish beard."

"That could be from his Christian mother."

"It could. But look at him. He obviously doesn't feel that he's a Moor."

"Nor a Christian, damn it."

"Oh, come off it, Sebastián. How often have you been to mass in the last twenty years?"

"As little as possible," Copons admitted.

"And how many of the Church's commandments have you broken since you've been a soldier?"

Copons gravely counted them off on his fingers.

"All of them," he concluded somberly.

"And does that stop you being a good soldier to your king?"

"Of course not."

"Well, then."

Diego Alatriste continued studying the Moor Gurriato, who was sitting with his feet dangling over the side of the galley as he contemplated the sea. This, apparently, was the first time the Moor had been on a ship, and despite the swell that had been buffeting them ever since they left behind them the cross of Mazalquivir, his stomach had remained steady; the same could not be said of some of the other men. The trick, it seemed, was to place some saffron paper over the heart.

"He's certainly not one to complain," said Alatriste. "And he adapts well too."

Copons grunted.

"You're telling me. I just vomited up some bile myself." He gave a crooked smile. "I obviously didn't even want to take *that* with me from Oran."

Alatriste nodded. Years before, he had found it difficult to adjust to the harsh galley life: the lack of space and privacy, the worm- and mouse-eaten hard-as-iron ship's biscuits, the muddy, brackish water, the cries of the sailors and the smell of the galley men, the itch and discomfort of clothes washed in salt water, the restless sleep on a hard board with a shield as pillow, your body always exposed to the sun, the heat, the rain, and the damp, cold nights at sea, which could leave you either with congestion or deafness. Not to mention the sickness when there was bad weather, the wild storms, and the dangers of battle, fighting on fragile boards that shifted beneath your feet and threatened to throw you into the sea at any moment. And all of this in the company of galley men, who were hardly the noblest of brotherhoods: slaves, heretics, forgers, criminals condemned to the lash, bearers of false witness, renegades, tricksters, perjurors, ruffians, highwaymen, swordsmen, adulterers, blasphemers, murderers, and thieves, who would never pass up the chance to throw dice or shuffle a greasy pack of cards. Not that the soldiers and sailors were any better, for whenever they went on land—in Oran, they'd had to hang a man to teach the others a lesson—there wasn't a chicken run they didn't plunder, an orchard they didn't pick clean, wine they didn't filch, food or clothes they didn't steal, a woman they didn't enjoy, nor a peasant they didn't abuse or kill. For, as the saying goes: Please God, leave the galley to some other poor sod.

"Do you really think he'll make a soldier?"

Copons was still looking at the Moor, as was Alatriste. The latter shrugged.

"That's up to him. For the moment, he's seeing a bit of the world, which is what he wanted."

Copons gestured scornfully in the direction of the rowing chamber and then tapped his nose eloquently. Given the stench from all that humanity crammed together on the rowing benches, among coils of rope and bundles of clothes, not to mention the stink from the bilge, it would have been hard to breathe were it not for the wind filling the sails.

"I think 'seeing the world' might be a slight exaggeration, Diego."

"Time will tell."

Copons was leaning on the gunwale, clearly still suspicious.

"Why have we brought him with us?" he asked at last.

Alatriste shrugged.

"No one brought him. He's free to go where he likes."

"But don't you find it odd that he should have chosen us as his comrades, for no reason?"

"Well, hardly for no reason. And think about it. You don't choose your comrades, they choose you."

The captain continued looking at the *mogataz* for a while longer, then pulled a face.

"Besides," he added thoughtfully, "it's still early days to be calling him our comrade."

Copons considered these words, then grunted again and said nothing more for a while.

"Do you know what I think, Sebastián?" said Alatriste.

"No, damn it, I don't. I never know what you're thinking."

"That something in you has changed. You talk more than you used to."

"Really?"

"Yes, really."

"It must be Oran. I spent too long there."

"Possibly."

Copons frowned, then removed the kerchief he wore around his head and wiped the sweat from his neck and face.

"And is that good or bad?" he asked after a pause.

"I'm not sure. It's just different."

"Ah."

Copons was scrutinizing his kerchief as if it held the answer to a complicated question.

"I'm just getting old, I suppose," he muttered at last. "It's age, Diego. You saw Fermín Malacalza. Remember what he used to be like—before?"

"Yes, of course. I suppose his pack just got too heavy for him. That's what it must be."

"Yes."

I was at the other end of the ship, near the awning, watching the pilot comparing quadrant and compass. At seventeen, I was a bright, curious youth, interested in acquiring all kinds of knowledge. I retained that curiosity for most of my life and it later helped me make the most of certain strokes of good fortune. As well as the art of navigation, of which I gained a useful if rudimentary grasp while on board ship, I learned a lot of other things in that closed world: everything from finding out how the barber tended wounds—they didn't heal as quickly at sea, what with the damp air and the salt—to studying the dangerous varieties of humankind created by God or the Devil—I began these studies in Madrid as a mere child, continued them in Flanders as a schoolboy, and completed them on the king's galleys as a graduate—the kind of men who might well say, like the galley slave in these lines written by don Francisco de Quevedo:

I'm a scholar in a sardine school,
And good for nothing but to row;
From prison did I graduate,
That university most low.

From a distance, I contemplated, among the galley men, sailors, and soldiers, the Moor Gurriato sitting impassively on the side of the ship, staring at the sea, and Captain Alatriste and Copons, who were still talking beneath the trinquet sail at the far end of the gangway. I should say that I was still very shocked by our visit to Fermín Malacalza. He was not, of course, the first veteran I had known, but it had given me much to think about, seeing his wretched existence in Oran, poor and invalided out of the army after a lifetime of service, with a family to bring up and no hope that his luck would change, his only future being to rot like meat in the sun or to be taken captive along with his family if the Moors ever seized the town. And, depending upon one's profession, thinking is not always the most comfortable of occupations. When I was younger, I had often recited these lines by Juan Bautista de Vivar, which pleased me greatly:

A soldier's time, which is so full of strife,
Of war and weapons, fire and blood,
May yet still teach us—by all that's good—
To make the very best we can of life.

And sometimes, when I would ardently recite these to the captain, I would catch an ironic smirk on his face; not that he ever said anything, for he was of the view that no one learns from being told. You must remember that when I was in Oudkerk and Breda, I was still a green young lad, eager for novelty, and what, for others, meant tragedy and life at its cruelest—accustomed, as I was, like so many Spaniards, to enduring miseries from the cradle up—was to me a fascinating experience, part game and part adventure. At seventeen, however, with my character more formed and better educated, and my wits sharper, certain disquieting questions would slip into me like a good dagger through the gaps in a corselet. The

captain's ironic smirk was beginning to make sense, and
the proof is that, after visiting Malacalza, I never again
recited those verses. I was old enough and intelligent
enough to recognize the ghost of my own father in that
remnant of a man, and, sooner or later, in that of Captain
Alatriste, Copons, and myself. None of this changed my
intentions. I still wanted to be a soldier, but the fact is
that, after Oran, I wondered if it would not be wiser to
think of the military life as a means rather than as an
end, as a useful way of confronting—sustained by the
rigor of a discipline, a rule—a hostile world I did not
yet know well, but which I sensed would require everything that the exercise of arms or its results could teach
me. And by Christ's blood, I was right. When it came to
facing the hard times that came later, both for poor, unfortunate Spain and for me, as regards to loves, absences,
losses, and griefs, I was glad to be able to draw on all of
that experience. And even now, on this side of the frontier of time and life, having been certain things and
ceased to be many more, I am proud to sum up my existence, and those of some of the loyal and valiant men I
knew, in the word "soldier." Even though, in time, I came
to command a company and made my fortune and was
appointed lieutenant and later captain of the king's
guard—not a bad career, by God, for a Basque orphan
from Oñate—I nevertheless always signed any papers

with the words Ensign Balboa—my humble rank on the nineteenth of May in sixteen hundred and forty-three, when, on the plains of Rocroi, along with Captain Alatriste and what remained of the last company of Spanish infantry, I held aloft our old and tattered flag.

5. THE ENGLISH SAETTIA

We were sailing eastward, day after day, across the sea known to those on the other shore as Bahar el-Mutauassit, in the opposite direction from that taken by the Phoenicians, the Greeks, the gods of antiquity, and the Roman legions when they set sail for old Spain. Each morning, the rising sun lit up our faces from the prow of the galley and each night, it sank behind us, in our wake. This filled me with pleasure, and not just because at the end of the voyage lay Naples—that soldier's paradise and bounteous treasure chest of all Italy's delights. No, when the galley, propelled by the rhythmic strokes of the rowers, slid across waters smooth as a blade of burnished steel, it seemed to me that the blue sea with its red sunsets and calm, windless mornings was weaving secret connections with something that crouched in my mind like a sensation or a dormant memory. "This is where we came from," I heard Captain Alatriste murmur once as we passed one of those bare, rocky islands, so typical of the Mediterranean, on top of which could be seen the ancient columns of some pagan temple. It was a very different landscape from the León mountains of his childhood or from the green fields of my Guipúzcoa or the rugged peaks of Aragon where Sebastián Copons' soldierly ancestors, leaping from rock to rock, had been born and bred. Copons, by the way, stared at the captain in bewilderment when he heard him speak these enigmatic words. I, however, understood that he was referring to the distant, beneficent impulse that—via language, olive trees, vines, white sails, marble, and memory—had arrived at the distant, unsuspected shores of other seas and other lands, like the ripples set off by a precious stone dropped into a pool of still water.

We had traveled from Oran to Cartagena with the other ships in the convoy and, having taken on fresh supplies in that city praised by Cervantes in his *Journey to Parnassus*—"We finally reached the port / to which the men of Carthage gave their name"—we weighed anchor, along with two galleys from Sicily, and, once past Cabo de Palos, set sail east-northeast and in two days reached Formentera. From there, passing Mallorca and Menorca on our left, we headed for Cagliari, in the south of Sardinia, where, eight days after leaving the Spanish coast, we arrived safe and sound and anchored near the salt marshes. Then, sails hoisted and with fresh supplies of water and dried meat, we passed Cape Carbonara and, taking a south-easterly direction, sailed for two days to Trapani in Sicily. This time we kept a sharp eye open, with good lookouts posted on the tops of the trinquet mast and mainmast, because—this being the Mediterranean's slender waist and therefore a natural funnel through which passed all the nations that frequented it— these waters were full of ships traveling between Barbary, Europe, and the Levant. We were on the watch both for enemy ships and for any possible Turkish, Berber, English, or Dutch ships that we might capture, although, on that occasion, neither Christ nor our purses were in luck, for we encountered neither foe nor easy prey. Trapani, built right on the coast, is spread out along a narrow cape and has a reasonable harbor, although its many reefs and sandbanks meant that our pilot was never without a curse on his lips or the sounding lead in his hands. There, we parted from our convoy and continued on alone, rowing against the wind, until we reached Malta, where we were to deliver dispatches from the Viceroy of Sicily and four passengers—Knights of the Order of Saint John who were returning to that island.

I was still very intrigued by the Moor Gurriato, who, by then, appeared to be as accustomed to galley life as if he had been working on one since he was born. He seemed so patient and resigned, with his shaven head and bare muscular back (whenever the galley master gave the order "shirts off"), that if it hadn't been for the absence of shackles on his ankles—Biscay boots we called them—you would have taken him for just another slave. He ate, like the others, from a wooden bowl and drank the same murky water or watered-down wine from the wooden goblet—the *chipichape*—attached to his bench. He was also respectful and disciplined. He applied himself vigorously to the hard task of rowing, urged on by the galley master's loud whistles and hard lashes—for the galley master did not distinguish between voluntary backs and forced ones—and never protested or looked for excuses not to carry out his duties. Whether standing up—when the order came to row till they dropped—or seated and leaning back as he pulled on the oars when the rowing was easier, he would chant the same songs they all did to keep the rhythm right. And although he did not become close friends with anyone—he was the only free man on his bench, which he shared with a Spanish convict and two Turkish slaves—he was nonetheless a good comrade, well liked by his companions. The fact that he got on well with both the Christian and the Turks was significant, because if, one day, we were to fall into the hands of the Berbers or the subjects of the Ottoman Empire, the testimony of the Turks, pointing him out as a volunteer who had renounced his religion—or whatever other accusation they chose to make—would be more than enough for him to be skewered without the benefit of fat or lard to ease his passing. However, the Moor Gurriato seemed unperturbed by this possibility. He slept between the benches like his colleagues, happily engaged in mutual delousing sessions, and when, in rough weather, a soldier or sailor, so as not to get drenched at the heads in the prow, would, instead, quite without consideration, do as the galley slaves did and relieve himself next to the rower nearest the sea—always the worst place to sit—the Moor, having more freedom of movement, would throw a bucket attached to a rope into the sea, fill it with water, and wash the deck clean. He treated his companions as considerately as he did everyone else, chatting to them if it fell to him to do so, although he was not, on the whole, a great talker. We thus discovered that he spoke not only Spanish and Moorish Arabic, but could also speak Turkish—picked up, we learned later, from Turkish janissaries in Algiers—as well as the lingua franca that was spoken from end to end of the Mediterranean, a mishmash of all the languages.

I would go over to him occasionally, driven by curiosity, and we would talk, and thus I learned more details of his life and about his desire to see the world and stay close by Captain Alatriste's side. I never got to the bottom of that strange loyalty, for he never explained, as if constrained by a strange modesty. However, the truth is that, in the events that followed, his deeds never gave the lie to his intention, but rather the reverse. As I said, I was astonished at how easily he adapted to that life and, as I discovered, to the many other lives it fell to him to live while in our company; for, although I prided myself on being a brave lad, I would have found life as a galley man very hard to take.

> *At first, I trembled, wanting to withdraw,*
> *But time and custom taught me:*
> *All's within their cure.*

What I couldn't stand was the boredom. I had grown used to the promiscuity in which we lived, to the stench, the discomfort, and the noise, but I could not get used to the hours of idleness, which, in the cramped space of that floating piece of timber, were entirely wasted, so much so that I would even greet with excitement any sail we spotted as a chance for a hunt or a fight, or would feel pleased when the sky grew dark, the wind began to howl in the rigging, and the sea turned gray, with the prow bucking and the storm harrying us. At such moments, everyone else on board would be praying and crossing themselves and commending themselves to God and making pious promises that, later, once back on dry land, they were most unlikely to keep.

To fill the tedium, I continued to apply myself to reading, a habit greatly encouraged by the captain, who often

led by example, for, unless he was talking to me or Sebastián Copons or other comrades, he could usually be
found sitting snugly in one of the ship's embrasures with
one of the two or three books he always carried in his pack.
One, which I remember with particular gratitude, for I
read and reread it on that voyage, was Miguel de Cervantes' *Exemplary Novels*. The colloquy between the dogs
Ciprión and Berganza and the characters in *Rinconete and
Cortadillo* made me laugh out loud, to the amazement of
sailors, soldiers, and galley men alike. Another book that I
read with great pleasure, even though I found it sourer in
style and rather short on ideas, was a very old and dog-
eared tome, printed in Venice in the previous century, and
titled *Portrait of the Lively Andaluza*. Since it was a work
of a somewhat scabrous nature, the captain was reluctant
at first to place it in my hands, and only did so when he discovered that, unbeknownst to him, I was reading it anyway.

"After all," he concluded, resigned, "if you're old
enough to kill and be killed, you're old enough to read
whatever you choose."

"Amen to that," said Copons, who hadn't read a single
book in his entire life and had no intention of doing so.

Six or seven leagues before we reached Cape Passero, with
the rowers taking turns, our galley changed direction. We

had come across a Dalmatian tartane carrying dates, wax, and leather from the Kerkennah Islands to Ragusa. Its crew, once they were near enough to talk, told us that a three-masted pirate saettia and a smaller ship had called in at the island of Lampedusa to be careened. They had spotted them at dawn the previous day when they approached to take on water, and the saettia looked very like the one in which, for a month now, some English pirates had been patrolling the sea between Cape Bono and Cape Bianco, stealing everything they could lay their hands on, and which had so far eluded both the galleys of Malta and of Sicily. When the tartane sailed on, a council of war took place under the awning of our ship and, given that the wind was now a fair easterly one, perfect for the *Mulata* to unfurl her two lateen sails and do a good league an hour, we headed south-southwest, in the direction of Lampedusa, ready to knock seven bells out of those bastards, if, that is, they were still there.

As I have mentioned before, there was nothing unusual about Englishmen or Dutchmen venturing ever farther into Mediterranean waters and frequenting the ports of Barbary and even of the Turk, because what interested them was persecuting Spain and the other Catholic nations. This was an obligation to which the men of fair Albion had been applying themselves with zeal, smuggling and pirating with few interruptions, since the days of the

Virgin Queen Elizabeth—and I use the word "virgin" purely as an epithet, not as a proven fact. I refer to that red-haired bitch whom our poets, among them the Cordoban Góngora, viewed as the very worst of our enemies:

> *More she-wolf than lascivious queen,*
> *Wife and daughter-in-law to many,*
> *Vile, libidinous, and mean.*
> *And to whom Cristóbal de Virués dedicated these*
> *eloquent lines:*
> *Ungrateful queen, unworthy of the name,*
> *Cast out from God—a Jezebel —*
> *O why disturb this holy armèd peace?*
> *And make a Christian peace a hell?*

And whose death—for, thank Heaven, that hour comes round for everyone—was greeted by Lope, our Phoenix, with this fitting epitaph:

> *Here lies Jezebel,*
> *The new Athalia;*
> *Harpy of th'Atlantic gold,*
> *Of oceans, the cruel fire.*

And while we're on the subject of the English, I should point out that the people who behaved most shamelessly and outrageously in the Mediterranean were not the Turks or the Berbers, who tended to keep punctiliously to any agreements made between nations, but those pitiless, drunken dogs come from their cold seas on the hypocritical pretext of making war on the papists, and who behaved not like corsairs, but like pirates, buying complicity in ports such as Algiers and Saleh. So bad were they that even the Turks viewed them unkindly, because they blithely plundered everyone, regardless of cargo or flag, under the protection of their sovereigns and their traders, who, while they dissembled in public, in private encouraged their raids and pocketed the profits. I said "pirates," and that is the word that fits them; for in the old usage, "corsair" was an ancient, traditional, and respectable occupation: a group of private individuals who, granted a patent—royal permission to plunder the enemies of the crown—would set sail for their own private profit, on the understanding that they would pay their quint to the king and be ruled by certain laws agreed among the nations. In this respect, we Spaniards, apart from a few corsairs from Mallorca, the Cantabrian coast, and from Flanders, played an almost exclusively military role: cruel and ruthless, yes, but always acting under the flag of the Catholic king and in keeping with all ordinances; rigorously punishing any treaty violations and any excesses or abuses practiced against neutral nations. For reasons of reputation and conduct—and because, centuries before, we had experienced corsairs on our own shores in Spain—the corsair acquired a very bad name indeed; it was, after all, war by other means, and war waged by soldiers or by sailors was one thing, but it seemed murky and ungentlemanly when carried out by privateers. There was the added misfortune that, while our enemies would resort to anything to sap our strength on sea and land, our Spanish corsairs—apart from our intrepid Catholics from Dunkirk, the scourge of the English and the Dutch—gradually dwindled away for lack of crews, because of the difficulty or inconvenience of obtaining royal permission, or because, if it was granted, the profits were minimal, sucked dry by a bureaucratic tangle of taxes, corrupt functionaries, and diverse other parasites. One must not forget the sad end of the Duke of Osuna, Viceroy of Sicily and later of Naples—a close friend of don Francisco de Quevedo, and to whom we will return later—the terror of both Turks and Venetians, the father of our Spanish corsairs, and implacable bane of our enemies, a man whose triumphs and good fortune aroused such envy that, ultimately, it brought him discredit, prison, and death. And naturally, with such antecedents, when for reasons of politics and war, Philip IV and the Count-Duke of Olivares wanted to arm a fleet of corsairs again—even promising that the booty would be shared out among the Basque regiment, and that the king would renounce his quint—many privateers, wary, skeptical, or ruined, preferred not to get drawn in.

Lampedusa is a bare, scrubby, depopulated island situated some fifteen or sixteen leagues southwest of Malta. Our lookouts, who, from their vantage points could see for about fifteen miles, spotted it late in the afternoon, and to ensure that the corsairs, if they were still there, did not, in turn, spot us—the pilot warned that there was a watchtower in the south of the island—Captain Urdemalas ordered the two masts to be struck, and we continued on our way, sailless and rowing very gently, so that we could approach unseen and not before nightfall. While we were thus engaged, making the necessary arrangements to seize the corsair ship before it slipped from our grasp, the pilot, who knew those waters, told us that the island was used by both Muslims and Christians as a port, and that fugitive slaves from both sides took refuge there, and that there was a small, easily accessible cave containing an ancient image of Our Lady with the Child in her arms, painted on canvas with a wooden backing, where people left offerings of dry biscuits, cheese, bacon, oil, and the odd coin. The strange thing was that near the cave lay the tomb of an anchorite whom the Turks venerated as a great saint, and where they also left offerings (although not, of course, of bacon). And this was so that when any runaway slaves reached the island, they would have something to eat, for there was water to be had from a nearby well, which, although brackish and unpleasant, served its purpose. And whatever the religion of the slave arriving there, he would never touch the offerings left by those of the other faith, but would respect both their faith and their needs. For in the Mediterranean, where it was a case of "I'll do the same for you one day," these lines by Lope fitted like a glove.

> *When it comes to fathers*
> *No one can be sure.*
> *But when we say "Our Father,"*
> *We're sons of Adam pure.*

The fact is, as I say, that with sails struck and rowing slowly, we reached Lampedusa from the northeast while the sun was setting on the starboard side and the darkness was helping us in our enterprise. The last thing we saw before the light went was a column of smoke, an indication that, whether or not it was the saettia, someone was on the island. And with night almost upon us and any brightness reduced to a fine red line on the horizon, we were then able to see the occasional fire burning. This encouraged us greatly, and we began to prepare for action, feeling our way in the gloom, for Captain Urdemalas had given orders that no lights should be lit on board, nor was anyone to raise his voice; even the galley master was ordered not to use his whistle. And so we proceeded in near silence across the dark sea before the moon had risen, and the only sound was the hoarse, guttural breathing—a kind of long-drawn-out *uuuh, uuuh, uuuh*—from our oarsmen keeping a steady rhythm and the splash of forty-eight oars striking the water.

"Landing party, to your posts! All weapons unloaded and woe betide anyone who fires a shot!"

When this murmured order reached them, the twenty men crouched and waiting on either side of the galley were already heading toward ladders at the stern. The skiff and the rowboat that would take them to land had been lowered. We had made our approach in the darkness with great stealth, rowing slowly and silently, masts and lateen yards lowered so that we would not be silhouetted against the night sky. The pilot was lying facedown on the ram at the front of the galley, with a sailor next to him reciting the depth of the water according to the knots on the sounding lead. Spanish galleys had a very shallow draft and were subtle and light as the wind; they could sometimes get close enough in for people to land without even getting their breeches wet, although not in this case. As a precaution, our men would travel the final stretch in the skiff and the rowboat. The disembarkation point was very narrow, and we didn't want to get the harquebus fuses or the gunpowder wet.

"Take care, Íñigo," whispered Captain Alatriste. "And good luck."

He placed his hand briefly on my shoulder, and Copons squeezed the back of my neck. Then they moved off and went down the ladder to the skiff on the starboard side. Busy donning my steel corselet, I only muttered a belated "Good luck" when they were out of earshot. The squad of harquebusiers was split into two groups, one under the command of Ensign Muelas and the other with Captain Alatriste in charge, leaving Sergeant Albaladejo to watch over the sixty soldiers left on board. As the men settled into the boats, we could hear them talking in low voices, muttering oaths whenever anyone pushed or stepped on someone else. Otherwise, there was only the sound of the oars being fitted into the rowlocks and the metallic clink of weapons, muffled by the rags they were wrapped in. The plan was for the harquebusiers to disembark on the sands of a tiny bay which, according to the pilot, lay directly ahead, on the eastern side of the island. The mouth of the bay was only one hundred and fifty paces wide, but it was free of any reefs or rocks that might get in our way in the dark. The squad would land there, then cross the island in a southwesterly direction, spread themselves out around the area where the corsairs were encamped, in order to fire on them and prevent them escaping into the countryside or gaining access to the tower and the one well of water. Meanwhile, at first light, the *Mulata*, rowing silently around the island, would close off their exit via the sea and, having bombarded them with cannon shot, would then set about boarding the vessels. Toward midnight, taking advantage of the very thin crescent moon, two sailors, who were excellent swimmers—one of them was a certain Ramiro Feijoo, a remarkable diver who later became famous for holing a Turkish vessel in the siege of La Mamora—had set off in the smaller of the boats to reconnoiter the large bay or port in the south of the island. When they reached its easternmost point, they were able to confirm that there were indeed two ships—one a saettia and the other perhaps a tartane or a felucca—and that the saettia did not appear to be ready to set to sea, for she was heeled over, as if beached or in the process of being careened by its crew.

"To your oars, men," said Captain Urdemalas once the skiff and the rowboat had disappeared into the night. "Set to without a noise or a word. Prepare and arm the pavisades."

The oars moved in the water while we arranged mattresses, shields, and *pedreros* along the ship's edge, and the master gunner and his assistants positioned the three cannons at the prow. Then, as soon as the small boats had returned and been secured with a towline, our captain issued new orders, the helmsman held the rudder firm, and, still in silence, with no shouts or whistles, the oarsmen turned the ship around. And thus, as quietly as possible, we turned until the pole star was behind us and our prow was pointing toward a fairly low rocky point, whose dark mass rose up nearby. Then, with the pilot keeping a close eye on both the sounding lead and the shore—in case we should hit a sandbank or an unexpected rock—we followed the coast of Lampedusa southward.

About six or seven paces away, a rabbit, ears erect, looking all around, poked its head out of a burrow. In the hesitant dawn light, Diego Alatriste watched the rabbit and rested his chin on the butt of his harquebus, which was ready and loaded with gunpowder and with a bullet in the barrel. The harquebus was wet, as were the scrub, stones, and earth on which he had been lying for more than an hour now, his clothes damp from the last of the night dew. The only dry things were the harquebus pan and the key—wrapped in a waxed cloth—and the slow match, which was rolled up in his pack. He shifted slightly to ease his numb legs and grimaced in pain. The old wound in his hip, acquired four years before—from Gualterio Malatesta near the Plaza Mayor in Madrid—ached whenever he had to remain still for too long in the damp. For a moment, he considered the idea that he was no longer up to night dews and dawns spent out in the open air, although, lately, he'd had plenty of experience of both. He was tempted to think that his was a truly scurvy profession, but he dismissed the idea. He might have entertained the thought if he'd had another profession to turn to, but he didn't.

He looked at his comrades, lying as still as he was. All he could see of Sebastián Copons, crouched behind some bushes, were his espadrilles. Then he glanced up at the stone tower that stood out against the gray overcast sky. They had walked a mile to get there, taking the utmost care not to be heard, and had encountered two sentinels at the tower, one asleep and one dozing. He didn't get a chance to find out if they were English or not because Copons and Ensign Muelas had silently slit their throats in the dark, *ris, ras*, before they could open their mouths to say anything, in English or in any other language. Then, forbidden to move, speak, or light their fuses until the time was right— the wind might carry the smell down to the beach—the twenty men had spread out around the bay that acted as the island's port and which they could now see in the early light. The bay was large enough to hold eight or ten galleys; about half a mile wide at its mouth, it formed a kind of clover leaf with three smaller coves leading off it. In the middle of the largest and sandiest of those coves lay a saettia, half heeled over and held in place by three anchors as well as by cables holding it fast to the beach itself and to the rocks to the east. It had a large open deck with no rowing benches and a high stern, the kind of ship that depended entirely on sail power, leaving more space for artillery along the sides. It had three sails, one square mainsail and two lateens, with the lateen yards lowered and tied down on deck. It also had four cannons on either side, although, at that moment, they were all on the side of the ship that was tilted over. The crew was clearly engaged in careening the hull, either to repair damaged strakes, because of faulty caulking or because they were rotten, or to scrape off the barnacles, a crucial task on a pirate ship, which needed speed and clean lines if it was to attack and flee unimpeded.

The saettia was not alone. Nearby and to the west of the same cove, a felucca was anchored, its prow facing into the gentle breeze blowing off the land. It was smaller than the saettia, lateen-rigged, with the trinquet sail raked forward to the prow. It didn't look like a corsair ship and had no artillery; perhaps it had been seized by the crew of the saettia. The decks of both ships appeared to be deserted, but there was a small fire on the beach around which a few men could be seen moving about. A clumsy error, thought

Alatriste, all that smoke and flames visible at night. Typical of the arrogant English, if that's what they were; for, despite their proximity, with the breeze in the opposite direction, he could barely hear their voices. He had a clear view of them, though, and of the four men posted at the far end of the bay, on a rocky promontory, next to one of the saettia's cannons, ready to defend the entrance to the bay from inopportune visitors. However, the sea was empty as far as the horizon, and there was no sign yet of the *Mulata*, which, Alatriste hoped, for his sake and for that of his nineteen companions, would soon be approaching the bay.

The rabbit came out of its burrow, froze when it saw a tortoise hauling itself phlegmatically along, then hopped away and disappeared into the bushes. Diego Alatriste changed position again, rubbing his sore leg. It was a shame to see that rabbit running around, he thought, rather than roasting on a spit. Watching those corsairs enjoying their breakfast, he suddenly felt very cold and devilishly hungry. He looked across to his right, where Ensign Muelas was lying next to the well, and they exchanged a wordless glance. The ensign shrugged and gazed out at the empty sea. For a moment, Alatriste wondered what would happen if the galley did not appear and they were left there to their fate. It wouldn't be the first time. He counted the corsairs he could see on the beach: fifteen in all, although there might be others out of sight, not counting the four standing by the cannons and others who might be on board the ships. Too many to keep at bay for very long with their harquebuses—they had six rounds per man, just enough for the initial attack. Once those were spent, it would be a question of swords and daggers. So Captain Urdemalas had better keep his promise.

He noticed with unease that two men had left the group around the fire and were climbing the slope that led up to the tower and the well. Not good, he thought. They must be coming to relieve the two dead sentinels or to fetch water; it didn't much matter which, because they were heading straight for him. This either complicated matters or would perhaps simply precipitate them. And still no sign of the galley. 'Od's blood. He looked to Ensign Muelas for instructions. He had spotted the two men as well. Alatriste saw him rub one fist on the back of the other and then bend one finger over his own harquebus: the signal to light their matches. Alatriste put his hand into his pack, took out flint, steel, and slow match, and lit the latter. While he was removing the waxed cloth, he blew on the match and attached it to the serpentine, screwing it into place, and noticed that his companions were all doing the same, and that the breeze was carrying threads of acrid smoke toward the men coming up the hill. At this point, however, it made no difference. He placed a little gunpowder in the pan and calmly raised the harquebus, resting it on a large, flat stone, and aimed at a point between the two men approaching without fixing on one in particular. Out of the corner of his eye, he saw that Muelas was doing the same; it was up to Muelas, as commander of the squad, to decide who should begin the dance. And so Alatriste waited, his finger off the guard, breathing slowly so as to keep from shaking, until the two corsairs were so close he could see their faces. One had long hair and a bushy beard and the other, a burlier figure, was wearing a leather-lined helmet on his head. The bearded man looked English and was wearing the ankle-length breeches favored by that race. They were each armed with a musket and two scimitars and were talking, unaware of any danger. A few foreign words reached Alatriste's ears, but then the talking stopped, because the bearded man had pulled up short about fifteen paces away, sniffing the air and looking around, an expression of alarm on his face. Then Ensign Muelas fired a shot that blasted off half the man's head, and Alatriste, taking that as a signal, shifted the barrel of his harquebus to the left, aimed at the burlier of the two, who had half turned to run away, and felled him with one shot.

The other eighteen Spaniards were a select group, experts in their field, which is why they were there. The ensign didn't have to give any order or signal while he and Alatriste were recharging their harquebuses. (This took as long as the time needed to say two Hail Marys or two Our Fathers, which some men actually did.) Copons and the others were already making the bay and all around echo with a volley of well-directed shots aimed both at the men on the beach and at those guarding the cannons. Of those four, three were killed outright, and one of them dived into the water. As for those on the beach, just out of sight, Alatriste saw only two fall, while the others ran for cover. They—along with some men who appeared on the deck of the saettia—were quick to react and began returning fire with harquebuses and muskets. Fortunately, those shots fell short, and since the cannons were all on the wrong side of the ship, they couldn't be used to fend off any attack, from land or sea. Like his comrades, who only put the match to the powder when they were sure of a hit, Alatriste tried to make good use of the five bullets he had left, firing them off as the corsairs on the beach—a boat containing reinforcements was approaching from the saettia—were advancing up the slope, doubtless having first calculated the likely number of their ambushers and taking shelter behind rocks and shrubs as they came nearer. Alatriste counted more than thirty, which was not many if the galley arrrived in time, but a lot if he and his comrades ran out of ammunition and had to fight with swords. For this reason, he rationed out his bullets as best he could; he hit another corsair, who dropped to the ground somewhere out of sight, and finally, when he came to his last bullet, he aimed it at a man who was only eight or so paces away, shattering his leg. It made a noise like a branch breaking. Then he laid down his harquebus, unsheathed his sword, and waited, resigned, for them to come to him. A glance told him that Ensign Muelas was lying dead by the well. And he was not the only one. He could see, too, that the bushes in which Copons was hiding were waving wildly about, while the butt of his gun rose and fell amid the sound of blows and crunching noises and curses. Copons was perhaps now regretting having left Oran, for he was fighting for his life. Alatriste heard voices nearby shouting something in English. He could expect little mercy from them, and so he looked up at the gray sky, took a few deep breaths, and gritted his teeth. Bloody galley, he muttered, as he stood, sword in one hand and dagger in the other. Then, at the east end of the bay, the *Mulata* hove into view, rowing hard.

The galley was traveling swiftly through the calm waters of the bay toward the saettia. The galley master's whistle set the rhythm for the oarsmen who, chests gleaming with sweat, were putting their all into their work, now standing up between the benches, now sitting down, giving heart and soul to their rowing, the tempo punctuated by the metallic clank of manacles and shackles and the lash of the whip, cracking through the air and tickling backs and making no distinction between Moors, Turks, heretics, or Christians. The hoarse hum of voices, half moan, half gasp, was like the stertorous breathing of a dying man. And meanwhile, sixty soldiers and fifty sailors, armed to the teeth and spoiling for a fight, were crowded together on the *arrumbadas*—the raised fighting platforms round the edge of the boat and at the prow—impatient to begin. For even knowing that the day would bring more honor than profit, not even the most errant idler wanted to be left behind. The four Knights from Malta who were traveling as passengers—one French, one Italian, and two from Castile— had also asked Captain Urdemalas' permission to join the troops, and there they were, armored like knights of old, in their elegant red surcoats bearing the white cross, which they wore in combat. They would merely have cut a ridiculously fine figure were they not known throughout Christendom as fearsome warriors.

"Row! Row! Row!" we were shouting, keeping pace with the whistle and the lash. "Board them! Board them!"

There were good reasons for this ardor of ours, given that our enemies were probably cruel and insolent Englishmen, who, not content with plundering us in the Indies, were now trying, through threats and bullying, to make a space for themselves in our backyard. We could also hear firing coming from the land and knew that any one of those shots might take the life of a comrade. That is why we were so loud in our encouragement of the rowers, and I myself—may God forgive me, if he pays heed to such trifling things—would have gladly picked up a whip myself and lashed the rowers' backs to make them row still faster.

"Board them! Board them!"

And thus, from the moment we rounded the point, we headed unhesitatingly straight for the saettia, with Captain Urdemalas screaming orders and curses into the ear of the helmsman. From the mouth of the bay, as we approached, we saw that the saettia, because of the way it was anchored, was sideways on to the wind, while, at its stern and some distance off, the felucca had its prow pointing toward the beach. If the saettia had had her cannon ready on the seaward side, she could—given our angle of approach—have done us considerable damage. However, in her current state—slightly listing and held fast by anchors and cables— she was, fortunately for us, unable to make use of her artillery. We watched the motionless, defenseless vessel gradually grow in size before us through the thin smoke given off by the linstocks held in readiness by the master gunner and his assistants as they crouched behind the cannons and culverins on the prow. The sailors in charge of the *pedreros* had meanwhile taken up positions above the cordage room and along the sides of the galley. There were barely any harquebusiers on board, for almost all were on land, but we were nonetheless bristling with pistols, pikes, half-pikes, and swords, and were, as I say, more than ready to use them. I had gotten into the habit, like so many soldiers, of tying a kerchief about my head so that my hair didn't get in the way when I was fighting or so as to be able to pull on a helmet, and on this occasion I was wearing a corselet attached at the sides with chains so that I could easily pull it off if I fell into the sea, as well as carrying a small wooden shield covered in leather. With my dagger tucked in my belt and my short, wide sword in its sheath, I needed nothing more. Squeezed in among my fellows in the gangway on the starboard side near the prow—for no one crossed the ram until the cannons and the other weapons had been fired—I thought about Angélica de Alquézar as I always did before going into battle, and then I crossed myself as did nearly everyone else, in readiness to board the saettia.

"There they are, the dogs!"

Yes, a dozen or so men had appeared at the rail and, in a trice, had raked us with musket fire. The bullets, fired in haste, whistled over our heads, into the sides of the galley or into the sea, but before our enemies could seek shelter to reload, our gunner and his assistants dealt them a direct blow with a shot from the cannon, loaded with a sack of nails, bits of old chain, and bullets. The saettia's rail splintered, and there was a terrible sound of breaking shrouds and the creak of broken wood, causing considerable damage to the crouching musketeers. Now the English may have been good tacticians and even better artillerymen, but there was one thing they feared like the Devil, and that was what happened next, before they had time to recover from the shock: the Spanish infantry boarded the ship. For we Spaniards could fight on the deck of a ship as fiercely as if we were on land. Once our galley master and our helmsman had maneuvered the ram of the galley so delicately that it rested against the side of the saettia without damaging so much as a strake, we fell upon the enemy. Half of us, fifty or so men, just had time to hurry across the ram's two feet of narrow planks, before the *Mulata* drew back a little and, going around the stern of the saettia, passed between that and the felucca, so that the *pedreros* on our port side could rake that deck with stones, just in case. Then, very adroitly, she turned as she approached the beach, so that the *pedreros* on the other side could pelt the corsairs there before landing the rest of our men, who waded through the waist-high water, yelling: "Forward for Spain! Attack! Attack!" As the saying goes:

With sword or cutlass, dagger or knife,
I'll kill the first who threatens my life.

The truth is that I could not really pay much attention to that part of the maneuver, for, by then, I had jumped down from the ram onto the listing hull of the saettia. Slipping awkwardly on the grease and begriming my clothes with pitch, I managed to get onto the deck. There, I took out my sword and, together with my comrades, fought as best I could. The enemy was indeed Englishmen, or so it seemed. We made short work of a few of the fair-haired fellows and finished off the occasional wounded sailor whose blood was running in streams to the other side of the deck. One group tried to take refuge behind the mizzenmast and behind the piles of canvas and rolls of cable there; but though they fired on us with their pistols, killing some of our men, we nevertheless hurled ourselves upon them, ignoring their shouts and boasts, for they wielded their weapons very arrogantly, challenging us to come near. Oh, we came near, all right, enraged by their impudence, capturing their refuge, and mercilessly putting them to the sword on the poop deck, from which some, seeing that no quarter would be given, threw themselves into the sea. We were so athirst for blood that there was not enough meat to sink our teeth into, and so I did not fight with any man in particular, apart from a blue-eyed fellow with long sideburns armed with a carpenter's ax, with which he cut through my shield as if it were wax, and, for good measure, left me with a dent in my corselet and a bruise on my ribs. I threw down my shield, recovered myself as best I could, and assumed a crouching position, intending to go for his guts, but it was difficult fighting on that tilted deck. Then one of the Knights of Malta happened by and sliced off the fellow's head above the eyebrows, leaving me with my opponent with his brains hanging out, his soul in Hell, and his body in the sea. I looked around in search of someone else to stick my sword in, but there was no one. And so I went down with a few other men to take a look below-decks, pilfering what we could while we hunted for anyone who might be hiding there. I had the grim satisfaction of finding one such sea dog, a big freckled Englishman with a long nose, whom I discovered huddled behind some barrels of water. He crept out, ashen-faced, and fell to his knees, as if his legs would not support him, saying, "No, no," and crying, "Quarter, quarter." Once deprived of the strength that sheer numbers give them and when they are not in that gregarious frame of mind bestowed on them by wine or beer, many inhabitants of that "brave" nation swallow their arrogance with true Franciscan humility as soon as things turn sour. On the other hand, when a Spaniard finds himself alone and cornered and sober, he is at his most dangerous, for like a furious beast he strikes out madly, blindly, with neither reason nor hope, with not a thought for Saint Anthony or for the Holy Virgin. But to return to the Englishman in the hold, I was not, as you can imagine, in the sweetest of moods, and so I went over to stick my sword in his throat and finish him off. And I was just raising my weapon, determined to send the rascal off to Satan along with the Anglo-Saxon whore who bore him, I remembered something that Captain Alatriste had once said to me: "Never plead for your life with the man who has vanquished you, and never deny life to someone who pleads for it." Well. We are as we are. And so, restraining myself like a good Christian, I simply kicked him in the face and broke his nose. *Croc*, it went. Then I bundled him upstairs onto the deck.

I found Captain Alatriste on the beach, along with the other survivors of the attack, Copons among them. They were dirty, exhausted, battered, but alive. And that was some achievement, for as well as Ensign Muelas and the four other men who had been killed, there had been seven wounded—two of whom died later, on board the galley— proof of just how fierce the fighting had been on land. To those losses had to be added three dead and four wounded during the boarding, including our master gunner, who died when a harquebus blew away half his jaw, and Sergeant Albaladejo, who was blinded when a musket was fired at him at point-blank range. This was no small price to pay for a saettia that was worth at most three thousand *escudos*, but this was tempered by the thought that we had slit the throats of twenty-eight pirates—almost all of them Englishmen, along with a few Turks and some Moors from Tunis—and had taken nineteen prisoners. We had also seized the felucca, and, according to the royal ordinances, we soldiers and sailors would receive a third of the value of its cargo. The felucca was a Sicilian ship that the English had captured four days earlier. We freed eight crew members from the hold, and they said enough for us to be able to reconstruct events. The captain of the saettia, a certain Robert Scruton, had sailed through the Strait of Gibraltar in a square-rigged ship and with an English crew, resolved to make his fortune by smuggling and pirating out of the ports of Saleh, Tunis, and Algiers. Their ship proved too heavy for the light Mediterranean winds, and so they had captured a large saettia, which was faster and more suited to the job, and with that they had spent eight weeks scouring the seas, although without seizing any vessel that brought them the wealth they coveted. The felucca, which was taking wheat from Marsala to Malta, had realized that the saettia was a pirate ship, but, unable to escape it, had been forced to shorten sail. The pirates, however, drew alongside so clumsily—a combination of heavy swell and poor helmsmanship—that the saettia itself came off worst, for its starboard side was holed. That is why, being so close to the island, the English had decided to carry out repairs there; indeed, they had already completed them when we attacked, and that very day were considering setting sail again to sell the eight Sicilians and the felucca and its cargo in Tunis.

Having heard the witnesses and verified the information, the trial was deemed to be over. The sentence was clear. The saettia had not been issued with a corsairs' patent or with any other document recognized among honest nations. For example, the Dutch, who, although they were our enemies because of the war in Flanders, were treated by us as prisoners of war when we captured them in the Indies or in the Mediterranean, and our policy was to allow those who surrendered to return home, to relegate to the galley those who fought on once they had struck their flag, and to hang any captains who attempted to blow up their ship rather than hand it over. These were the polite customs practiced by civilized nations, which even the Turks were happy to follow. However, at the time, we were not at war with England—the felucca was from Syracuse in Sicily, which was as much ours as Naples and Milan were—and so their sailors had no right to proclaim themselves corsairs and to plunder the subjects of the king of Spain: they were mere pirates. Captain Scruton's avowals that he had been issued patents in Algiers and had signed agreements authorizing him to sail those waters made no impression whatsoever on the stern tribunal watching him, all the while mentally measuring up his neck, while our galley master—bearing in mind that the Englishman came from, of all places, Plymouth—prepared his very finest noose. And when the felucca and the saettia—the latter crewed by some of our men—set sail the following morning thanks to a northwest wind that threatened rain, Captain Robert Scruton, a subject of His Royal Highness the King of England, was left hanging from a rope from the watchtower of Lampedusa, with a notice at his feet—written in Castilian and in Turkish—which read: An Englishman, a thief, and a pirate.

The other eighteen men—eleven Englishmen, five Moors, and two Turks—were put to the oars and there they stayed, rowing their hearts out for the king of Spain, until the vicissitudes of both sea and war put paid to them. As far as I know, a few were still alive when, eleven years later, the *Mulata* sank during the naval battle of Genoa against the French, with the galley slaves chained to their benches, because no one bothered to free them. By then, none of us was on board, nor was the Moor Gurriato who, with the new influx of rowers, had more time on his hands, thus providing me with more opportunities to talk to him, as I will recount in the following chapter.

6. THE ISLAND OF THE KNIGHTS

I was impressed by both the appearance and the recent
history of Malta, the island of the corsair Knights of Saint
John of Jerusalem. The fearsome galleys of the religion, as
we called them, were the scourge of all the Levant, for
they patrolled the seas pursuing Turkish vessels and seizing valuable merchandise and numerous slaves. Hated by
all Muslims, the Knights of Saint John were the last of the
great military orders of the Crusades, and their members
owed obedience only to the pope. After the fall of the Holy
Land, they settled in Rhodes, but when they were expelled
from there by the Turks, our emperor Charles V gave them
Malta in exchange for a symbolic annual payment of one
Maltese falcon. That gift, the fact that we were the most
powerful Catholic nation in the world, and their proximity to the viceroyalties of Naples and Sicily—the latter

sent aid during the great siege of fifteen hundred and sixty-five—forged strong bonds between the order and Spain, and our galleys often sailed together. Besides, many of the Knights of Malta were Spanish. The knights took a vow to fight Muslims wherever they were. They were hard, spartan men who knew they would receive no mercy if taken prisoner, and for this reason, they so scorned their enemy that their galleys were under orders to attack even if they were one ship against four. Given these circumstances, it is easy to understand why the Order of Malta looked to Spain as its main defender and support, for we were the only power that gave no quarter to Turks and Berbers, whereas other Catholic nations made pacts with them or brazenly sought alliances. The most shameless of these were the ever ambivalent Venice and, of course, France, who, in her struggle with Spain, had gone so far as to allow her galleys to travel in convoys with the Turks and for Barbarossa's corsair fleet to overwinter in French ports while they plundered the Spanish and Italian coasts, capturing thousands of Christians.

You may consider, then, my state of mind when, having passed the the Dragut Point and the formidable fortress of St. Elmo, the *Mulata* cast anchor in the great harbor between Fort St. Angelo and the Sanglea peninsula. From there we could view the scene of the dreadful siege that had taken place sixty-two years before, an episode that

made the name of the island as immortal as that of the six
hundred knights of various nations and the nine thousand
Spanish and Italian soldiers and citizens of Malta who, for
four years, fought off forty thousand Turks, of whom they
killed thirty thousand, battling for every inch of land and
losing fort after fort in bloody hand-to-hand combat, until
all that remained were the redoubts of Birgu and Sanglea,
where the last survivors fought to the end.

As old soldiers, both Captain Alatriste and Sebastián
Copons regarded these places with the respect of men who
could all too easily imagine the tragedy played out there.
Perhaps that is why they were so silent from the moment
we got into a felucca to cross the large harbor to reach the
Del Monte gate until we passed under its two small towers and entered the new city of Valetta, named in memory
of the Grand Master Jean Parisot de la Valette, who had it
built after leading the defense of Malta during the siege.
I remember walking through the city's dusty but well-laid-
out streets flanked by houses with shuttered balconies and
roof gardens, with, as our guide, a Maltese boatman, whom
we paid for his services. We viewed everything with almost religious awe, first following the city wall straight to
the cathedral, then turning to the right toward the sump-
tuous palace of the Grand Master of the Order and the
lovely square in front of it, with its fountain and its column.
Then we reached the moat surrounding Fort St. Elmo,

whose impressive star-shaped bulk loomed above. And next
to the drawbridge, where the red flag bearing the eight-
pointed cross of the order was flying, our guide, whose
father had fought in the siege, told us in a mixture of Italian, Spanish, and lingua franca how his father had helped,
along with other sailors from Birgu, in taking volunteer
knights—Spanish, French, Italian, and German—from St.
Angelo to the besieged St. Elmo, and how every night they
broke the Turkish blockade—by boat or by swimming—
to replace the terrible losses of the day, and how the knights
knew full well that this was a one-way journey and that
they were going to certain death. He also told us how on
the last night, they had been unable to cross the Turkish
lines, and the volunteers had had to turn back, and how, at
dawn, those who were besieged with Grand Master La
Valette watched from the forts of Sanglea and St. Michael,
as a tide of five thousand Turks overwhelmed St. Elmo in
a final assault on the two hundred knights and soldiers, almost all of them Spaniards and Italians. Worn down,
beaten, and wounded after five weeks of fighting day and
night, battered by cannon shot, the knights continued to resist among the rubble. He concluded his tale by describing
how, injured and unable to go on fighting, the last of the
knights withdrew, without once turning their backs on the
enemy, to the final redoubt of the church, killing and dying
like cornered lions. However, when they saw that the Turks,
enraged by the price they had been forced to pay for vic-

tory, showed no mercy to the wounded they came upon, the knights strode out into the square again, prepared to die like the men they were. So it was that six of them—one Aragonese, one Catalan, one Castilian, and three Italians—fought their way through the enemy throng to the sea, where they hoped to be able to swim to Birgu. Alas, they were taken prisoner in the water. And so angry was Mustafa Pacha— he had, after all, lost six thousand men in St. Elmo alone, including the famous corsair Dragut—that he ordered the knights' corpses to be crucified and he himself cut a cross on each chest with his scimitar. Then he set them on the water and let the current carry them across to the other side of the harbor, where Sanglea and St. Michael continued to resist. Finally, he bought all the captives, stood them on the city walls, and ordered their throats to be cut. The Grand Master responded to this barbarous act by killing all his Turkish prisoners and firing their decapitated heads into the enemy camp.

That was the story told us by our guide, and when he had finished, we stood for a moment in silence, thinking about what we had just heard. Then Sebastián Copons, who was leaning on the sandstone balustrade and frowning down into the moat surrounding the fort, suddenly said to Captain Alatriste:

"We'll probably end up the same way one day, Diego... Crucified."

"Possibly, but I can assure you, we won't be taken alive."

"Not a chance."

These words shocked me, but not because the idea, however unpleasant, frightened me exactly. I understood what Copons and the captain were talking about, and I had good reason to know, by then, that almost all men are capable of both the very best and the very worst. The truth is that on the blurred frontier of those Levantine waters, human cruelty—and nothing is more human than cruelty—opened out so many disquieting possibilities, and not only on the part of the Turks. There were hard-to-explain resentments buried deep in the memory: old hatreds, family feuds, which the Mediterranean light, its sun and blue waters kept alive. For us Spaniards—born of ancient races, with a centuries-long and still-fresh history of killing Moors or killing each other—slitting the throats of Englishmen was not the same as dealing with Turks, Berbers, or the other people who lived on the shores of that sea. What did Captain Robert Scruton and his pirates have to do with us? They were mere intruders, and killing them in Lampedusa had been a mere formality, an act of family cleansing, a delousing before getting back to our proper business: Turks, Spaniards, Berbers, Frenchmen, Moriscos, Jews, Moors, Venetians, Genoans, Florentines, Greeks, Dalmatians, Albanians, renegades, and corsairs. We were all neighbors, living around the same courtyard. We were people of the same caste, with whom there was no reason why we shouldn't share a glass of wine, a laugh, a colorful insult, a macabre joke, before—viciously and imaginatively—crucifying each other or exchanging heads instead of cannonballs, with solid, good old-fashioned Mediterranean loathing. For one always slits a person's throat better and with more pleasure when one knows the person in question well.

We returned to Birgu at evening, when the dust in the air and the last rays of sun were tinging with red the walls of Fort St. Angelo, which looked as if they were made of molten iron. Before returning to the ship, we had walked for a long time through the steep, narrow streets of the new city, visiting the harbor of Marsamucetto on the west side of the island, and the famous auberges, or barracks, of Aragon and Castile, the latter with its beautiful staircase. For there is an auberge for each of the seven languages, as the Knights of the Order called them: the auberges of Aragon and Castile mentioned above, which, of course, belong to the Spanish nation; those of Auvergne, Provence, and France, belonging to the French nation; and those of Italy and Germany. On our way back, we ended up next to the moat of Birgu, where the taverns for soldiers and sailors are to be found in the old part of the city. And since there was still more than half an hour before the Angelus, when we would have to return to the galley, we decided to forgo yet another bowl of ship's gruel and, instead wet our whistles at our own expense and eat a meal fit for Christians. We duly installed ourselves in a small inn, around a barrel that served as a table, with a leg of mutton, some pork chops, a large round loaf of bread, and a pitcher of strong red wine from Mytilene, which reminded us of Bull's Blood. We were watching the people come and go: the swarthy men who looked and behaved like Sicilians and spoke a language that still contained words used by the Carthaginians, and the women, who were very beautiful but, out of modesty, avoided male company and, in public, swathed themselves in black or gray shawls because of strictures imposed by their relatives and husbands, who are as jealous as Spaniards, or more so—a legacy, no doubt, from the Moors and the Saracens. And there the three of us were sitting, our belts loosened, when some Venetian soldiers and sailors who were drinking nearby happened to buy from a passing peddlar some St Peter's stones, which are held in high regard in Malta—legend has it that the saint was shipwrecked there—because they are said to cure the bites of scorpions and snakes.

Then I did something unwise. I was not a skeptical youth, but I had my doubts on certain questions of faith, as I had been taught by Captain Alatriste. And with the insolence of youth, I could not repress a smirk when I saw

one of the Venetians proudly showing off to his companions the stone threaded on a cord he had bought. Unfortunately, he saw that smirk and took umbrage. He was clearly
not a very long-suffering fellow, for he strode over to me
with a snarl on his lips, one hand resting on the hilt of his
sword, and backed up by his companions.

"Apologize," Captain Alatriste muttered to me.

I shot him a sideways glance, taken aback by his abrupt
tone and by that order to retract the offense, although, when
I thought about it later, I realized he was quite right. Not
for fear of the consequences—although there were six of
them and only three of us—but because there really wasn't
time to get involved in a dispute, and because quarreling
with Venetians, and in Malta, really could prove serious.
Relations between us and Venice were not good; there were
frequent incidents in the Adriatic over matters of preemi-
nence and sovereignty, and it took very little to spark such
quarrels. And so, swallowing my pride, I gave a forced
smile intended to calm the waters and said, in the lingua
franca that we Spaniards used on those seas and in those
lands, something like: *"Escusi, signore, no era cuesto con
voi."* The Venetian, however, remained unappeased. On the
contrary, emboldened by what he believed to be this show
of meekness and by the difference in numbers, he pushed
back his hair—he wore it long, unlike we Spaniards, who
had been wearing our hair short since the days of Emperor

Charles—and heaped abuse on me in a scoundrely fashion, calling me a thief, which would be enough to enrage anyone, especially a proud lad from Guipúzcoa like me. And I was foolishly about to leap to my feet, when the captain, still impassive, grabbed my arm.

"He's just a boy and doesn't know the customs," he said very calmly and in Castilian, looking the Venetian straight in the eye. "But he'll gladly buy you a mug of wine."

Again, the man misinterpreted the situation, and thinking that my two companions were also backing down and made braver still by the presence of his colleagues, he pretended not to have heard the captain's words, and, unwilling to let go of his prey, namely me, he puffed himself up and said very insolently:

"*Scende, espagnuolo marrano, ca te volio amasar.*"

And he continued rubbing the hilt of his sword. Captain Alatriste, without any hint of emotion, removed his hand from my arm and glanced at Copons. Until then, Copons, as usual, had said nothing and simply kept a close eye on our boastful companions. At that point, however, he stood up.

"Lily-livered swab," he muttered.

"*Che cosa diche?*" asked the Venetian angrily.

"He says," replied the captain, also standing up, "that for all he cares, you can beat your whorish mother to a pulp, but not us."

. . .

And so began the incident between Spaniards and Venetians
that the history of Malta and the records of the time recall
as the Birgu riot, a detailed description of which would require more paper than exists in the whole of Genoa. For
having spoken those words, the captain took out his sword,
as did Copons and I, with such speed that, even though the
Venetian and his companions already had their hands resting on the hilts of their swords, the "lily-livered swab"—as
Copons had called him—stumbled backward with a cut to
one cheek inflicted by the dagger that had leaped like lightning from its sheath to the captain's left hand and from there
to the Venetian's face. And in less time than it takes to tell
it, the man nearest Copons found his upper arm skewered by
a sword, while I, light on my feet, took on the third. The latter jumped to one side, but nevertheless felt the blade of my
sword against his buffcoat, and even though it didn't pierce
actual flesh, that was enough to encourage him to keep a respectful distance.

Then matters got out of hand, because, at that moment, the Moor Gurriato appeared from nowhere—later,
I learned that he had been waiting for us in the shade, ever
since we had got into the boat to visit the new part of the
city—and, without more ado, lunged at the Venetian closest to hand and stuck a knife into the small of his back. The

tavern was at the bottom of the street that runs from the harbor esplanade up to the church near the moat surrounding Fort St. Angelo. It was an extremely crowded place, and at that hour was seething with soldiers and sailors heading back to the ships moored or anchored nearby. Attracted by the shouts of the wounded men and their comrades—who, although they had now unsheathed their swords, still did not dare to approach—more Venetians came rushing in, putting us in no little danger. And although we formed a defensive semicircle—in the manner of the old Spanish regiments—using stools and lids for shields and stabbing and slashing for all we were worth, things would have ended badly had not many of our comrades from the *Mulata*—also awaiting the moment to embark—unsheathed their swords too and taken our part without even asking the reason for the quarrel. For although galley men were not perhaps on the best of terms with Justice, they always, rightly or wrongly, helped their comrades, on the understanding that such help would one day be reciprocated. And they would as gladly fight constables and catchpoles as fellow Spaniards or foreigners, it being a point of honor, after any such ruckus, to give refuge on board to any soldier, sailor, or galley slave who sought it, as they might in a church, only with no higher authority to answer to than the captain of the ship.

And of course, given the kind of people we enlisted—

the cream of every house, you might say—in a matter of seconds, Birgu was transformed into Troy. Amid the shouts and screams of the innkeepers and tradesmen whose furniture and wares were being hurled to the ground, amid the knots of curious onlookers and excited children, we ended up with fifty or so Venetians doing battle with the same number of Spaniards. So great was the tumult that men from both sides came to offer reinforcements, for, as soon as news of the affray reached the ships, many disembarked, sword in hand, and from one or two vessels there was even the sound of musket fire. Fortunately for us, we Spaniards were popular in Malta, whereas the Venetians—seen as greedy, sly, and disrespectful, not to mention being guilty of conniving with the Turk—were hated even by the Italians, and so a number of Maltese men joined in, attacking the Venetians with sticks and stones, throwing some of them into the water and forcing others to dive in voluntarily to escape. Deaths and damage were inflicted, for in the old part of the city, even though no one knew or could remember the original reason for the dispute, there ensued a hunt for anything that so much as smelled of Venice, for a rumor had been put around that several men of that nation had offended against the honesty of certain Maltese women—always a good way to start a riot. In the process, several Venetian-owned shops were sacked by the populace and various pending accounts settled, and the day was summed up some seventeen years later by Giulio Bragadino, a Venetian and therefore not an entirely disinterested chronicler:

> *The subjects of the Serenissima suffered much ill-treatment during the night, with damage inflicted to their persons and their goods. . . . In order to avoid further mayhem, the Grand Master of Malta and the captains of galleys and other ships had to impose their authority, ordering soldiers and sailors to return to their ships and remain there on pain of death. The instigators were sought, but none were found, although it was noted that the Spaniards, who were suspected of having started the quarrel, were very quick to leave the scene.*

Nevertheless, the following morning, when the soldiers and sailors on the *Mulata* were being inspected, we got the most almighty telling-off from Captain Urdemalas, who really gave it his all, although there were some who were sure he must have been chuckling inside. He strode up and down from prow to stern, with everyone lined up along the corridors on port and starboard, all of us having been ordered to wear full body armor, which weighed about thirty pounds, and a helmet, which weighed another thirty, just to make us suffer, because all that metal really burned in the heat of the harbor where we were anchored. And he kept us standing there for a good long while after the awning had been removed from the galley, even though it was hellishly hot and there wasn't a breath of wind. It was a spectacle worthy of a painting, those lines of men with tragic, contrite faces, sweating cobs, and staring down at their feet— this was not modesty, but prudence—whenever Urdemalas passed us, fixing each one with a gimlet gaze. "You, gentlemen, are nothing but animals," he said loudly enough to be heard in Birgu. "A pack of delinquent braggarts who will be the ruin of me. However, before you succeed in doing so, I will, by my faith and on the souls of my ancestors, hang the lot of you if someone doesn't tell me who started the last night's fracas. Gadswoons I will. And I swear on myself and on Satan and on the mother who bore me that I'll hang twelve of you today from one yardarm if someone doesn't own up." Our captain said all this in a very loud, haughty voice that boomed around the harbor and up to the city walls. However, as both we and Urdemalas expected, we all kept as silent as if we were being stretched on the rack, standing firm beneath the bombardment, but winking at each other in the knowledge that sooner or later it would stop. And we were quite a sight lined up there, many of us with cuts and bruises, some sporting plasters, bandages, and dressings, others with an arm in a sling or with a black eye. Far from having had a day's leave to stretch our legs on

Malta, we looked as if we were fresh from boarding a Turkish galley.

When the signal for departure was given a day later—with all shore leave having been canceled—we weighed anchor without further incident, heading northeast around the coast of Sicily to Messina. For half of the voyage we had good weather, and the galley slaves were pleased because there was a favorable wind and they barely had to row. That same night—while on the port side—we could see a light in the distance that might as easily have been Cape Passero as the lighthouse at Syracuse—I had a long conversation with the Moor Gurriato. The two sails were creaking, and galley slaves, soldiers, and sailors, apart from those on watch, were all sleeping soundly on or between the rowing benches and in the embrasures, emitting the usual snores, groans, belches, and other nocturnal noises I will refrain from mentioning. My head ached and I couldn't sleep, and so getting up carefully, without disturbing anyone, I walked along the starboard side, crushing cockroaches underfoot as I went, hoping that the night breeze might clear my head a little. When I reached the bench normally occupied by the strokesman, I saw a familiar silhouette, faintly lit by the lantern at the stern. The Moor Gurriato was leaning on the rail, contemplating the dark sea and looking up at the stars, which the sails, by turns, revealed and concealed as the ship rolled. He couldn't sleep either, he told me when I asked. He had never been on a ship before embarking with us in Oran, and everything was very new and strange, and when he wasn't rowing, he spent many nights with his eyes wide open. It seemed a miracle to him that something so large, heavy, and complex could move safely over the sea in the night. Hoping to discover the secret, he watched the movement of the galley, the occasional faint light on the horizon, and listened to the whisper of the invisible water that glittered phosphorescently along the sides of the ship. He said that the words that the sailor on watch sang out in a monotonous voice every half-hour, when he turned the hourglass over, sounded to him like some magical incantation, like a spell or a prayer.

The hour just gone is good,
Better the one to come.
Next man's on watch,
Hourglass is turned.
We'll make good sailing
If God is willing.

It was then that I asked him about the cross tattooed on his cheek, and about the legend according to which his people had once been Christians, even long after the arrival of the Muslims in North Africa and the fall of Spain in the days of the Visigoths, with Tariq, Muza, and the treacherous Count Julian. These names meant nothing to him, he said, after a brief silence. But it was true that his father and grandfather had told him that his tribe, the *azuago* Beni Barrani, were different from other tribes, for they had never converted to the Mohammedan faith. After years of fighting in the mountains, they had lost almost all their Christian customs and become a people without a god and without a country. That was why other Moors did not trust them.

"And why do you have that cross on your cheek?"

"I'm not sure. My father used to say it was a mark that dated from the time of the Goths, to distinguish us from the other pagan tribes."

"The other day, you spoke of a bell hidden in the mountains."

"*Tidt*. It's true. A large bronze bell in a cave. I've never seen it, although I was told it had been hidden away for eight or even ten centuries, since the Muslims arrived. There were books, too, very ancient ones that no one could read anymore, from the days of the Vandals or before."

"Written in Latin?"

"I don't know what Latin is, but no one could read them."

A silence fell. I imagined those men, isolated in the

mountains, remaining faithful to a religion that gradually slipped through their fingers with the passing centuries, and repeating symbols and gestures whose meaning had long ago been forgotten. Beni Barrani, I remembered, meant "without a country." The children of foreigners.

"Why did you choose to come with us?"

The Moor Gurriato shifted in the dim light. He seemed embarrassed by the question.

"Fate," he said at last. "A man should travel while he can. Should go to distant places and return wiser. Perhaps that way he will understand better."

I leaned against the netting on the side of the ship and asked, genuinely interested:

"What is it that you need to understand?"

"Where I come from, and by that I don't mean the mountains where I was born."

"But why?"

"Knowing where you came from will help you to die."

There was another silence, broken by the routine words exchanged by the man on watch at the prow and the helmsman, the former indicating to the latter that the way ahead was clear. Then we heard only the creak of the yardarms and the murmur of the water under the galley.

"We spend our life on the edge of death," the Moor Gurriato added after a while, "but many people do not know that. Only the *assen*, the wise men, know it."

"Are you a wise man? Or do you want to be?"

"No, I am simply a Beni Barrani," he responded calmly, unhesitatingly. "I haven't even seen with my own eyes the bronze bell or the books no one can read. That is why I need other men to show me the way, like that magic needle you have over there."

He gestured toward the stern, doubtless toward the binnacle, where in the half-dark we could see the face of the sailor on watch caught in the glow from the compass light. I nodded.

"I see. So that's why you chose Captain Alatriste to make that journey with."

"Yes."

"But he's just a soldier," I objected. "A man of war."

"True, he's an *imyahad*, a warrior. That's why I tell you he is wise. He looks at his sword each morning when he opens his eyes and again each night before he closes them again. He knows he will die and he is prepared. Do you understand? That makes him different from other men."

The word "die" soon took on urgent meaning. Until around dawn, the wind had been moderate and favorable, but then it began to blow very hard, becoming a stiff northeasterly that threatened to carry us too near the coast. The galley slaves were whipped awake, the oars lowered into the water, and with everyone rowing, we gradually pressed ahead into the choppy, churning water, while the spray drenched the rowers. It was pitiful to see them half naked and soaked to the skin, lungs bursting as they rowed. Sailors and cabin boys were rushing from one side to the other, blaspheming and praying in about equal measure, while the privileged few took shelter in the stores or the infirmary or the captain's cabin. We soldiers took our chanooo, oquccxcd together in the embrasures, clinging to each other, some of us vomiting or cursing each time the galley pitched into the heart of a wave and the water flooded everything. The blankets and bits of canvas we threw over ourselves were of little use because to the great swell was added a hard, cold rain that ended up sousing us all, and the wind was far too strong for us to put up the awning.

By sheer oar power—five or six were broken that day— we managed to travel about a league, although it took us all morning. And when the galley master mentioned the possibility of a few soldiers lending a hand at the oars if things got really bad and there was a risk of us being blown onto the shore, it was curious to hear the chorus of protests, arguing that they were men-at-arms and therefore gentlemen, and that they wouldn't dream of taking up an oar unless, God forbid, the king condemned them to the galleys. Some even said that they would rather be drowned like newborn kittens but with their honor intact than be saved with their honor diminished, and that they would rather be chopped into pieces than see themselves brought down, even for a moment, to the vile condition of galley slaves. And so, for the time being, there was no further discussion, and everything continued as before, with us soldiers crammed in the embrasures, shivering and soaked, spewing and praying and cursing the universe, and the galley slaves rowing as hard as they could, beneath the lash of the galley master and his assistant.

By midafternoon, fortunately for us all, the wind swung round to the southeast, and we could pull in the oars. Then, with the mainsail lowered and the wind behind us, a small trinquet sail was hoisted, and that put us back on course. The problem was that a fierce, stormy rain was still falling, enough for a second Flood, and thus, lashed alternately by rain and gusts of wind, with lightning playing in the distance and with everyone crowded in the stern so as not to weigh down the prow, we approached the Strait of Messina at a speed, according to the pilot's calculations, of four miles for each turn of the hourglass. To make matters worse, it was black night, and that made it difficult to verify our position, and somewhere ahead of us lay Scylla and Charybdis, which, in bad weather, had been the worst place in the world and the terror of sailors since Ulysses' day. However, the heavy seas and the exhaustion of the

galley slaves meant that we could neither beat to windward nor keep our distance. And that was the situation as
we were about to enter the narrow funnel of the strait—
unable to turn back even if we had wanted to—when some
of the men swore that they could see a light on land, and
the pilot and Captain Urdemalas, after much consultation,
decided to take a chance, uncertain as to whether it was the
fire in the Messina tower or the lighthouse about two
leagues to the north. And so, leaving the trinquet sail
raised, the oars were brought out again. The galley master
tried hard to make his whistle heard above the wind howling in the rigging, and the galley slaves, the Moor Gurriato included, began to row, while the helmsman, battling
against the rolling of the ship, struggled to keep the bow
pointing toward the distant light. Our hearts in our mouths
and clinging on as best we could, we were plunging into
darkness and far faster than we wanted, hoping that we
wouldn't be wrecked on a sandbank or a rock. And that is
precisely what would have happened if something had not
occurred that many claimed was a miracle and others
thought was merely the luck of the sea. For the light on the
tower suddenly went out, perhaps doused by the sheer
quantity of rain, when we were, according to the pilot,
very near the city of Messina. The wind had rolled around
to the northeast again, and there we were in the dark, with
the sea a little calmer, looking for the harbor mouth. And

had a flash of lightning not lit up the fort of San Salvador a mere pistol shot ahead of us, forcing the helmsman to fling the rudder hard in the other direction, we would have crashed straight into it and been lost just when we had salvation within our grasp.

7. SEE NAPLES AND DIE

The night sky glowed red, Vesuvius infusing everything as far as one could see with that strange, ghostly light, even the moon rising on the other side of the city. The outline of Naples, its buildings, hills, and towers, the land and the sea, were thus eerily lit from two different angles, creating crazy shadows, a landscape as unreal as that in the canvases Diego Alatriste had watched burn—real fire consuming painted fire—during the sacking of Flanders.

He took a deep, pleasurable breath of the warm, salt air as he unhurriedly put on his belt with sword and dagger. He wasn't wearing a cape. Despite the lateness of the hour—the Angelus bell had rung—the temperature was still very pleasant. That, along with the remarkable nocturnal light, lent the city a certain melancholy enchantment. A poet like don Francisco de Quevedo would have written a few good—or bad—lines of verse about it, but Alatriste was no poet; his only poetry was his scars and a handful of memories. And so he donned his hat, and, after looking both ways—dark nights in remote places like that were not safe even for the Devil—he set off, aware of the sound of his own footsteps, first on the dark stones of the paved road and then, muffled, on the sandy soil of Chiaia. As he strolled along, keeping an eye out for any shadows that might be hiding among the fishing boats moored by the sea, he could see, black against the red at the far end of the broad beach, the hill of Pizzofalcone and Uovo castle with its feet in the calm sea. Not a single window was lit, and there were no torches in the streets. Not a breath of wind either. The ancient city of Parthenope was sleeping wrapped in fire, and Alatriste smiled to himself beneath the broad brim of his hat, remembering. That same light, which only occurred when the old volcano stirred into life, had lit many of his youthful adventures as a soldier.

That was seventeen years ago, he thought. He had first come to Italy in sixteen hundred and ten, after being caught up in the horror of the Morisco problem in the mountains and on the beaches of Spain. As a soldier on the corsair galleys—*leventes,* the Turks called them—with plenty of booty from the Greek islands and the Ottoman coast within the grasp of any man with balls enough to go after it, the six years of his first term in the Naples regiment had been among the best years of his life. His purse had always been full between voyages, there were the inns and taverns of Mergellina and Chorrillo, Spanish plays put on at the courtyard theater, good wine, even better food, a healthy climate, and garrison life in the nearby villages, beneath vine trellises and leafy trees, in the company of pleasant comrades and beautiful women. There he had met a future grandee of Spain who was serving on the Neapolitan galleys as a volunteer—which was how young noblemen made a name for themselves—the Count of Guadalmedina, the son of the man who had been his general in Flanders at the time of the siege of Ostend.

Yes, Guadalmedina. While he walked along the shore, Alatriste wondered if, there in his palace in Madrid, Álvaro de la Marca would know that he was back in Naples. Always supposing that the count, friend and confidant of Philip IV, gave a fig for the fate of the man who, in sixteen hundred and fourteen, in the Kerkennah Islands, had carried him, wounded, on his shoulders and borne him back through the waist-high water to the ships, with the Arabs hot on their trail like dogs. But too many things had happened between then and now, including sword fights at night outside a certain house in Madrid and a few hard blows to the face by the River Manzanares.

"A pox on him!"

The curse bubbled up from inside, and he turned away

with an impatient click of his tongue. The thought of Guadalmedina, whom he hadn't seen since the skirmish at El Escorial, troubled his mind and his pride. To soothe both, he thought of more pleasant things. For heaven's sake, he was in Naples, surrounded by all the delights of Italy, in reasonable health, and with a few coins clinking in his purse. He had good comrades there too. As well as Sebastián Copons—whom he was very glad to have rescued—there were others who knew how to eat and drink well, comrades with whom a man could happily share his cape. One such was Alonso de Contreras, the oldest of his friends, for with him, when he was barely thirteen, he had enlisted as a drummer boy in the regiments heading for Flanders. Alatriste and Contreras had met up again ten years later in Italy, then in Madrid, and now once again in Naples. Brave Contreras was the same as ever: valiant, talkative, and somewhat boastful, although this surface appearance could prove misleading and dangerous for those who did not know him. He still held the rank of captain and had become quite famous since Lope de Vega wrote a play about him—*The King with No Kingdom*. He had served on the Maltese galleys during their attacks on the Morea coast and in the Aegean, and while he had never been exactly rich, he had always had more than enough to spend. The Duke of Albuquerque, Viceroy of Sicily, had just given him the command of the Pantelaria garrison, an island halfway to Tunis, as well as a small frigate to go pirating in if he got bored. As Contreras put it, he was no more a king than when Lope had made him one, but it was a pleasant posting that brought with it regular pay and responsibility.

Alatriste continued along the beach. Just before he reached Pizzofalcone, he walked up the hill to his left. At the top, and after going through a gate that remained open all night near the port of Chiaia, he plunged back into the city streets, taking the usual necessary precautions. On the corner of two streets, the lights from a tavern fell across his path. Inside, he could hear the strumming of a guitar, Spanish and Italian voices, and the laughter of men and women. He was tempted to go in and drink half a pitcher of wine, but he decided against it. It was late, he was tired, and it was still some way to the large area known as the Spanish quarter where he had his lodgings. Besides, he had drunk enough to quench his thirst—and, by God, it wasn't only his thirst he had quenched that night—and he only drank to the very dregs when the demons were dancing in his heart and in his memory, and that was not the case tonight. His most recent memories were closer to Heaven than to Hell. The idea made him smile again, and when he smoothed his mustache, he could still smell on his fingers the perfume of the woman whose house he had just left. It was very good, he thought, to be alive and back in Naples.

"*Non è vero,*" said the Italian.

Jaime Correas and I looked at each other. Fortunately, neither of us was carrying weapons—in the gaming house, they made you leave them at the door—because otherwise we would have knifed the insolent fellow right there and then. Those words may not have been offensive to Italians, but no Spaniard would let them pass without immediately putting hand to sword. And the gambler knew very well where we were from.

"You're the one who's lying in his teeth," I said.

And I stood up, furious to have my word doubted. I grabbed a jug, which I resolved to break and smash in the man's face at the slightest provocation. Correas did the same, and we stood there next to each other, with me facing the gambler and my comrade facing the eight or so very surly individuals who were sitting around the table. This wasn't the first time we had found ourselves in such situations, for as I mentioned elsewhere, Correas was not really one for the quiet life and was accustomed to gambling until the sun came up. He had picked up bad habits in Flanders and become an expert in cheating, gambling, and whoring, and a regular in gaming dens and brothels. He was one of those lost boys who lives his life very close to the edge and who, if he doesn't learn the error of his ways, usually ends his days either on the wrong end of a knife, rowing in the king's galleys, or with a rope around his neck. As for me, what can I say? I was the same age, I was his friend, and I was certainly no saint. And so we strode around like two brave fellows, wielding our swords and wearing our hats at a jaunty angle, through those parts of Italy of which we Spaniards had been the masters, more or less, ever since the old kings of Aragon had conquered Sicily, Corsica, and Naples, and since the Great Captain's armies and then Emperor Charles' regiments had kicked out the French. And all this despite the popes, Venice, Savoy, and the Devil.

"You're a lying dog," said Correas, hammering the final nail into our coffin.

A silence had fallen of the kind that bodes no good, and I cast a soldierly eye about me: things looked very black indeed. The villain in question was a cardsharper, a Florentine, while the others were Neapolitans, Sicilians, or God knows what, but none of them, as far as I could see, were Spaniards. What's more, we were in a dingy cellar in the Piazza dell'Olmo, opposite the fountain and a long way from the Spanish quarter. The only good thing was that they were all apparently as weaponless as we, unless they had a knife or sword concealed beneath their clothes. I privately cursed my friend who, once again, with his foolish insistence on playing cards in a disreputable hole like that was responsible for getting us into this mess. Not that this was the first time, but it looked likely to be the last.

The gamester, for his part, remained perfectly calm. He was a past master of the gaming arts and accustomed to such difficulties while plying his worthy trade. His appearance was hardly reassuring: he was extremely thin, disguised his bald head with a very bad wig, wore thick gold rings on his fingers, and the points of his waxed mustache reached almost to his eyes. He could have passed for a comic actor in a play were it not for the threatening look in his eyes. With a sly air and the falsest of smiles, he glanced at his fellow villains, then indicated the cards spread out on the table begrimed with wine and candle wax.

"Voacé a fato acua," he said coolly. *"A perduto."*

I looked at the cards placed faceup, more annoyed because they took us for fools than because of the trick itself. The kings and the sevens with which he claimed to have won had more marks on them and were more dog-eared than a preacher's Bible. Even a child of two would have noticed, but the reprobate, seeing that we were greenhorns, had thought us more innocent than babes.

"Pick up our money," I whispered to Correas, "and let's get out of here."

My companion didn't wait to be told twice. He quickly put the coins we had lost—like the boobies we were—back in his purse. Still with the jug in my hand, I did not take

my eyes off the sharper or his consorts for an instant. I was
still working out moves in my head, as Captain Alatriste always advised me to do: before you get into a fight, he said,
plan your escape route. It was ten paces and a dozen steps
to the door where our weapons were. In our favor was the
fact that, to avoid getting the owner of the den into trouble with the law, the regulars did not usually attack you
there and then, but out in the street. This meant we had a
clear run as far as the square. I racked my brains to remember which church to take refuge in should it come to
a sword fight. Santa Maria Novella and Montserrate were
the nearest.

In the end, we had no difficulty in leaving, which surprised me somewhat; nevertheless, you could have cut the
silence with a knife. At the top of the stairs, we collected
our knives and swords, gave a coin to the boy in charge,
and went out into Piazza dell'Olmo, looking back all the
time, because we could hear footsteps behind us. The rosy-
fingered dawn—to use the old cliché—was just appearing
behind the mountain crowned by the castle of San Martino
and lighting our drawn and sleepy faces, the faces of ne'er-
do-wells after a night of too much wine, too much music,
and too much gaming. Jaime Correas had not grown much
taller since Flanders, but he had broadened in the shoulders and acquired a prematurely thick beard as well as a
sword so long that its point dragged along the ground. He

indicated with a jerk of his head that the Florentine, along with three of his consorts, was coming after us. He asked me softly if we should run or unsheathe our swords. I sensed that his preference would be to take to his heels. This somewhat cooled my ardor, for I was in no fitter state than he was to be exchanging sword thrusts. Besides, according to the viceroy's edict, anyone caught fighting in the street and in broad daylight would be sent straight to Santiago prison if he was Spanish and to Vicaria prison if he was Italian. And so there I was, with the Florentine and his followers at my back, hesitating, like the *miles gloriosus* I was, between two tactics, that of playing the hero, shouting "Forward Spain!" and all that, or of imitating that speedy creature, the hare—after all, courage does not necessarily exclude prudence. Then Correas and I had a miraculous vision, in the form of a squad of Spanish soldiers come to relieve the guard at the smaller of the harbors. And so, without more ado, we joined our compatriots and left those Italian rascals stopped in their tracks, although they did take a long hard look at us, so that they would be able to recognize us later on.

I adored Naples, and even now, when I think back to my time as a young man in that city—which was like a world unto itself, as large as Seville and as beautiful as paradise—the mere memory draws from me a smile of pleasure and nostalgia. Imagine me then, a young, handsome Spaniard—fighting beneath the flag of the famous infantry whose nation was the world's greatest power and greatest scourge—living in a delicious place like that: *"Madono, porta mangiare! Bisogno prosciutto e vino! Buongiorno, bella signorina!"* Add to this the fact that, in Italy, with the exception of Sicily, the women walked the streets during the day without a cloak, showing their ankles, and with their hair caught back in a net or covered only by a mantilla or a light silk scarf. And we Spaniards, unlike the mean French, the squalid English, or the brutish Germans, still had a certain reputation in Italy, for although we were arrogant and boastful, we were also perceived as disciplined, brave, and free with our money. And despite our fierce nature—to which the popes of Rome could attest—we got on extraordinarily well with the Italians, especially in Naples and Sicily, where people had no difficulty in speaking Castilian. Many Italian regiments—we had some with us in Breda—spilled their blood beneath our flag, and they were never considered traitors by their fellow countrymen or by their historians, but rather its faithful servants. It was only later on, when Spain sent not just the captains and soldiers who kept the French and Turks at bay, but a deluge of tax collectors, judges, scribes, and other shameless bloodsuckers, that our great deeds gave way to unscrupulous domination, to the rags, banditry, and poverty that would give rise to riots and bloody uprisings, like the one in sixteen hundred and forty-seven led by Masaniello.

But let us go back to the prosperous, fascinating Naples of my youth, and add to this the restless company of my comrade Jaime Correas. We would hang around convents, like would-be suitors to the nuns, although we spent Fridays and Saturdays with the local roughs down by the harbor, bathing in the sea on hot nights or else visiting any balcony or shuttered window likely to conceal the eyes of some woman willing to be courted. Then there were the taverns—whose sign, in Italy, was a sprig of bay—the gaming dens, and the brothels. Although, as regards the latter, I was as restrained as my companion was unbuttoned, because whereas Jaime would go with any whore who said "What lovely eyes you have," I, fearful of the diseases that can afflict both health and purse, would keep out of the way, drinking wine and engaging in polite conversation, restricting myself to more peripheral activities, which, while pleasurable, carried little risk. And because—all credit to Captain Alatriste—I had been brought up to be a discreet and generous lad, and because people prefer a clock that tells the time to one that merely shows it, I was always well thought of in the elegant inns near Chiaia beach, in the bawdy houses in Via Catalana or the Mandraccio or Chorrillo taverns. The ladies there were fond of me and found my youth and my discretion rather touching; some even occasionally ironed—and starched—my cuffs, collars, and shirts. The other fellows who grazed in the same pastures all addressed me as "friend" and "comrade," for they knew, too, that thanks to my experiences at the captain's side, I was, by profession, a swordsman, quick to unsheathe both sword and dagger, and light on my feet as well. That and having money to spend always gives one a good reputation among ruffians, roughnecks, cutthroats, ne'er-do-wells, and others of the same tribe.

"There's a letter for you," said Captain Alatriste.

In the morning, when he finished guard duty in Castelnuovo, he had passed by don Francisco's sentry post and picked up the sealed letter bearing my name. It was now lying on the table in our room in the inn of Ana de Osorio in the Spanish quarter. The captain was looking at me, saying nothing, standing at the window where only half his face and one tip of his mustache were lit from the light behind. I went slowly over to the letter, as if approaching enemy territory. I recognized the writing at once. And I swear to God that, despite all the time that had passed, despite the distance, my age, and everything that had happened since that intense and terrible night at El Escorial, I felt an almost imperceptible twinge in the scar on my back, as if I had just felt on it the brush of warm lips after the touch of cold steel, and my heart stopped for a second, only to begin again, this time beating wildly. Finally,

I reached out my hand to pick the letter up, and then the captain looked me straight in the eye. He seemed about to say something, but instead, after a moment, he grabbed his hat and belt—with sword and dagger attached—walked straight past me and left me alone in the room.

Señor don Íñigo Balboa Aguirre
Company of Captain don
Justino Armenta de Medrano
of the Spanish Infantry in Naples

My dear soldier,

It has not proved easy to find you, although, even far from Spain, I am still kept in touch with what goes on there through relatives and acquaintances. That is how I learned that you had returned to the army in the company of that Captain Batistre or El-Triste, and that, not satisfied with slitting the throats of heretics in Flanders, you have now turned your attentions to the Turk, always, of course, in support of our universal monarchy and of the one true religion, which does you credit as a valiant, hardworking gentleman.

If you think that I am living here in exile, you are quite wrong. New Spain is a novel and exciting place, full of possibilities, and my uncle don Luis' name and

connections are as useful here as they were at court,
even more so, given that letters take such a long time
to come and go. I need say only that his position
remains unchanged, indeed he has grown in prestige
and fortune, despite the false accusations leveled at
him last year, in relation to that incident at El
Escorial. I hope to see him fully rehabilitated soon in
the eyes of the king, our lord, for he still has
influential friends and family at court. I have good
reason to believe this, too, for we have enough powder
for a countermine, as you might say in your soldier's
jargon. In Taxco, where I live, we produce the best and
most beautiful silver in the world, and a large part of
the silver carried on the fleets to Cádiz and Spain
passes through my uncle's hands; that is, through
mine. As Father Emilio Bocanegra would say—and
I'm sure you will remember that saintly man as
fondly as I do—the ways of the Lord are unknowable,
especially in our Catholic homeland, which is the
bulwark of the faith and of so many fine virtues.

As for you and me, a lot of time has passed and
many things have happened since our last encounter, of
which I remember every moment and every detail, as,
I hope, do you. I have grown within and without, and I
would like to compare such changes at closer quarters;
and so I hope very much that we will meet face-to-face

on some not too distant day, when this period of
difficulties, voyages, and distances is a mere memory.
But as you well know: I am good at waiting.
Meanwhile, if you still harbor the same feelings for me
as when I knew you, I demand an immediate response
in your own hand, assuring me that time, distance, and
the women of Italy and the Levant have not erased
from you the marks left by my hands, my lips, and my
dagger. If not, then damn you, and I wish for you the
worst evils in the world, imprisonment in Algiers, a
spell on the galleys, and impalement by a Turk.
However, if you are still faithful to she who has not yet
killed you, I swear I will reward you with
unimaginable torments and joys.

As you see, I think I still love you, but don't rely
on that or on anything else. You will only find out
when we are once more face-to-face, looking into
each other's eyes. Until then, stay alive and avoid
any unpleasant mutilations. I have interesting plans
for you.

Good luck, soldier. And when you attack your
next Turkish galley, call out my name. It pleases me
to think that I and my name have been on the lips of
a brave man.

Yours,
Angélica de Alquézar

After a moment's hesitation, I went out into the street. I found the captain—doublet unfastened, hat, sword, and dagger on a stool beside him—sitting at the door of the inn, watching the passersby. I was holding the letter in my hand and generously held it out to him. He didn't even want to look at it; he merely shook his head.

"The name Alquézar has always brought us bad luck," he said.

"She's my business," I replied.

I saw him shake his head again abstractedly. He seemed to be thinking about something else. The inn was on Three Kings Hill, and he had his eyes fixed on the junction of our street with that of San Matteo. In between two miserable little shops, one selling coal, coke, and kindling and the other tallow candles, some mules, tethered to rings on the wall, were liberally sprinkling the ground with their droppings. The sun was high, and the washing hung out to dry was dripping down onto our heads and creating alternating rectangles of light and shade on the ground.

"She wasn't only your business when you were in the dungeons of the Inquisition or when we boarded the *Niklaasbergen*." The captain was speaking softly, as if thinking out loud rather than talking to me. "Nor was she in the cloisters at Minillas or in El Escorial. She implicated friends of ours. People died."

"She wasn't the problem. She was used."

He turned slowly to face me and then glanced at the letter in my hand. I looked away, embarrassed. Then I folded up the letter and put it in my pocket. Some of the sealing wax had stuck to my nails, like dried blood.

"I love her," I said.

"I heard you say that once in Breda, when you'd received just such a letter from her."

"Now I love her more."

He said nothing for some time. I leaned one shoulder against the wall. We were watching the various people pass by: soldiers, women, kitchen hands, servants, and errand boys. The whole quarter, built by private individuals in the previous century at the instigation of the Viceroy don Pedro de Toledo, housed most of the three thousand Spanish soldiers in the Naples regiment, for there was only room for a few in the barracks. The rest lodged there, as did we. It was an unlovely, architectural mishmash of a place, but it served its purpose. There were no public edifices, only inns, hostels, and tenements with rooms to rent, in buildings of four or even five stories that took up all the space. It was, in short, a vast urban military base populated by soldiers either just passing through or garrisoned there, and where we all lived cheek by jowl. Some were married to Italian women or to women who had come over from Spain and had children. We lived alongside the locals who rented out lodgings, fed us, and, in short, made a living, and not a bad one, from what the military spent. On that day, as on every day, while the captain and I were talking at the door to the inn, women were calling to one another from their windows above, old people were leaning out to take the air, and loud voices, Spanish and Neapolitan, echoed around inside the houses. Some small ragged boys were shouting in both languages as they pursued a poor, tormented dog up the hill; they had tied a broken jug to its tail and were chasing it and calling it a Jew.

"There are some women . . ." the captain began, then stopped, frowning, as if he had forgotten the rest of the sentence. For some unknown reason, I felt irritated, insolent. Twelve years ago, in that same Spanish quarter, my former master—with too much wine in his belly and too much anger in his heart—had killed his best friend and marked the face of a woman with a dagger.

"I don't think you're in a position to give me lessons about women," I said, slightly more loudly. "Especially not here, in Naples."

Touché. His green eyes were lit by an ice-cold flash of lightning. Anyone else would have been afraid of that look, but I wasn't. He himself had taught me to be afraid of nothing and no one.

"Nor in Madrid," I added, "with poor Lebrijana crying her eyes out while María de Castro . . ."

Now it was my turn to leave a sentence unfinished, rather

uncertain as to how to continue, for the captain had slowly gotten to his feet and was still looking at me hard, from very close, with eyes that were the same color as the wintry water in the canals in Flanders. I brazenly held his gaze, but swallowed hard when I saw him smooth his mustache.

"Hmm," he said.

He thoughtfully studied the sword and dagger on the stool beside him.

"I think Sebastián is right," he said after a moment. "You've grown too fast."

He picked up his weapons and unhurriedly buckled them on. I had seem him do this a thousand times, but on that occasion, the clink of steel made my skin prickle. Finally, in utter silence, he donned his broad-brimmed hat, which cast a shadow over his face.

"You're quite the man now," he added. "Capable of raising your voice and, of course, of killing. But capable, too, of dying. Try to remember that when you talk to me about certain things."

He continued to fix me with the same hard, cold stare, as if he had just seen me for the first time. And then I did feel afraid.

The washing festooning the narrow streets resembled shrouds floating in the darkness. Diego Alatriste left behind

him the broad, paved Via Toledo, with torches blazing
at every corner, and made his way into the Spanish quarter, whose steep, straight streets rose up the gloomy slope of
Sant'Elmo hill. You could just make out the castle above,
still vaguely lit by the fading, distant reddish light from
Vesuvius. Having stirred into life in recent days, it was falling
asleep again. A brief wisp of smoke hovered over the crater
now, and its red glow was reflected only faintly on the clouds
and on the waters in the bay.

As soon as he felt safe among the shadows, he allowed
himself to throw up, grunting like a pig. He remained there
for a while, leaning his head against the wall and holding
his hat in one hand, until the world around him stopped
spinning and a bitter clarity of mind replaced the vapors
from the wine he had drunk—a lethal mixture of Greco,
Mangiaguerra, Latino, and Lacrima Christi. This was
hardly surprising given that he had spent all evening and
part of the night alone, going from tavern to tavern, avoiding any comrades he met on that *via crucis*, and only opening his mouth to ask for more wine, which he drank like a
German—or like the man he was.

He looked behind him, toward the brightly lit Via
Toledo, in case there should be any importunate witnesses.
He had sent the Moor Gurriato away with a flea in his
ear, and he would probably now be sleeping in the modest
barracks in Monte Calvario. There wasn't a soul in sight,

and so only the sound of his own footsteps accompanied him when he put on his hat again and set off, orienting himself down the dark streets. He crossed Via Sperancella, making sure the hilt of his sword was easily accessible and keeping to the middle of the street to avoid any unfortunate encounters on porches or at corners, and then he continued until he reached the arches where the street narrowed. Turning right, he walked as far as the small square and church of the Trinità degli Spagnuoli. That area of Naples brought him good memories and bad, but it was the latter that had been stirred into life again that very afternoon. Despite the years that had passed, they were still there, fresh and vivid, like mosquitoes refusing to drown in a glass of wine. And no thirst, however great, could ever drink them down.

It wasn't just that he had killed a man and scarred a woman's face. It wasn't a matter of remorse or of some ache that could be relieved by going into a church and kneeling down in front of a priest, in the unlikely event that Diego Alatriste would enter a church other than to seek refuge there, with the law at his heels. He had killed many people during his forty-five years of life and knew that he would kill many more before the time came when he would have to pay for all his misdemeanors. No, the problem was of quite a different order, and the wine had helped him first to digest it and then to vomit it up. It was the chilling certainty that every step he took in life, every sword thrust to left or right, every scrap of money earned, every drop of blood that spattered his clothes, all formed a kind of damp mist, a smell that clung to his skin like the smell of a fire or a war. The smell of life, of the passing years with no turning back, of the uncertain, hesitant, crazy, or resolute steps he took, each one of which determined the steps that would follow and that did not allow for any change in direction. It was the smell of resignation and impotence before a certain and irrevocable destiny. Some men tried to disguise the smell with fantastical perfumes or to ignore it by averting their gaze, while others steadfastly breathed it in, facing it head on, aware that every game, even life and death, had its rules.

Before he reached the church of San Matteo, Diego Alatriste took the first street on the left. The inn of Ana de Osorio was only a few steps away and was always lit up at night by the candles that burned before the three or four wall niches dedicated to the Virgin and to various saints. When he reached the door, he looked up from beneath the brim of his hat at the dark sky between the houses and the washing hung out to dry. Time changes some places and leaves others untouched, he thought, but it always changes your heart. Then he muttered an oath and went slowly up the unlit stairs that creaked beneath his boots. He opened the door to his room, fumbled around for flint and steel, and lit an oil lamp hanging from a nail on a beam. When he unbuckled his belt, he threw his weapons angrily down on the floor, not caring who he might wake up, then went in search of the demijohn of wine he kept in a corner and quietly cursed again when he found it empty. That afternoon, the serenity he had felt on being back in Naples had vanished with a brief conversation in the street down below and with the realization, once again, that nobody goes through life unscathed, and that with just a few rash words, a lad of seventeen could become a mirror in which one saw one's own face reflected, along with the never forgotten scars and the kind of disquieting memories that can only be avoided by those who have not lived enough. Someone had written somewhere that traveling and books led to wisdom. This was true, perhaps, for some men, but in the case of Diego Alatriste, they led to a table in a tavern.

A couple of days later, I found myself involved in a curious incident, which I will describe just to show you that, despite the grand airs I put on and everything I had experienced during those years, I was still very much a babe newly weaned. I was returning in the small hours from guard duty next to what we called the Alcalá tower, near Uovo castle. Apart from the vague reddish glow in the sky above the volcano on the other side of the city, and its reflection in the waters of the bay, it was black night, and as I walked up Santa Lucia, past the church, near the fountains and next to the little chapel there, which was adorned with ex-votos depicting babies, legs, and eyes made from wax and brass, as well as bunches of withered flowers, medallions, and almost anything else you care to name, I saw a woman on her own, her cloak wrapped about her. Being there at that hour, I thought, meant that she was either very devout or was craftily setting her nets. Anyway, on the premise that to a young falcon all flesh is good, I slowed my pace, trying to get as good a look at her as I could in the dim light of the small oil lamps burning on the altar. She seemed quite a handsome woman, and as I approached, I could hear the rustle of silk and the smell of amber. This, I thought, meant that she was no mere cheap prostitute, and so I showed more interest, trying to get a glimpse of her face, which was almost hidden by her mantilla. What parts I could see were very pleasing, and the whole even more so.

"*Svergognato anda il bello galante*," she said very charmingly.

"I'm not forward at all," I responded calmly, "but no man could remain indifferent before such beauty."

I was encouraged by her voice, which was young and clear and Italian, not like the voices of so many of our proud compatriots, whether Andalusian or not, who worked in Italy and made out they were of the highest nobility, but always addressed potential clients in plain Castilian. I was standing in front of her now and could still not see her face, although her figure, which pleased me greatly, was silhouetted against the glow from the lights on the little altar. Her mantilla seemed to be made of the finest silk, and from the little I could see of the rest of her, I was tempted to buy the whole bale.

"*Tan sicura crede Lei tener la sua caccia?*" she asked slyly.

I may have been young, but I was not entirely a fool. When I heard those words, I was sure: she was a clearly a lady of the night, albeit dressed like a lady of quality. She was not at all like the ordinary whores, trulls, drabs, and stales who hung about on street corners, the kind who swore they would faint at the sight of a mouse, but didn't turn a hair to see half a company of harquebusiers arrive for business.

"I'm not on the hunt," I said simply, "I've just come off duty, and I feel more like sleeping than anything else."

She studied me in the dim light, weighing me up. I assume my youth was evident in my face and my voice. I could almost hear her thinking.

"*Spagnuolo e soldato bisogno,*" she concluded scornfully. "*Più fanfaronata che argento.*"

There she touched a sore point. "*Bisogno*" was the nickname given to the poor new Spanish soldiers who arrived in Naples as innocent as Carib tribesmen, unable to speak the language, apart from the word *bisogno*—"I need." And, as I say, I was very young. Anyway, somewhat piqued, I patted my purse, which contained three silver carlins, one piece of eight, and the odd smaller coin. I was forgetting, of course, don Francisco de Quevedo's sage advice: "When it comes to women, choose the cheapest."

"*Mi piace il discorso,*" said the lady pirate with great aplomb.

And without more ado, she took my hand and tugged at me gently. Her hand was small and warm and young. That assuaged my fear that she might simply be putting on a youthful voice and that, beneath the disguise, I would find a haggard old whore trying to pass herself off as a sweet virgin re-created with needle and thread. I still hadn't seen her face though. Then I decided to undeceive her, saying that I had no intention of going as far as she was offering to go. However, fearing—fool that I was—to offend her with a brusque negative, I remained somewhat ambiguous. And so, when I told her that I was going back to my inn, she bemoaned my lack of manners in allowing her to return to her house unaccompanied; besides, her house was right there, in Pizzofalcone, at the top of those steps. A woman alone and at night, she said, must avoid any unfortunate encounters. As a final flourish, she allowed her mantilla to slip a little, as if by accident, to reveal a firm mouth, very white skin, and the kind of dark eyes that pierce and kill in a trice. And so there was nothing more to be said, and we walked along, arm in arm, with me breathing in her amber perfume, listening to the rustle of silk, and thinking, with every step, and despite all my experiences to date, that I was merely accompanying a woman through the streets of Naples and that nothing bad could possibly come of it. I even doubted, in my innocence, that she really was just a strumpet. It even occurred to me that she was perhaps merely a capricious young girl, a strange miracle of the night, out on a youthful adventure or some such thing. You see how very stupid I was.

"Vieni qua, galantuomo."

These words, spoken in a whisper, were accompanied by a caress to my cheek, which did not displease me. We reached her house, or what I took to be her house, and the sweet girl removed a key from under her cloak and opened the door. I may have been losing what little sense I had, but I noticed at once how sordid the place was and that put me on the alert. I tried to say good-bye there and then, but she again took my hand. We had walked up the steps that go from Santa Lucia to the first houses in Pizzofalcone— the large barracks I lived in years later had not yet been built—and once through the door, we entered a deep, dark, musty hallway. She clapped her hands, and an old, sleepy-eyed serving woman arrived bearing a light and led us up more stairs to a room furnished only with a mat, two chairs, a table, and a straw mattress. That room dispelled all my fantasies, for this was clearly not a private house, but a place where flesh was bought and sold, one of those places that abound in fake mothers, shopkeepers selling their own nieces and some very distant cousins. As the poet says:

The comely widow dressed in black
Swears to everyone, it's said,
That fearing to see her husband's ghost
She much prefers to share her bed.

Anyway, she removed her mantilla and revealed a reasonably attractive face, although rather more heavily made up and less youthful than it had seemed to me in the dark. She started telling me a long unlikely tale about a jewel a female friend of hers had pawned, and about a cousin or brother of one or the other, and about some money that she needed desperately, it seemed, in order to save the honor of both ladies, and I don't know what else, all very pertinent no doubt. I, meanwhile, hadn't even sat down and was still standing there, with my hat in my hand and my sword in my belt, waiting for her to finish speaking in order to deposit a few coins on the table, in payment for wasting her time, and leave through the same door I had entered. However, before I could put that thought into action, the door opened again and, just as if we were in a farce by Quiñones de Benavente, the villain of the piece made his entrance—and "made his entrance" exactly describes the act, the moment, and the character.

"Gadzooks!" quoth the villain.

He was Spanish and dressed as a soldier, and bore himself very proudly, although he clearly had nothing of the military about him, and the closest he had ever got to a Lutheran or a Turk had been in the theater. Otherwise, he was like a character straight out of a book, all bluster and bravado, swearing by Christ's wounds and affecting a false Andalusian accent as if he had just arrived hotfoot from Seville. He had the inevitable waxed mustache proper to all swashbucklers, and having stalked into the room, he immediately struck a bold pose, legs astride, one fist on his waist and the other on the hilt of a sword seven spans long. He pronounced his *g*'s like *h*'s and his *h*'s like *j*'s—a sure sign of unassailable bravery—and was, in short, the very image of the pimp who takes young girls and lives off the fruits of their hard labor while he boasts of having killed no end of men and of how he regularly hands out beatings and larrupings before he's even had breakfast, roughs up whores in the presence of their very own bullyboys, makes mincemeat of catchpoles, holds his tongue on the rack, and enjoys the admiration, respect, and affection of his fellow ruffians. And Lord knows what else.

"God's teeth!" he spluttered, frowning furiously, then added in a voice that echoed round the room: "I've told you before, señora, that for the sake of my honor, you must never bring another man into this house!"

And he continued in the same vein for some time, declaiming as if from a pulpit, thundering against the treachery and scandal brought on him by his dam, declaring that, even captive in Algiers, he would not have suffered such humiliations, and warning that his sword was very sharp, by God. Because when the rage took him and his bile was up, by all that's holy, he could as lief kill two as two hundred. He was within an ace of marking that trollop's face with the sign of the cross so that she would learn once and for all that Cannibals and Gorillas like him (he meant, of course, to say Hannibals and Attilas) would not put up with such excesses, and if anyone should abuse his good faith and try to put horns on his head, his wrath would be terrible to see, and woe betide the Turk in question if he, too, wasn't man enough to dispatch seven men at once and put them well beyond the help of surgeons. By the Eternal Father and the mother who bore him, et cetera, et cetera.

While this jewel of the scoundrelry babbled on, I, after

my initial surprise, stayed where I was, my back to the wall, hat in hand and sword in sheath, saying nothing, but waiting to see when he would finally get to the point. And so I had the leisure to observe that the poor sinner, who took her role very seriously, like someone who knows both words and music, stood looking troubled and contrite and fearful, wringing her hands in great sorrow, and occasionally interposing excuses and pleas, while her better half, without ceasing to rain down words on her, would now and then raise his hand from his hip as if to slap her, only to hold back at the last moment. And he did all this without once looking at me.

"So," said the pimp, coming at last to the nub of the matter, "we'll have to reach some arrangement; otherwise, I can't be answerable for my actions."

I stood where I was, thoughtful and motionless, silently studying him, while I pondered what Captain Alatriste would do in my situation and in my shoes. However, as soon as I heard the words "arrangement" and "actions," I moved away from the wall and lunged at the villain so quickly that I had put my hand to my dagger, unsheathed it, and slashed his face before he could cry "God save me." I didn't see much else of what happened, or only out of the corner of my eye: the braggart collapsing with a gash above his ear, his whore rushing to his aid with a yelp of horror, and then, fleetingly, the steps of the stairs in the house and then those of Santa Lucia, which I took four at a time and in the dark, risking falling and cracking my head open, as I fled as fast as my young legs would carry me. For as the saying goes—and quite right too—it's every man for himself and the Devil take the hindmost.

8. THE CHORRILLO INN

Captain Alonso de Contreras was drinking from a fountain, cupping the water in his hands. Then, drying his bristling mustache on the sleeve of his doublet, he looked across at Vesuvius, whose plume of smoke was melting into the low clouds on the far side of the bay. He took a deep, satisfied breath of the cool breeze blowing along the dockside, where his frigate, ready to set sail, was moored alongside two galleys belonging to the pope and a square-rigged French vessel. Beside him, Diego Alatriste drank too, and then they both continued their walk toward the imposing black towers of Castelnuovo. It was midday, and the sun and the breeze were drying the rivulets of blood beneath their feet, the blood of eight Morisco corsairs who had been beaten to death in the early hours of that morning, almost as soon as they stepped off the galleys that had captured them five days earlier off Cape Colonna.

"I hate to leave Naples," Contreras said. "Lampedusa is so small, and in Sicily, I have the viceroy on my back. Here, I feel free again, I even feel younger. I swear to God, this place could rejuvenate anyone, don't you agree?"

"I suppose so, although I think it might take rather more than that to rejuvenate us."

"Yes, you're right. It's as if time were traveling posthaste, and speaking of post, I've just come from don Francisco's, and someone said there was a letter for you. I've just had a letter myself from Lope de Vega. Our protégé Lopito will be coming to Naples at the end of the summer. Poor lad, eh? And poor Laura. Dead from a fever after only six months of marriage. God, how time flies! That trick we played on her uncle seems like only yesterday, and yet it's a whole year ago."

Alatriste said nothing, his thoughts elsewhere. He was still looking at the dark stains that ran from the quay to the customhouse. The men from whose bodies that blood had flowed had landed along with the other captives, a total of twenty-seven corsairs from Algiers, all of them Moriscos, captured on board a brigantine that had plundered a number of ships along the coasts of Calabria and Sicily, among them a Neapolitan vessel every single member of whose crew—from captain to cabin boy—was put to death for flying the Spanish flag. When the prisoners were being taken off, some of the recent widows and orphans were on the quay along with the crowd that usually gathered for the arrival of galleys. Such was the public anger that, after a brief consultation with the bishops, the viceroy agreed that those who were prepared to die as Christians would be hanged in three days' time without suffering any further torture, but those who refused to accept the one true religion would be handed over to the people clamoring to mete out justice there and then. Eight of the Moriscos, all of them *tagarinos*—Spanish Muslims from the same Aragonese village, Villefeliche—spurned the priests waiting for them on the quayside and affirmed their faith in Islam. It therefore fell to some Neapolitan boys, the urchins of street and port, to beat them to death with sticks and stones. At that hour, after the bodies had been displayed beneath the lantern on the quay and on the tower of San Vicente, what was left of them was being burned, amid much celebration, on the other side of the smaller harbor in La Marinella.

"By the way," Contreras said, adopting a confidential tone, "they're preparing another raid on the Levant. I know this because they've asked me to lend them Gorgos, my pilot, and have spent days consulting my Universal Map, which details these coasts, inch by inch, or almost. And while I'm honored that they should do so, I'm angry too. I haven't seen my magnum opus since Prince Filiberto asked to borrow it in order to make a copy. And whenever I demand it back, those bloodsuckers dressed in black, like cockroaches, put me off with excuses, Devil take 'em!"

"Galleys or sailing ships?" asked Alatriste.

With a sigh of resignation, Contreras put thoughts of his map to one side.

"Galleys. Ours and those belonging to the knights, I understand. The *Mulata* is one of them. So you have a campaign to look forward to."

"A long one?"

"Fairly. They say one month or two, beyond the Mayna channel, possibly even as far east as the Dardanelles, where, as I recall, you would need no pilot."

Alatriste pulled a wry face in response to his friend's broad smile. They left the harbor and proceeded along the esplanade between the customhouse and the imposing moat surrounding Castelnuovo. The last time Alatriste had seen the Dardanelles was in sixteen hundred and thirteen, when the galley he was sailing in was captured by the Turks near Cape Troya, with many dead and the lateen yard bristling with arrows. Gravely wounded in one leg, he had been liberated along with the other survivors when they were within sight of the fortresses overlooking the strait, where the Turkish ship was in turn captured.

"Do you know who else is going?" he asked, raising one hand to the brim of his hat, to greet a few acquaintances— three harquebusiers and a musketeer on guard at the postern leading to the ramp up to the castle. Contreras did the same.

"According to Machín de Gorostiola, who told me the news, there will be three of our galleys and two belonging to the knights. Machín is embarking with his Basques, which is how he knows."

They reached the esplanade, where carriages and cavalry and an animated crowd were still heading toward the palace square and Trinità dei Spagnuoli, on their way back from the burning of the Moriscos. A dozen or so young lads marched alongside them. They were carrying on a broom handle the tattered, bloody tunic of a corsair.

"The *Mulata*," Contreras went on, "will be carrying extra troops. I believe Fernando Labajos will be on board along with twenty good, experienced harquebusiers, all of them from your company."

Alatriste nodded, pleased. He got on well with Lieutenant Labajos, a tough, efficient veteran, accustomed to life on the galleys. As for Captain Machín de Gorostiola, he commanded a company made up entirely of Basques from Vizcaya, sturdy, long-suffering men, cruel and unrelenting in combat. It looked set to be a serious expedition.

"That's fine by me," he said.

"Will you take the boy?"

"I suppose so."

A downcast Contreras twirled his mustache.

"I'd give anything to come with you, because I do so miss the good old days, my friend. Do you remember how

the Turks used to call us the Catholic king's corsairs? And
how we would fill our hats to the brim with silver coins?
Ah, all those famous battles and beautiful whores! Dear
God, I'd give Lampedusa, my Knights Hospitaller's habit,
and even the play Lope wrote about me, just to be thirty
again. What times, eh, those of the great Duke of Osuna!"

They grew serious at the mention of the unfortunate
duke's name, and said nothing more until they reached
Via dei Macellai, opposite the gardens belonging to the
viceroy's palace. The great Duke of Osuna was the same
don Pedro Téllez Girón, under whom Alatriste had fought
in Flanders, during the siege of Ostend. He was later made
Viceroy of Naples and then of Sicily; together with the
Spanish galleys he had sown terror throughout the seas of
Italy and the Levant during the reign of Philip III, and he
gained the respect of Turks, Berbers, and Venetians alike.
His private life may have been outlandish, scandalous, and
mad, but he was an efficient statesman and met with great
success as a soldier, always eager for glory and for booty,
which he later squandered. He surrounded himself with
the best soldiers and sailors and made many men at court,
including the king, very rich indeed. However, the dazzling
rise of his star inevitably aroused a great deal of resent-
ment, envy, and hatred, and, after the king's death, the
duke's life ended in ruin and imprisonment. Submitted to
a trial that never reached a conclusion, refusing to defend

himself because, he maintained, his exploits spoke for themselves, the great Duke of Osuna, sick and sad, had died a miserable death in prison, to the applause and joy of the enemies of Spain, in particular Turkey, Venice, and Savoy, whom he had held at bay when the black flags bearing his ducal coat of arms had victoriously ravaged the Mediterranean. His last words were: "If I have served God as well as I have served my king, then I have been a good Christian." Don Francisco de Quevedo had been a close friend—indeed, his friendship with Diego Alatriste dated from that same period in Naples—and he was one of the few who had remained faithful to the duke even in his misfortune. He wrote some of his finest sonnets by way of an epitaph. These lines for example:

> *Although his country has denied him praise,*
> *His deeds will always be his best defense;*
> *Imprison'd by Spain, he died—poor recompense*
> *For one who conquer'd Fortune all his days.*

And this other poem, which reflected, better than any history book, the reward that our wretched Spain all too often gave to its best sons:

> *Though he annulled the marriage of the sea and Venice*
> *And crushed the waves beneath the keels of Spain,*

Making shake both Cyprus Isle and Greece,
This conquerer was conquered by the Law's thin cane!

"Speaking of your young companion," Contreras said suddenly, "I have news of him."

"Of Íñigo?"

"The very same. But I doubt very much that the news will please you."

And having said that, Contreras brought Diego Alatriste up to date. In one of those coincidences so common in Naples, a certain acquaintance of his, a chief constable, had been interrogating a ne'er-do-well who frequented the Chorrillo Inn. At the first turn of the screw, the man in question, who was not made of the sternest of stuff and a bit of a blabbermouth, had given tongue, without even taking a breath, to everything he knew about man and God. Among other things, he mentioned that a certain Florentine gambler, a regular customer at such places and more astute than brave, was recruiting villains in order to recover—in blood and via an ambush—a gaming debt incurred in Piazza dell'Olmo by two young soldiers, one of whom was lodged at Ana de Osorio's inn in the Spanish quarter.

"And are you sure he was referring to Íñigo?"

"'Od's blood! The only thing I'm sure about is that one day I'll have to meet my Maker, but the description and the fact that he's lodging at the inn fit like a glove."

Alatriste somberly smoothed his mustache and instinctively placed his left hand on the hilt of his sword.

"And this happened at the Chorrillo, you say?"

"The very place. Apparently, the Florentine frequents the taverns in that area."

"And did the snitch give the Florentine's name?"

"Yes, Giacomo Colapietra. A rogue and a rascal apparently."

They walked on in silence, Alatriste frowning beneath his hat, which cast a shadow over his cold, green eyes. When they had gone only a short way, Contreras, who was watching him out of the corner of his eye, gave a chuckle.

"By my troth, my friend, I'm sorry to be leaving tonight. I would swear that the Chorrillo is about to become a very interesting place indeed!"

As it turned out, it was our room at the inn that was about to become a very interesting place, for shortly before the Angelus, when I was just about to go out on the town, Captain Alatriste came in with a loaf of bread under one arm and a bottle of wine under the other. I was accustomed to guessing his thoughts and his mood, and as soon as I saw the way he threw his hat down on the bed and unbuckled his sword, I knew that something, and certainly nothing pleasant, was troubling him.

"Are you going out?" he asked, seeing me dressed in my street clothes.

I was, it must be said, rather smartly turned out in a shirt with a Walloon collar, a green velvet waistcoat, and a fine cloth doublet—the latter bought at the sale of Ensign Muelas' effects after his death in Lampedusa—breeches, stockings, and silver-buckled shoes. And on my hat, I had a new green silk ribbon. And I said that, yes, I was going out, that Jaime Correas was waiting for me at an inn in Via Sperancella, although I spared the captain the details of our expedition, which included a visit to an elegant gaming den in Via Mardones, where they played hard at cards and dice. This would be followed by a supper of roast capon and cherry tart accompanied by a little good wine at the house of the *Portuguesa*, a place near the fountain of the Incoronata, where there was music and you could dance the canario and the pavanne.

"And what's in that purse?" he asked, seeing me close it and put it away in my pocket.

"Money," I said curtly.

"It looks like a lot of money for one night."

"How much I take with me is my business."

He stood looking at me thoughtfully, one hand on his hip, while he digested my insolent riposte. It was true that our savings were shrinking. His savings, which he had placed with a goldsmith in Via Sant'Anna, were just enough to pay for our lodgings and to help out the Moor Gurriato, whose sole wealth was the silver earrings he wore. The Moor had not yet received his first pay and, as a new soldier, he only had the right to stay in the barracks and eat whatever the troops ate. As for my money, about which the captain never asked, there had been a number of drains on my purse of late, so much so that I needed a fair wind at the gaming table if I was not to end up stone broke.

"And I suppose getting knifed to death on a street corner is your business too."

My hand, which had reached out to pick up my sword and my dagger, stopped halfway. I had spent many years by his side, and I knew that tone of voice.

"Are you referring to a possibility, Captain, or to one particular knife thrust?"

He did not reply at once. He had opened the bottle of wine and poured himself a mugful. He drank a little and looked at the wine, assessing the quality of what the innkeeper had sold him. Apparently satisfied, he took another sip.

"There are many reasons for getting yourself killed, but getting yourself killed in the street over a gaming debt is, quite simply, shameful."

He was speaking slowly and calmly, still looking at the wine in his mug. I was about to protest, but he raised his hand to stop me.

"It is," he concluded, "unworthy of a real man and of a soldier."

I scowled. For while the truth may hurt a Basque, it never breaks him.

"I have no debts."

"That's not what I've heard."

"Whoever told you that," I retorted, "is a lying Judas."

"What's the problem, then?"

"What problem are you referring to?"

"Explain to me why someone would want to kill you."

My surprise, which must have been written all over my face, was entirely genuine.

"Kill me? Who?"

"A certain Giacomo Colapietra, a Florentine gamester, a regular at the Chorrillo and the Piazza dell'Olmo. He's currently hiring the services of some ruffians with sharp knives to finish you off."

I took a few steps about the room, stunned. I wasn't expecting such news. A wave of embarrassment rose up my body.

"It isn't a debt," I said. "I've never had any debts."

"Tell me what happened, then."

I explained as briefly as I could how Jaime Correas and I had been halfway through a card game with the Florentine when he tried to cheat us by using marked cards, and how we had left without giving him the money he claimed we owed him.

"I'm not a child, Captain," I said.

He looked me up and down. My account did not seem to improve his view of the affair. While it was true that the captain was often quite happy to drink everything that was put in front of him, it was equally true that he had never been seen with a deck of cards in his hand. He despised those who risked money that, in his profession, could either pay for a life or for the sword that took that life away.

"You're not yet a man either, it seems to me."

That really angered me.

"No one has the right to say that to me," I said, my pride injured. "And I won't give that right to anyone."

"*I* have the right to say it."

He was looking at me as coldly as the ice that used to crunch under our boots in the winters in Flanders.

"And you," he added after a silence as heavy as lead, "will give me that right."

This wasn't a statement, it was an order. Struggling to find a response that would not prove too humiliating, I glanced at my sword and my dagger as if appealing to them for help. Like the captain's weapons, they both bore scratches and dents on blades and guards. And I had scars on my body too, although not as many as him.

"I've killed . . ."

Several men, I wanted to say, but held back, out of

shame. It sounded like an empty tavern boast spoken by a ruffian.

"Who hasn't?"

He was regarding me ironically, scornfully, in a way that made my gorge rise.

"I'm a soldier," I protested.

"Even a deserter can say he's a soldier. The gaming dens and taverns and whorehouses are full of them."

This comment enraged me almost to the point of tears. It was unfair, a dreadful thing to say, especially since the man saying it had seen me by his side at the Gate of Lost Souls, at the Ruyter Mill, in the barracks at Terheyden, on board the *Niklaasbergen*, on corsair galleys, and in twenty other places.

"You know I'm not one of them," I stammered.

He looked down at the floor, as if aware that he had gone too far. Then he took another sip of wine.

"Those reluctant to accept another's advice are very prone to err," he said, barely raising his lips from his mug. "You are not yet the man you think you are, nor the man you should be."

That was the final straw. Almost mad with rage, I turned my back, buckled on my sword and dagger, picked up my hat, and headed for the door.

"Not, at least, the man *I* would like you to be," he added. "Or the man your father would have liked you to be."

I paused on the threshold. Suddenly, for some strange reason, I felt above him, above everything.

"My father . . ." I began, then pointed to the bottle of wine on the table. "At least he died before I saw him so drunk he couldn't tell a fox from a rabbit."

He took a step toward me, just one. He had a murderous glint in his eye. I stood firm, holding his gaze, but he stayed where he was, looking at me hard. Then I slowly closed the door behind me and left the inn.

The following morning, while the captain was on guard at Castelnuovo, I took my trunk and moved into the barracks in Via Monte Calvario.

From don Francisco de Quevedo
to don Diego Alatriste y Tenorio
Company of Captain Armenta
de Medrano Naples Regiment

My dear captain,

Here I am, still at court, loved by the great and spoiled by the ladies, enjoying the good favor of everyone who counts, although time does not pass in vain and I find myself ever more unsteady on my legs and unable now to walk at an amble. The one cloud on my horizon is the appointment of Cardinal Zapata to the post of Inquisitor General. My old

enemy Father Pineda is constantly pestering him to
include my works on the Index of Prohibited Books.
However, God will provide.

The king is as kind as ever and continues to
perfect himself in the art of hunting (of all kinds),
as is only natural in a man in the full flower of
youth. The count-duke, meanwhile, rises a little
higher with each shot fired by our second
Theodosius; and so everyone is happy. However,
the sun shines on both kings and commoners: my
ancient aunt Margarita is about to pass on to a
better life, and I have reason to believe that her
last will and testament will contain something
that will raise me a little higher too. Otherwise,
there is not much to tell after January's bankruptcy,
except to say that the Treasury is surrounded
by the usual folk, that is to say, by everyone, and a
few more besides, not counting the Genoans and
those Portuguese Jews of whom the count-duke
is so fond; for it is always far more galling to
see a banker thrive than the Turk. As long as
the galleons from the Indies continue to arrive
punctually, carrying in their holds large
quantities of silver and that other sweet blond
metal, everything will continue the same in
Spain: bring me some wine, roast me some pork,

*for as long as I can eat and drink, the maggots
must fast.*

*Of the mudhole that is Flanders I say nothing,
because in Naples, among others of the same
profession, I am sure you receive more than enough
information about that. Suffice it to say that here the
Catalans continue to deny the king the money he
needs for the war and barricade themselves behind
their privileges and their laws, and many predict a
bad outcome for such obstinacy. Regarding a new
war, which, with Richelieu in the Palais du Louvre,
seems inevitable sooner or later, any domestic
troubles here would suit France perfectly, for as
they say, the Devil looks after his own. With respect
to your adventures on the wine-dark sea, whenever
some brief report is published here about what our
galleys have been up to, I imagine that you were
involved in every escapade, putting Turks to the
sword, and that pleases me. May the Ottoman
bite the dust, may you win both laurels and booty,
and may I see and savor it all, and drink to your
health.*

*Now, because books are always a source of
consolation, I am sending with this letter a copy of
my* Dreams *to distract you when you are not at war.
The ink is still fresh, for Sapera the printer has only*

just sent it to me from Barcelona. Give it to our
young Patroclus, who, I know, will find it an
edifying read, since, according to the censor Father
Tomás Roca, it contains nothing that offends
against the Catholic faith or against good custom,
and you, I am sure, will be as pleased about
that as I am. I trust that Íñigo remains in good
health by your side, prudently accepts your counsel,
and bows to your authority. Send him my warm
regards and tell him that my negotiations at court
on his behalf are progressing well, and with a
favorable wind behind them, and if all goes to
plan, his entry into the ranks of royal courtiers
is as good as guaranteed as soon as he returns to
Madrid a fully accredited miles gloriosus. Tell him
that, as well as adorning his mind with my words,
he must not neglect those of Tacitus, Homer, and
Virgil; for even were he to don the armor of Mars
himself, in the tumult of this world, the pen is still
mightier than the sword, and of considerably
more comfort too, swans being higher up the scale
than ducks.

There are more matters at hand about which I
cannot tell you in a letter, but all will be well, and
God will shed his light on us and bring us good
fortune. Suffice it to say that I have been questioned

lately about my Italian experiences under the great
and much-missed Osuna. However, it is a delicate
business and its telling requires great tact, and the
time for that is not yet ripe. By the way, there is a
rumor going around that an old and dangerous
friend of yours, whom you left in the hands of the
law, was not executed secretly as was first thought.
Rather (and this is between you and me and has yet
to be confirmed) he bought his life by providing
valuable information about certain affairs of state. I
do not know what stage these negotiations have
reached, but it might be a good idea to glance over
your shoulder now and then if you hear someone
whistle.

I have more things to tell you, but I will leave
them until my next letter. I end this one with
regards from La Lebrijana, whose tavern I
occasionally visit to honor your absence with
one of those dishes she prepares so well and with
a pitcher of San Martín de Valdeiglesias. She
remains a handsome woman, with a fine figure and
a still finer face, and is as devoted to you as ever.
Other habitués also send their regards: Father
Pérez, Master Calzas, the apothecary Fadrique,
and Juan Vicuña, who has just become a
grandfather. Martín Saldaña appears to have

recovered at last, after spending almost a year
hovering on the frontier between this life and the
next—thanks to that cut you dealt him in the
Rastro—and is once again to be seen out and
about in the streets with his staff of office, just as
if he had never left. I meet Guadalmedina at the
palace occasionally, but he always avoids any
mention of your name. There is much talk lately of
him being sent to England or to France as
ambassador.

Take great care of yourself, dear captain. And
look after the boy so that he may enjoy many long
and happy years.

A warm embrace from your friend,
Francisco de Quevedo

It was late afternoon, and, as usual, the Chorrillo was beginning to get lively. Diego Alatriste sauntered around the
small crescent-shaped piazza, observing the people sitting
outside the taverns, of which there were many, gathered
around the establishment that gave the square its name—
a famous inn that brought a flurry of old memories. The
name, Chorrillo, was a Spanish version of the Italian Cer-
riglio, which was the name of an inn situated near the
Santa Maria Novella church, and whose reputation for good

wine, food, and pleasure dated from the previous century. Almost since the legendary days of Pavia and the Sack of Rome, the place had been frequented by soldiers and by men hoping to enlist, or so they said, and many rogues, ruffians, and hired blades were to be found among that rabble. Indeed, the term *chorrillero* or *churrullero* was commonly used in Naples and in Spain to refer to the kind of Spanish soldier, whether pretend or real, who worked harder at throwing dice and emptying wineskins than sticking a sword in a Turk or knifing the odd Lutheran. The type, in short, who would sigh "Ah, what battles we've seen, comrade, and what wine we've drunk!"—and only the bit about the wine was true.

Alatriste greeted a few acquaintances, but did not stop. Despite the warm weather, he was wearing a short gray cape over his doublet; this was in order to conceal the pistol he had stuck in the back of his belt. At that hour and given his intentions, this was an understandable precaution, although the presence of the pistol was not directly related to the villainous faces to be seen about the place. There were still a couple of hours of daylight left, a time of day when all kinds of idlers would arrange to meet: braggarts and bullyboys of the criminal classes, regular inmates of the Vicaria prison or the military prison of Santiago, who would spend their mornings on the steps of Santa Maria Novella, watching the women going in to mass, and their evenings and nights in the various taverns, discussing the conditions of such and such an enlistment or—revealing the field marshal inside every Spaniard— mulling over stratagems and tactics and declaring how a certain battle should have been won or why another was lost. Almost all were Spanish and had been brought to Naples either by the army or a need to earn some money, and all were so proud and fierce that, even if they had been mere cobblers back home, here they boasted of their high lineage. It was the same with many Spanish whores, who arrived by the cartload, calling themselves Mendoza or Guzmán, so that even their Italian colleagues ended up demanding to be treated as *signora*. This gave rise to the Italian word *spagnolata*, used to describe any kind of pomposity or boastfulness.

> *In Córdoba and fair Seville,*
> *I've property a-plenty.*
> *My parents, born into the gentry,*
> *Are lords of all Castile.*

There was also no shortage of natives of the region, as well as Sicilians, Sardinians, and people from other parts of Italy. They formed a panoply of cutpurses, counterfeiters, gamesters, cape-thieves, deserters, ruffians, and other scum, gathered together to exchange blasphemies, per-

juries, and other such nonsense. The name of Chorrillo in
Naples could have taken its rightful place among such il-
lustrious locations as the steps in Seville, the Potro in Cór-
doba, La Sapienza in Rome, or the Rialto in Venice.

Leaving the inn behind him, Alatriste strode across this
noble venue and went up an alleyway known as the steps
of the Piazzetta, so narrow there was barely room for two
men wearing swords to pass. The smell of wine from the
drinking dens, from which came the buzz of conversation
and the tuneless singing of drunkards, mingled with the
stench of urine and other filth. And when the captain
stepped aside to avoid treading in some of that filth, he
inadvertently got in the way of two soldiers coming down.
They were dressed in Spanish style, although unostenta-
tiously: hats, swords, and boots.

"Why don't you damn well go and get in someone else's
way," one of them muttered angrily in Castilian, and made
as if to continue down the steps.

Alatriste slowly, almost thoughtfully, smoothed his
mustache. Both were military men in their late thirties.
The man who had spoken was short and stocky and had a
Galician accent. He was wearing expensive gloves, and his
clothes, although of a sober cut, were made of good cloth.
The other man was tall and thin and had a melancholy air
about him. Both wore mustaches and plumed hats.

"I would be delighted to do so," he replied simply, "and
in your company too, if you have no other engagements."

The two men had stopped.

"In our company? Whatever for?" asked the shorter man brusquely.

Alatriste shrugged, as if the answer were obvious. Indeed, he thought, there was no other possible response. There was always one's wretched reputation to consider.

"To discuss a few of the finer points of fencing. You know the kind of thing: length of step, keeping the blade in line, feint and riposte, et cetera."

"Upon my oath," murmured the short man.

He did not say "upon my oath as a gentleman," as was usual among those who were very far from being gentlemen. Alatriste saw that both men were studying him carefully and that they had noticed the scars on his face as well as the sword at his waist and, in his belt, the dagger on whose hilt his left hand was resting almost casually. They couldn't see the pistol, hidden beneath his cape, but it was there. He sighed to himself. This was not part of his plan, but if that was how things were, then so be it. As for the pistol, he hoped not to be obliged to use it. He had brought it more as a threat than as a precaution and had another purpose in mind for it.

"My friend is not in the best of moods," said the taller of the soldiers in a conciliatory tone. "He has just met with a problem."

"What I have met with is my affair," said the other man gruffly.

"Well, I'm sorry to say this," replied Alatriste coolly, "but if he doesn't mend his manners, he'll soon have another problem to deal with."

"Be careful what you say," said the taller man, "and don't be deceived by my companion's appearance. You would be very surprised to know his name."

Alatriste, who had not taken his eyes off the shorter man, shrugged again.

"Well, then, to avoid confusion, he should either dress in accordance with his name or choose a name in accordance with his dress."

The other two men looked at each other, uncertain what to do, and Alatriste moved his hand away from the hilt of his dagger. They had the manners of decent people and did not appear to be men who would knife you in the street or in the back. And they were certainly not the kind to queue up on payday at the arsenal to collect their four *escudos*. Beneath their soldiers' clothes one could sense that they were refined folk, clean and serious, employed by some noble or general, or else the venturesome sons of good families who were spending some time in the army to add luster to their reputation. Flanders and Italy were full of them. He wondered what had thrown the shorter, stockier man into such a rage. A woman perhaps. Or some bad luck at the card table. Whatever the motive, he really didn't care: everyone had their own problems.

"Anyway," he said, offering an honorable way out, "I have an urgent matter to attend to."

The taller man seemed relieved to hear this.

"We ourselves are on duty in two hours' time," he remarked.

He, too, had a Spanish accent, but somewhat harsher, from the north somewhere, Asturian perhaps. And the tone in which he said these words sounded genuine and dignified and far from being an excuse. The matter could have ended there had his companion shared his conciliatory mood. He was looking at Alatriste with the dark tenacity of a hunting hound who, furious at having lost a fox, is intent on attacking a wolf.

"There's plenty of time."

Alatriste again stroked his mustache. He sensed that this was not a good situation to be in. Exchanging sword thrusts with one of those men, or with both, could get him into trouble. He would like to leave things as they stood, but this was not easy. Wounded honor on both sides complicated matters. And he was beginning to find the other man's obstinacy irritating.

"Right, let's not waste words," he said resolutely.

"Bear in mind," said the tall man in the same reasonable tone, "that I couldn't possibly leave my companion alone. You would have to fight me as well. And then, of course, should there be . . ."

"Enough talk," the other man announced, interrupting him and facing Alatriste. "Where shall we go? To Piede-gruta?"

Alatriste gave him a hard look, as if taking his measure. Now he really did feel like sticking a foot of steel in the guts of this importunate conceited little cockerel. Damn it. It would be over in a trice. And he would finish off his companion as well, two for the price of one. That way, at least, he would make them pay for the trouble they had caused him.

"The Porta Reale is nearer," he suggested. "And there's a discreet little meadow there, just crying out for someone to fall down dead in it."

The taller man gave a resigned sigh.

"This gentleman will require a witness," he said to his companion. "We don't want people saying that we mur-dered him between us."

A distracted smile flickered across Alatriste's lips. That was very reasonable, and considerate too. Duels were for-bidden in Naples by royal ordinance, and any transgressor would go straight to prison, or to the gallows, if there was no one to speak up for him. It was, therefore, best to keep to the rules, especially if there were people of quality in-volved. It would, he concluded, be a matter of killing one—the shorter man—and leaving the other more or less unscathed, so that he could report that the fight had been fair and square. Although, if there were no witnesses at all, he could just kill them both and vanish.

"We can sort that out on the way there, if you would be so kind as to wait for me for a moment." He pointed up the steps, where the alleyway turned to the right. "I have some business to sort out."

After exchanging a somewhat bemused glance, the two men nodded. Then calmly turning his back on them—life had taught him on whom it was safe to turn his back and on whom it was not, and he just hoped that he was right on this occasion—Alatriste went up the last few steps. He could hear the Spaniards following behind; they seemed in no hurry he noticed, and he felt pleased to be dealing with such reasonable people. He went around the corner and through an archway that was as narrow as the rest of the street; there he found a tavern sign. Having first checked that he was in the right place and giving no further thought to his startled companions, he adjusted his hat and made sure that sword and dagger were in position should he need them. Then he fastened the buffcoat he was wearing under his cape, felt for his pistol, and went inside. It was one of the seamier places in Naples: a courtyard with an arcade along which the tables were placed. Chickens pecked about on the dirt floor. There were about twenty or so rather rough-looking customers, Italians to judge by their appearance. At some of the tables, cards were being played, watched by the occasional onlooker, who might simply have been enjoying the game or else was spying on the cards of their accomplice's unwitting opponent, a trick known as "Claramonte's mirror."

Alatriste went discreetly over to the innkeeper, greased his palm with a silver coin, and asked which player was Giacomo Colapietra. A moment later, he was standing by a table where a very thin individual, all skin and bones, wearing a wig and sporting a waxed mustache, was drinking and shuffling the cards. He was accompanied by a couple of nasty-looking toughs, the kind who carry sword and shield and whose collars are frayed and stiff with grease.

"Could you and I have a private word?"

The Florentine, who was just then separating the kings from the jacks, looked up and peered at him inquisitively. Then he curled his lip.

"*Nascondo niente a mis amichis,*" he said, indicating his companions.

His breath stank of cheap watered-down wine. Alatriste glanced at the aforementioned *amichis*. Obviously Italian. A bold front, but pure pasteboard inside. He needn't worry too much about them, even if they were carrying swords. The Florentine was the only one without a sword, although a dagger a span and a half long hung from his belt.

"I understand you're hiring men who know how to handle a knife, Signor Giacomo."

"*Non bisogno nessuno più.*"

The expression on Alatriste's face was like a sliver of glass.

"I'm not making myself clear. Those men are being hired to kill a friend of mine."

Colapietra stopped shuffling the cards and glanced at his comrades. Then he took a more careful look at Alatriste. A smug smile appeared beneath his waxed mustache.

"I've been told," Alatriste went on impassively, "that you have paid for a nasty surprise to be sprung on a certain young Spaniard very close to my heart."

When he heard this, Colapietra burst into scornful laughter.

"*Cazzo,*" he said.

Then, simultaneously sly and threatening, he made as if to get up along with his companions, but was stopped in his tracks. Alatriste had whipped the pistol out from beneath his cape.

"Sit down, all three of you," he said calmly and slowly, when he saw that they had grasped the idea. "Or I'll shit on your whorish mothers. *Capisci?*"

Silence had fallen all around, but Alatriste kept his eyes fixed on the three ruffians, who had turned as pale as wax.

"Keep your hands on the table and away from your swords."

Still not looking behind him, so as not to reveal any

lack of confidence, he put the pistol in his left hand and rested his right hand on the hilt of his sword, just in case he needed to unsheathe it in order to make his way to the door. He had already worked out an exit strategy, including his retreat back down the steps. Should things get out of hand, he had only to get as far as the Chorrillo, where there would be no shortage of helping hands. He could, of course, have taken someone with him, Copons or the Moor Gurriato—who was longing to render him just such a service—or some other comrade who would gladly have backed him up. However, the theatrical effect would not have been the same. Therein lay the art.

"Now listen, you bastard."

And pressing the barrel of his pistol to the ashen face of the gambler—who had dropped his cards on the floor—Alatriste brought his mustache very close to his and then quietly, precisely, and unequivocally detailed just what he would do to Colapietra, to his innards, and to those who had engendered him, if any friend of his came to any harm. Even a fall in the street or a stumble would be enough for him to come and settle accounts with the Florentine, whom he would hold responsible, even for cases of diarrhea or fever. And he, Diego Alatriste by name, resident in the Spanish quarter at the inn of Ana de Osorio, would have no need to hire anyone else to wield the knife, largely because people usually hired *him* to do such dirty work. *Capisci?*

"So, listen well. I'll always be here, or else waiting on some dark corner, to slit you open. Do you understand?"

Shaken, Colapietra nodded briefly. The futile dagger at his waist only accentuated his pathetic air. Alatriste's cold, pale eyes, only a few inches from his, seemed to rob him of speech. His wig had shifted to one side and you could smell his fear—damp and acrid. The captain decided against tormenting him further with the barrel of the pistol. One could never foresee what would make a man mad.

"Is that clear?"

As clear as day, said Colapietra's silent nod. Moving away a little, the captain shot a sideways glance at the Florentine's consorts. They were as still as statues and had, with angelic innocence, kept their hands on the table. One would have said that apart from stealing from their mothers, murdering their fathers, and prostituting their sisters, they had never done anything wrong in their whole sinful lives. Then, without lowering the pistol or removing his hand from the hilt of his sword, in a silence in which one could hear the flies buzzing and the chickens pecking, Alatriste left the table. Then, without entirely turning his back on them and keeping a close eye on the other customers, who sat frozen and dumb, he made his way to the door. There he bumped into the two Spaniards, who had followed him and witnessed the whole episode. He was surprised to see them there, for so concentrated had he been on his own affairs, he had quite forgotten them.

"Right, to business," he said, ignoring the expression of amazement on their faces.

The three went out into the street together, the other two men still speechless, while Alatriste lowered the hammer on his pistol and put it back in his belt, under his cape. Then he spat on the ground, between his boots, looking angry and dangerous. The cold anger that had been building up in him since his encounter with these two men, plus the tension of that scene in the tavern, required some outlet. His fingers itched impatiently when he touched the guard of his sword. Christ's blood, he thought, imagining the coming fight. Maybe there was no need to go to the Porta Reale in order to set the bells ringing and resolve the matter. At the first surly word or gesture, he decided, he would take out his dagger—the street was too narrow for swordfights—and stick them like pigs right there, even if this did bring down upon him the law and the viceroy himself.

"By my oath," said the taller man.

He was staring at Diego Alatriste, as if seeing him for the first time, and his companion was doing the same. The latter was no longer frowning, but seemed, rather, pensive and curious.

"Do you want to go ahead with this?" the taller man asked his comrade.

Without answering, the latter kept his eyes fixed on

Alatriste, who held his gaze, meanwhile making an impatient gesture as if inviting him to set off to some place where they could resolve their argument. The other man did not stir. Instead, after a moment, he removed his right glove and held out his hand—frank and bare—to Alatriste. "I'd rather be basted like a runaway slave," he said, "than fight a man like him."

9. THE CATHOLIC KING'S CORSAIRS

The Turk ran up the flag of peace and took in his sails without a fight. It was a black caramusal with a long hull and a high stern: a two-masted merchant ship that our five galleys had prevented from making full use of the speed of her sails by cutting her off from both land and sea. It was our third capture since we had been keeping watch over the channel between the islands of Tinos and Mykonos, a much-frequented route on the way to Constantinople, Chios, and Smyrna. And the moment we came alongside and sent on board a group of infantrymen, we could see that it was a very good catch indeed. Crewed by Greeks and Turks, it was carrying oil and wine from Candia, soap and leather from Cairo, and other things of value, and, as passengers, it was carrying some Jews from

Salonica—the sort who wear yellow turbans—and they were well provided with silver coins. That day we used our fingers more than our swords, for we spent half an hour plundering the ship, and everything we touched stuck to our fingertips. When one soldier from another galley either fell or threw himself into the water to avoid the officers who were trying to impose order, he preferred to drown rather than give up his ill-gotten gains. The caramusal was a Turkish vessel, and so, as a worthy prize, we sent it off to Malta with the Greek crew and a few of our soldiers. The two renegades (whom we hoped the Inquisition would deal with later), eight Turks, three Albanians, and five Jews were shared out among the five galleys and set to the oars. The Hebrew race not being built for rowing, one of the Jews died two days later, either because he was ill or because he could not bear to see himself a miserable slave. The others were later ransomed for less than a thousand *sequins* by the monks of Patmos, who later released them, as they usually did, and charged them interest. For although the Patmos monks spoke Greek, they counted money in Genoese.

The two renegades were allocated to the *Mulata*. One was Spanish, from Ciudad Real, and in an attempt to improve his lot, he gave us some interesting information of which I will tell you more in due course. First, though, I should say that our campaign was proving highly profitable. Back on board, our hair once again slick with tar, our skin with salt, and our clothes with brine, we had set off with three galleys from Naples—the *Mulata*, the *Caridad Negra*, and the *Virgen del Rosario*—all newly careened and well provided with supplies and soldiers for a voyage of two months through the Aegean and along the Anatolian coast, on whose islands lived Greeks dominated by the Turks. Once we had left Capri behind us, we met up with two Maltese galleys—the *Cruz de Rodas* and the *San Juan Bautista*—off Fossa di San Giovanni and sailed with them in convoy as far as the small islands off Corfu. From there, having taken on salt meat and fresh water, we followed the Morea coast past Kefalonia and Zante, which belonged to the Venetians, and then skirted around the island of Sapienza and took on more water at the mills of Coron, where the Turkish artillery fired on us from the town, but missed. After that, we headed east along the Mayna channel and past Cape St. Angelo, where we entered the limpid waters of the archipelago, blue in the gulf and crystalline green on the shores, in order to do as Vélez de Guevara proclaimed in *The Terror of the Turks*:

> *I sailed on the sea of Levant*
> *In search of the arrogant Turk,*
> *The one who, defying our Spain,*
> *Must die, or be punished with work.*

I was particularly moved when we sailed past the gulf of Lepanto, where Spanish galley crews were in the habit of lining up on the landward side of the ship and saying a prayer in memory of the many Spaniards who died there, fighting like furies, when the fleet of the Holy League destroyed the Turkish fleet in the battle of fifteen hundred and seventy-one. I was also moved, although in a different way, when we passed the island of Sapienza and the town of Modon, which belongs to the Turks, for I remembered reading the name of Modon in the Captive's Tale in the first part of *Don Quixote*, never imagining that I would one day set to sea as a soldier, just as Cervantes did, and see the very lands and seas where he fought in his youth—not much older than I was at the time—until he found himself in Lepanto and on board the galley *Marquesa*, on "the most memorable occasion that the centuries, past and present, have ever seen, or that future centuries can hope to see."

But I promised to tell you about the information vouchsafed by the Spanish renegade captured on the caramusal. We did not know it then, but what he told us would dramatically affect our future and cost the lives of many valiant men. In order perhaps to ameliorate his fate at the hands of the Inquisition and to improve his situation on the galley—for he had been given one of the worst places on the rowing benches—the renegade asked to speak to Captain Urdemalas, saying that he had something of great import to tell him—in private. Having given an account of his life—full of the usual lies—he revealed something that our captain found quite unbelievable: a great Turkish vessel was preparing to set sail from Rhodes to Constantinople, carrying both rich merchandise and people of quality, among them a woman who was either a relative or a wife of the Great Turk, or was being sent to him as a wife—the renegade was unsure on this point. And, as we soon found out—for there are no secrets on a galley—the Spanish renegade advised Captain Urdemalas that if he wanted further information, he simply had to turn the screws on the master of the caramusal, who was also a renegade and had been assigned the same rowing position. The master of the caramusal was originally from Marseilles but, on being circumcised, had changed his name to Ali Masilia. As became clear, the Spaniard had a few scores to settle with him, and this was the perfect way to do so.

Given the potential importance of this information, Ali Masilia was duly put to torture. He was full of bravado at first, declaring that he knew nothing and that, besides, there wasn't a Christian alive who could make him talk. However, the first turn of the screw by the galley overseer, who threatened to make the renegade's eyes pop out of their sockets, was enough to make him change his tune; indeed, he proved so loquacious and eager to cooperate that Captain Urdemalas, fearing that his shouts would be heard by everyone, took him below and shut himself up with him in the food store. From there he emerged shortly afterward, stroking his beard and smiling from ear to ear. That afternoon, taking advantage of the windless conditions and the flat calm sea, we hove to about half a league to the north of Mykonos. There, the skiffs were lowered into the water, and the various officers met under the awning on board the *Caridad Negra*, which was our flagship, captained by don Agustín Pimentel, great-nephew of the old Count of Benavente, and to whom the Viceroy of Naples and the Grand Master of Malta had entrusted the expedition. In attendance were his galley captain, Machín de Gorostiola—who was also captain of the infantry on board—the chaplain, Father Francisco Nistal, and the chief pilot, Gorgos, a native of Ragusa, who had sailed with Captain Alonso de Contreras and who knew those waters like the back of his hand. Representing the other galleys were our own Captain Urdemalas and the captain of the *Virgen del Rosario*, a pleasant, talkative Valencian called Alfonso Cervera. The Maltese galleys sent their respective officers too, a gentleman from Mallorca called Brother Fulco Muntaner from the larger of the galleys, the *Cruz de Rodas*, and a Frenchman, Brother Vivan Brodemont, from the *San Juan Bautista*. And when the meeting ended, and before they had even returned in the skiffs to their respective galleys, the joyful rumor was already making the rounds of our small squadron that there really was a richly laden Turkish vessel traveling from Rhodes to Constantinople, and that we were in a good position to board it before it entered the Dardanelles. This made us howl with joy, and it did one good to see and hear all the soldiers and sailors on every galley cheering and wishing each other good luck. That same evening, before prayers were said, orders were issued to give the galley men some Candian wine, salt cheese from Sicily, and a few ounces of bacon, after which the whips cracked from prow to stern and the five galleys set off into the night with the slaves breaking their backs, rowing as hard as they could, like a pack of wolves scenting prey.

Dawn found me, as usual, in the embrasure on the starboard side toward the stern, watching the light gradually filling the horizon and observing the pilot performing his first rituals of the day. It was still very early, and the oarsmen were sleeping on their benches or in between them, because we were now under full sail, with the canvas and the rigging creaking gently, being pushed along by a reasonable northeaster which, with the galley keeping close to the wind, was carrying us along on our desired course, with the oars stowed and the ship heeling to starboard. Almost all the soldiers and sailors were asleep as well, while the cabin boys on watch, high up on masts and yards, scanned the horizon for sails or land, keeping a particularly close eye on the spot where the sun would come up, because the dazzle could conceal a dangerous enemy presence. I still had my blanket over my shoulders, for I slept with it wrapped about me, along with all the other men, and if I had put it down on the deck, it would have walked on its own so full was it of bedbugs and lice. I was leaning on some netting, which was damp from the night air, admiring the pinks and oranges of the dawn sky and wondering if one of the many sayings I had learned on board would hold true: red sky at night, sailor's delight; red sky in the morning, sailors take warning.

I glanced along the side of the galley. Captain Alatriste was already awake, and from afar I saw him shake out his blanket and fold it up. Then he leaned over the side and, using a bucket attached to a rope, scooped up some seawater and washed his face with it—drinking water being far too precious a commodity to use for washing—before rubbing his skin briskly with a rag so that the salt didn't stick to his skin. He took some hardtack from his pouch, dipped it in a little of the wine he shared with Sebastián Copons—they never drank it all at once, but rationed it out—and began eating, staring out to sea. When Copons, who was sleeping beside him, began to stir and raised his head, the captain broke the hardtack in two and gave him half. Copons chewed in silence, holding the biscuit in one hand and rubbing the sleep from his eyes with the other, while the captain surveyed the scene around him. When he noticed that I was near the stern, observing him, he looked away.

We had spoken little since Naples. The bitterness of our last conversation still rankled, and during our last days on shore, we had scarcely seen each other because I was staying at the military barracks in Monte Calvario, along with the Moor Gurriato, and I avoided the inns and taverns where the captain might go to eat and drink. This, however, allowed me to get to know the Moor better. He was back on board the *Mulata*, not, this time, as an unpaid oarsman, but with a wage of four *escudos* a month. We shared the same food and billet, and had already had occasion to fight alongside each other, albeit only briefly, during the capture of a samequin crewed by Albanians and Turks, which we came across within sight of the island of Milos. Since we were in the Argentera passage and therefore at risk of hitting a sandbank, we boarded using a skiff. Not that the escapade brought us much profit, for the ship was only carrying untanned hides; however, we returned with twelve men to put to the oars and with no losses on our side. Aware that Captain Alatriste was watching from a distance, I was among the first to jump aboard the samequin, followed by

PIRATES OF THE LEVANT

the Moor Gurriato, and I tried hard to distinguish myself in the eyes of everyone else, being the one to cut the sheets so that no one would tally them aft, and then fighting my way over to where the ship's master was standing, surrounded by the members of his crew, all of whom were wielding pikes and scimitars—although not with much enthusiasm, it must be said, for they had flagged visibly when they saw us boarding. When I managed to reach him, I dealt him such a blow to the chest that he almost died on the spot, just as he was about to open his mouth and ask for quarter, or so it seemed to me. I thus returned to the galley having earned the good opinion of my comrades, feeling prouder than a peacock and looking out of the corner of my eye to see if Captain Alatriste was watching.

"I think you should speak to him," said the Moor Gurriato.

He had just woken up and was lying next to me, his beard unkempt, his skin greasy from sleep and from the damp dawn air.

"Why? To ask his forgiveness?"

"No," he said, yawning. "I just mean that you should speak to him."

I gave an impudent laugh.

"If he has something to say, let him say it."

The Moor Gurriato was meticulously cleaning between his toes.

"He's older than you and wiser. That's why you need him. He knows things that you and I don't. On my soul, it's true."

I laughed again, smugly this time, as proud as a cockerel at five in the morning.

"That's where you're wrong. It's not like it was before."

"What was it like then?"

"Like looking at God."

He eyed me with his usual curiosity. This was one of his most appealing characteristics, that of giving absolute attention even to the tiniest and apparently most insignificant detail. He appeared to find everything interesting, from the composition of a speck of dust to the complex workings of the human heart. He would ask a question, listen to the reply, and then give an opinion, if required, very seriously and frankly, and without any pretense at discretion, wit, or bravery. He faced the good sense, stupidity, or ignorance of other people with equanimity and possessed the infinite patience of someone determined to learn from everything and everyone. Life is written in every thing and every word, he said once, and the wise man tries to read and listen in silence. This was a strange conclusion or philosophy to find in a man like him, who could neither read nor write, despite knowing Castilian, Turkish, and the Arabic of the Moors, as well as the Mediterranean

lingua franca, and for whom a few weeks in Naples had
been enough for him to begin to get a reasonable grasp of
Italian.

"And now he no longer resembles God?"

He was observing me with the same close attention. I
made a vague gesture toward the sea. The first rays of sun-
light were touching our faces.

"I've discovered qualities in him that I didn't see before,
and there are others that I can no longer see."

He shook his head almost sadly. Calm and fatalistic, he
came and went between Captain Alatriste and me, acting
as our one link on board, military duties apart. That rough,
brusque Aragonese, Copons, lacked the necessary subtlety
to ease the tension between us; his clumsy attempts at con-
ciliation always bumped up against my youthful obstinacy.
The Moor Gurriato was just as uneducated as Copons, but
he was more perspicacious. He had taken my measure, and
he was patient. He moved between us discreetly, as if providing contact were a way of repaying the strange debt
that he, in his complicated mind, believed he owed the
captain, the man he had met on that cavalcade on Wadi
Berruch. And he believed this all his life, until Nördlingen
that is.

"A man like him deserves respect," he commented, as
if concluding a long internal train of thought.

"So do I."

"*Elkhadar,*" he said, with a shrug of the shoulders. "Time will tell."

I thumped the netting with my fist.

"I wasn't born yesterday, you know. I'm just as much a man and a gentleman as he is."

He ran one hand over his smooth head, which he shaved each day with a razor and seawater.

"Ah, of course, a gentleman," he murmured.

He was smiling. His dark, gentle, almost feminine eyes glittered like the silver rings in his ears.

"God blinds those who want to lose," he added.

"Devil take God and all the rest."

"Sometimes we give to the Devil what he already has."

And having said this, he got to his feet, picked up a handful of oakum, and walked along the gangway to the ship's head, next to the ram, instead of doing as so many other men did and crouching between the timber knees at the sides of the ship. Because another of the Moor Gurriato's peculiarities was that he was as modest as the mother who bore him.

"We may be in luck," said Captain Urdemalas. "They say that the ship was still in Rhodes three days ago."

Diego Alatriste took another sip of the wine that Captain Urdemalas had ordered to be served beneath the faded and patched red-and-white striped awning at the stern. The wine was good—a white Malvasia rather like a San Martín de Valdeiglesias. Given Urdemalas' proverbial meanness—he was about as likely to spend a *maravedí* as the pope was to give up his piscatory ring—all of this augured well for interesting times ahead. Between sips of wine, Alatriste discreetly observed the other men. Besides the pilot, a Greek named Braco, and the galley master, there were Ensign Labajos and the three soldiers placed in charge of the eighty-seven infantrymen on board: Sergeant Quemado, Corporal Conesa, and Alatriste himself. Also present was the master gunner who had replaced the man injured in Lampedusa. He was a German who swore in Castilian and drank in Basque, but who was as adept at handling moyens, sakers, culverins, and swivel guns as a cook was his pots.

"It's a large ship apparently. A square-rigged galleass with no oars, but some artillery. The escort is a lantern galley manned by janissaries."

"They'll be a hard nut to crack," said the galley master when he heard the word "janissaries."

Captain Urdemalas scowled at him. He was in a bad mood because he had been suffering from appallling toothache all week and didn't dare place himself in the hands of the barber on board, or indeed in anyone else's.

"We've cracked harder ones than that," he snapped.

Ensign Labajos, who had already drunk his wine, wiped his mustache with the back of his hand. He was a young, thin swarthy man from Malaga, and good at his job.

"They're sure to put up a hard fight, and if they lose their prize passenger, they'll fight like men possessed."

Sergeant Quemado burst out laughing.

"Is the woman really the Great Turk's wife? I thought he never let them out of the seraglio."

"She's the favorite wife of the Pasha of Cyprus," Urdemalas explained. "His term there ends in a month's time, and he's sending her ahead with some of his money, servants, slaves, and clothes."

Quemado mimed mocking applause. He was a tall, lanky man, whose real name was Sandino. The nickname Quemado—Burned—dated from a highly profitable night attack on the island of Longos, which had involved sacking the town, setting fire to the Jewish quarter, and acquiring a booty of almost two hundred slaves. A petard had scorched his face while he was trying to blow in the door to the castle, but despite his unfortunate appearance, or perhaps because of it, he was always the joker. He was also rather short-sighted, although he never wore glasses in public. "When did you ever see Mars wearing spectacles?" he would say, half joking and half proud.

"She's a tasty morsel, then," he said.

"If we can capture her, yes," said Urdemalas. "Tasty enough to justify the whole campaign."

"Where are they now?" asked Ensign Labajos.

"They had to stop for some time in Rhodes, but now they've set sail again, or are about to."

"What's the plan?"

Urdemalas gestured to Braco the pilot, who unrolled a sea chart on the large plank that served as a table. The map showed the Aegean Islands, Anatolia, and the coasts of Europe. It went as far up as the Strait of Constantinople and as far down as Candia. Urdemalas ran his finger along the easternmost coast.

"Don Agustín Pimentel wants to capture them before they pass the Strait of Chios, so as not to cause any trouble for the monks and other Christian folk who live there. According to the chief pilot, Gorgos, the best place is between Nicalia and Samos. That's the most obvious route from Rhodes."

"Those are treacherous waters," said Braco. "There are shallows and rocks."

"Yes, but the chief pilot knows them well. And he says that if the galleass is being sailed by people who know where the sandbanks are, then the natural route to follow would be between the chain of islands and the mainland. It's more protected from the winds and safer."

"Yes, that would logical," said Braco.

Diego Alatriste and Corporal Conesa—a plump, stocky fellow from Murcia—were studying the map with great interest. They didn't usually get a chance to see such documents, and as subalterns, they knew how unusual it was to be invited to such meetings. Alatriste was an old dog though, and he could read between the lines. The ship they were planning to attack would be a major prize, and Captain Urdemalas needed everyone to know that. This way, he could be sure that the troops would find out the facts from good authority and be eager to put their all into the enterprise. Being in the right place at the right time and capturing the galleass would require them all to pull together, and soldiers and sailors who were aware of what was at stake would be more likely to obey than ill-informed or discontented ones.

"Do you think we can get there in time?" asked Ensign Labajos.

He showed his empty glass, in the hope that Urdemalas would summon his page to pour him some more wine. Urdemalas, however, pretended not to notice.

"The wind is in our favor," he said, "and, besides, we have the oarsmen. The Turkish galleass is a heavy sailing ship and will be traveling against the wind, and in calm weather the galley will have to tow her. The weather will turn cooler this evening, but we'll still have the wind in our favor. The chief pilot thinks we can catch up with them off Patmos or the Fournoi islands, and the other pilots and captains agree. Isn't that so, Braco?"

The Greek nodded as he rolled up the chart. Quemado

wanted to know what the Knights of Malta thought about the matter, and Captain Urdemalas said:

"Those bastards don't give a damn whether it's one galleass and one galley or fifty, whether they're carrying the wife of the Pasha of Cyprus on board or the wife of Suleiman himself. The merest whiff of booty is enough to set their mouths watering. The more Turks, the bigger the profit."

"What about the other captains?" asked Quemado.

"I don't know anything about the French captain. He's got knights with him, who are on their first expedition, as well as soldiers from France, Italy, Spain, and Germany. Brave men, as always. But I do know the captain of the *Cruz de Rodas*."

"Brother Fulco Muntaner," said the galley master.

"The one who was at the battle of Cimbalo and at Syracuse?"

"The same."

Some of those present raised their eyebrows, while others nodded. Even Alatriste had heard, through Alonso de Contreras, of that Spanish Knight of the Order of Saint John. At Cimbalo, after losing three of the Maltese galleys in a storm, Muntaner had dug himself in on an island along with his shipwrecked men, defending themselves like tigers against the Moors of Bizerta who disembarked en masse to capture them. Not that there was anything surprising about that, for not even the most optimistic knight expected mercy from the Mohammedans. This partly explains why it was that, at the battle of Lepanto, when the Maltese flagship was finally recaptured—it had been attacked and boarded by a swarm of Turkish galleys—only three knights were found alive, badly wounded, but surrounded by the corpses of three hundred enemies. Almost the same thing happened again in sixteen hundred and twenty, off Syracuse in Sicily, when the same Muntaner, by then in his sixtieth year, was one of only eighteen survivors on the Maltese flagship, after the bloody battle fought there between four Maltese galleys and six Berber galleys. The Knights of Malta, then feared and hated by their enemies, were tough professional corsairs, and Brother Fulco Muntaner was among the very toughest. Since the five galleys had met together in Fossa de San Giovanni, Alatriste had often seen him at the stern of the flagship, *Cruz de Rodas*, with his bald head, long gray beard, and face disfigured by cuts and scars, and had heard him haranguing the men in thunderous tones in his own Mallorcan tongue.

The proverb proved to be correct: that evening there was rain and, that night, there were occasional gusts of that promised northeasterly wind and more rain. The sea was so rough that, despite the lanterns lit on the stern of each ship, all five galleys lost sight of one another. However, we soon covered the forty miles separating us from the island of Nicalia, despite the battering weather. The sailors had to keep a constant eye on the sails, though, while everyone else, oarsmen included, crouched on the deck, numb with cold, sheltering as best we could from the spray. We proceeded thus until the wind turned to the southeast, and the following morning, which dawned peacefully, with remnants of the heavy rain moving off over the island's steep, rocky peaks, we found ourselves opposite Pope Point, where two of the ships in our convoy were waiting for us, while the other two arrived safely during the morning. Nicalia, which some call Ikaria—the island where Icarus fell into the sea—is a rugged place, and while many torrents rush down its rocks, there is no harbor at all. However, since both weather and sea were calm, we were able to go in close to land and happily fill casks, barrels, and kegs, for, given the number of people on board a galley, she is in constant need of fresh supplies of water.

According to our reckonings, the galleass would be sailing into the north wind and, we thought, would still be somewhere en route from Rhodes. In order to confirm this, Agustín Pimentel ordered four galleys to cover the strait between Nicalia and Samos, while the fifth went

south in order to find out more. One Spanish ship would
attract less attention than five galleys gathered together
like birds of prey on the hunt. Moreover, the Greeks who
lived on those islands seemed no better than the Ottomans,
for, having no schools, they were the most barbarous
people in the world, cowed by the cruelty of the Mohammedans and quite capable of selling us to the Turks
simply to gain favor with them. The *Mulata* was chosen
to be the scout, and so we set sail that night and by the
dawn watch had reached the deep, sheltered harbor of
Patmos, the best of the three or four good ports on the island, at the foot of the fortified Christian monastery that
dominates the harbor from above. We spent the morning
there, but the only people allowed to go ashore were Captain Urdemalas and the pilot Braco. As well as finding out
further information, they negotiated with the monks the
ransom of the Jews we had taken on board as oarsmen—
at least that was the pretext for the visit—although, for
some reason or other, an agreement was reached not to
free them until later, when we would leave them on
Nicalia. And so I did not have a chance to set foot on the
legendary island where Saint John the Evangelist was exiled by Emperor Domitian and where he dictated the
Apocalypse to his disciple Procoros. And speaking of books,
I remember that Captain Alatriste spent the day sitting in
one of the crossbow embrasures, reading the copy of

Dreams sent to him by don Francisco de Quevedo. It was a small octavo volume, which he usually carried in his pocket. And that same day, when he left it lying on his pack in order to go and deal with some matter at the prow, I picked up the book and, glancing through it, found this passage marked:

> *Truth and Justice came down to Earth: the first, being naked, found it most uncomfortable, as did the second, being rigorous. They wandered about for a long time, until Truth, out of necessity, fell silent. Justice, at a loss for what to do, roamed the earth, pleading with everyone; but seeing that no one took any notice of her and that everywhere her name was used to support tyrannies, she determined to flee back to Heaven . . .*

We soldiers and sailors spent part of that day resting, delousing each other and eating a meal of boiled chickpeas and a little salt cod—for it was a Friday—while the oarsmen, beneath the awning that protected the rowing benches, were given their usual ration of hardtack. The sun was very strong, and the heat so intense that tar was dripping down from the rigging. After midday, Captain Urdemalas and the pilot returned, looking very cheerful, having dined well with the monks and imbibed wine made from

honey and orange blossom—God curse them. Anyway, the
Turkish galleass, they were told, had not yet passed through
the strait, but had been seen, still with its galley escort,
sailing toward the isle of Longos, struggling against the
contrary wind, for it was a large and heavy vessel. And so,
in less time than it takes to say "knife," we had dismantled
the awning, weighed anchor, and set off, rowing hard to re-
join the other galleys.

For two days and nights, with lanterns extinguished and
eyes alert, we almost chewed our fingernails to the quick.
The sea was leaden and smooth, with no wind to bring
us that wretched galleass. Finally, a southwesterly wind
ruffled the surface of the sea, and our patience was rewarded, for the order came to clear the decks and prepare ourselves for battle. The five galleys were skillfully
deployed, being positioned almost, but not quite, out of
sight of each other, and covering an area of more than
twenty miles. A signal had been agreed on for when the
prize was spotted. Behind us lay the island of Fournoi, on
whose southernmost peak, from which one could see for
leagues around, we had posted four men with orders to
send up a smoke signal as soon as they spotted a sail. The
island had a long corsair tradition, for its name, which
means "oven" or "furnace," dates from the days when the

Turk Cigala used to have the hardtack for his galleys baked there. To the south, we had also posted a caïque—manned by our people, but rowed by Greeks who had been pressed into service—as a reconnaissance vessel that would not arouse any suspicions that the wolf was in the sheep pen. The unusual thing about the ambush was that, in order to get as close to the enemy as possible before engaging with them, and to avoid the galleass firing on us from a distance, we had made our ships look like Turkish galleys by shortening the mainmast, making the lateen yard seem stubbier and heavier, and lowering the topmast. Miguel de Cervantes, who knew a thing or two about corsairs and galleys, had written about this too.

In war there are a thousand ploys
Full of tricks and lying noise:
The thunder grumbles distantly,
Yet lightning strikes us instantly.

This disguise was completed with the Turkish flags and pennants we carried with us for just such occasions— as other ships would carry ours—and men wearing Ottoman clothes were placed in the most visible parts of the ships. Such tricks were part of the dangerous game that all the nations were playing on those ancient shores, the theater for this vast exercise in corsair chess and chance. For when there are eight or even ten cannons pointing at you, gaining time is of no small importance, even more so when they start firing and all you can do is row hard, grit your teeth until you're close enough to board, and pay them back for it in blood and guts. If England's encounter with the Armada in the English Channel had been a frank confrontation between two infantries, as at Lepanto, that day would be remembered quite differently now.

Anyway, whoever happened to be in the appropriate place donned a Turkish costume and was much mocked for it. I, thank God, escaped, but others—the Moor Gurriato was one, condemned to it by his appearance—had to put on baggy trousers, the long tunics or robes that the Turks call dolmans, all, as usual, very fancy, as well as bonnets, taffetas, and turbans. They formed a blue, white, and red rainbow, and their skins were so burned by the sun that all that was needed for them to be taken for real Turks was to start bowing to Mecca at the appropriate times. One even made fun of his own disguise, kneeling down and shamelessly invoking Allah, but when some of the Muslim slaves protested, angered by such blasphemy, Captain Urdemalas sternly reprimanded the wretch, threatening him with a public whipping if he upset the oarsmen. It was one thing, he said, to force them to row, but there was no need to insult them.

.   .   .

"Row hard, my lads! Harder, or they'll escape us!"

When Captain Urdemalas addressed the slaves as "my lads" this was a sign that more than one of them was likely to row himself to death and be whipped for his pains. And so it was. Keeping up the hellish rhythm set by the galley master's whistle, the crack of the whip on their bare backs, and the clink of their chains, the oarsmen alternately stood up and fell back, again and again, breathing so hard it seemed their lungs would burst, while the galley master and his assistant lashed them mercilessly.

"The dogs are ours! Keep it up and we'll have 'em!"

The long, slender hull of the *Mulata* seemed to fly over the rippling waves. We were to the south of the isle of Samos, whose bare, rocky coast we were leaving behind us on the port side. It was a luminous blue morning, marred only by a faint trace of mist on the strip of land to the east. The five galleys were in full pursuit with sails and oars working; two lay ahead of us, nearer to Samos, and another two behind, forming a line that gradually shrank as we converged on the galley and the galleass, which were trying desperately to escape through the strait between the island and terra firma or else find some beach on which to take shelter. The day, however, was ours, and even the most inexperienced soldier on board realized this. The northwest wind wasn't blowing hard enough to drive the large heavy galleass along, and its galley escort, of course, had to remain by its side. Meanwhile, our galleys, spaced about a mile apart and still quite far from each other, were visibly gaining on them. We had already begun our approach when, almost simultaneously, the men on the caïque and a tiny puff of smoke from the isle of Fournoi told us that the enemy ship's sails had been spotted. At first, the Turkish uniforms and the general appearance of our ships confused the new arrivals—later, we learned that they had mistaken us for galleys from Mytilene sent to escort them—and so they had kept their course unsuspecting. However, the scales soon fell from their eyes when they saw the way we were rowing and maneuvering the galley. And so the Turks tried to set course for the northeast, with the galleass to lee-ward of the galley, the latter trying to interpose itself and cover the larger ship's flight. The chase was as good as over. The Maltese flagship was already near the coast of Samos and would reach the strait first; the *Caridad Negra* had her ram pointing at the Turkish galley; and the *Mulata*, along with the *Virgen del Rosario*, and the *San Juan Bautista*, slightly to starboard of us, was heading straight for the galleass, whose three masts—trinquet, cross, and lateen—had now all filled with sail.

"Fetch your weapons and to your posts!" shouted Ensign Labajos. "We're going to board her!"

At the stern, the drumroll beat out the rallying call and the bugle sounded the attack. The corridors seethed with people preparing for battle. The master gunner and his assistants were readying the cannons in the central gangway as well as the *pedreros* mounted on the sides of the ship. The rest of us had padded the pavisades with shields, palliasses, blankets, and packs to protect us from Turkish fire, and we were now making our way in good order to the chests and baskets that had just been opened and from which we were taking our heavy weapons. The galley men were still rowing, drenched in sweat, their eyes starting from their heads, chains clanking, and to that sound, from prow to stern, was added the clank of all the metal armor and weapons being strapped on by the soldiers and the sailors who had been designated either to defend the galley or to board the other ship. All of this equipment was vital in close combat: breastplates, morions, shields, swords, harquebuses, muskets, pikes, and half-pikes with the end of the shaft greased so that the enemy could not grab hold of it. Smoke was rising from the harquebusiers' matchcords and the linstocks ready in their bowls of sand. The skiff and the other small boat were in the water, being towed along at the stern. The cook had put out the oven and any other fire on board, and the pages and cabin boys had washed down the deck with seawater so that neither bare feet nor espadrilles would slip. And at the stern, under the awning, along with the pilot and the helmsman, the captain was barking out orders: row, my lads, row, a quarter to port, damn it, now to starboard, row, you buggers, row, slacken that rope, tighten that halyard, row hard, the dogs are ours now, row or I'll have the skin off your backs, you wretches, yes, by God's teeth and the holy host, we're gaining on the bastards. Luther could not have put it better, for no one blasphemes like a Spaniard in a storm or in combat.

The fighting on the galleass was hard. We arrived first, just as the *Caridad Negra*, which was slightly closer to the island than we were, rammed the Turkish galley, and we heard the distant sound of firing and the shouts of Machín de Gorostiola and his Basques as they rushed on board. Meanwhile, every eye on the *Mulata* was fixed on the black portholes open in the sides of the galleass. There were six cannons on each side, and when the galleass saw that she could not avoid us, she turned two or three quarters to port and unleashed a volley that, even though it struck us only a glancing blow, took down our trinquet sail along with the four sailors who were, at that moment, hauling it in to secure it. Their guts were left hanging grotesquely from the rigging. Another such volley would have done much greater damage, because galleys have very fragile frames.

The experienced Captain Urdemalas, however, foresaw this, and, when the helmsman hesitated, he pushed him out of the way—indeed, he very nearly knifed him, for he had his sword in his hand—and flung the tiller to one side so that we were heading instead for the stern of the galleass, which, as I said, was as high as that of galleons and carracks, but which had the advantage of having no cannons, allowing us to get close without too much risk. The *Virgen del Rosario* bore the brunt of the second volley from the other side, and that, it seemed to us, was the better of two evils. After all, these things must be shared out among many, and Jesus Christ may have told us all to be brothers, but not to be arrant fools.

"Prepare to board!" roared Ensign Labajos.

We were almost within harquebus range, and if the oarsmen did their job well, the Turkish gunners would not have time to reload the cannons. I slung a small shield over my shoulder, and with my steel breastplate on and my helmet, and my sword in its sheath, I joined a group of soldiers and sailors holding grappling irons at the ready. At the prow, the sail on the broken yard had been taken in and stowed, and the mainsail was furled and at half-mast. The embrasures were packed with men bristling with metal. Another large group, gathered together around the felled trinquet sail and near the fighting platform atop the bow, was waiting for our artillery at the prow to fire so that they could occupy the foredeck and the ram. Among them I could see Captain Alatriste, who was blowing on the match-cord of his harquebus, and Sebastián Copons, who was, as usual, tying an Aragonese scarf about his head. I was wearing such a scarf too, on top of which I wore my helmet, which was very heavy and hellishly hot, but since we would be climbing upward to board the ship, it seemed advisable to protect one's bell tower from storks. When we were close to the galleass, my former master saw me there, as I had seen him, and before looking away, I noticed that he nodded to the Moor Gurriato, who was by my side. The Moor nodded back. "I don't need either of you," I thought, but that was all I had time to think because, at that very moment, the cannons in the gangway and the moyens on the prow fired off some chain shot to shatter the enemy ship's rigging and leave it without sails; *pedreros*, harquebuses, and muskets blasted them too, the latter filling the galley deck with smoke, which, in turn, was filled with Turkish arrows and lead and stone pellets that penetrated planks and flesh alike. We had no option but to grit our teeth and wait, which is what I did, crouched and afraid that a few of the many things falling on us would fall on me. Then the galley hit something solid that made the whole vessel shudder and creak. The galley slaves let go of the oars and, screaming, sought shelter among the benches. And when I looked up, I saw above our heads, among the clouds of smoke, the enormous stern of the galleass, which seemed to me as tall as a castle.

"Forward for Spain! Attack! Attack!"

Men were yelling furiously as they crowded onto the prow. No one was there simply because he had to be, apart from the oarsmen, of course; we knew that we had a prize here that could make us all rich. The grappling irons were thrown, and the lateen yard of the mainmast was lowered so that it rested on the side of the enemy ship for our men to climb along it. With the galley heeled slightly to starboard, the troops—and I was among the first—shinned up the ropes on the galleass as if they were a flight of steps. Lope Balboa, that soldier of our king, slain in Flanders with great pride and honor, would not have been ashamed of his son that day, watching me scale the high side of that Turkish galleass with all the youthful agility of my seventeen years, up to that place where your only friend is your sword, and where living or dying depends on chance, God, or the Devil.

As I said, the fighting was fierce and lasted more than half an hour. There were about fifty janissaries on board, who all fought valiantly and, grouped together at the prow, killed quite a number of our men. The janissaries, Christians by birth, had been taken as children by way of a tax or tithe and had then been brought up in the Islamic faith to show unthinking loyalty to the Great Turk. It is a point of honor among them to fight to the bitter end, and they do so with extraordinary ferocity. We had to fire on them several times at point-blank range with our harquebuses—and we did so gladly, for they had done the same to us through the portholes, hatchways, and grilles as we were climbing up. Then we had to go in with shield and sword to finish them off and seize the mainmast, which they defended like rabid dogs. I fought hard, although without letting myself get too carried away by the fury of the fighting, protecting myself with my shield and lunging forward, always looking around me, as the captain had taught me to, only taking a step when I knew it was the right moment to do so, and never retreating, not even when I felt Corporal Conesa's brains—blown out by a harquebus shot—spill onto the back of my neck. Beside me was the Moor Gurriato, scything his way through the crowd, and our comrades were not far behind. And so, step by step, sword thrust by sword thrust, we pressed the janissaries hard, driving them back as far as the trinquet sail and the prow itself. *"Sentabajo, cane!"* we screamed at them in lingua franca to get them to surrender. But by then, the men from the *Virgen del Rosario* and the *San Juan Bautista* were coming at them from behind, boarding at the prow, with the Spaniards shouting out the name of Santiago—Saint

James—and the Maltese Knights of Saint John. Once the three galleys came together, sentence had been read. The last of the wounded and exhausted janissaries, who had, until then, been hurling insults at us—such as *guidi imansiz*, which in Turkish means "infidel cuckolds," or *bir mum*, "sons of bitches"—suddenly changed their rhetoric, addressing us as *efendi* and *sagdic*, "sirs" and "skippers," and begging us to spare their lives *Alla'iche*, for the love of God. And once they finally threw down their arms, a large part of our squad set to busily scouring every corner of the ship and tossing bundles of booty down onto the decks of our galleys.

By God, we had a good day, stealing right, left, and center. For a while, permission was given to plunder freely, and we took our captains at their word, for the galleass was more than seven hundred tons and was carrying all kinds of merchandise: spices, silks, damasks, bales of fine cloth, Turkish and Persian carpets, quantities of gemstones, seed pearls, silverware, and fifty thousand gold coins, not to mention several barrels of arrack—a Turkish liquor—to which we all paid lavish homage. Smiling like Democritus himself, I stole along with the best of them, without waiting for the general share-out, and by God I deserved it, for I was one of the men who had made the Turks work hardest, and the first to stick my dagger in the mainmast as proof that I was there, for this brought both honor and the right to a larger share of the booty. Witness to how hard I fought were the seventeen Spaniards who died boarding the galleass, almost half of whom were on my side, as well as the various dents in my helmet and breastplate, and the whole bucket of water that was needed to wash the blood off me—other men's blood, fortunately. Captain Alatriste and Copons had boarded at the stern, fighting first with harquebuses and then with axes and swords, breaking down doors and pavises where the Turkish officers and some of the janissaries had barricaded themselves in, but I found out later that when Captain Alatriste asked the Moor Gurriato how things had gone on my part, the Moor summed up the situation very elegantly, saying that he would have had a hard time keeping me alive if I hadn't roundly dispatched everyone trying to stop him doing just that.

The men on the *Caridad Negra* and the *Cruz de Rodas* did their fair share of killing too. First one and then the other boarded the Turkish galley, and the ensuing battle was fierce and without quarter, for it happened that, as the *Caridad Negra* rammed the enemy vessel, taking with it all the oars on that side, a stone killed Sergeant Zugastieta, a jolly Basque, a valiant trencherman, and an even braver drinker, very popular among the other soldiers on the galley, who, as I explained, were all from the same part of Spain. And while the Basque people—and I speak as someone from Guipúzcoa—might sometimes be short on brains, we are always long on generosity and courage. They therefore leaped onto the Turkish galley, yelling *"Koarte-lik ez!"* and *"Akatu gustiak!"* and other such things, which, in our language meant that no mercy would be shown, not even to the captain's cat. And so everyone down to the last cabin boy was put to the knife and no attempt made to distinguish between those trying to surrender and those who were not. The only men left alive on board were the galley slaves who had survived the attack, of whom ninety-six were Christians, half of them Spaniards. You can imagine their joy at being liberated. Among them was one fellow from Trujillo who had spent twenty-two years as a slave, since his capture in sixteen hundred and fifteen, at the taking of Mahomet, and who, miraculously, was still alive, despite all that time at the oars. How the poor man wept and embraced us all!

For our part, we liberated fifteen young slaves from the hold of the galleass: nine boys and six girls, still virgins, the oldest being fifteen or sixteen. They were all fine-looking youths, Christians captured by corsairs on the Spanish and Italian coasts and being taken to be sold in Constantinople, where an all too foreseeable future awaited them, given the licentious nature of the people there. However, the most notable prize was the favorite wife of the Pasha of

Cyprus, who turned out to be a Russian renegade of about thirty. She had blue eyes and was tall and voluptuous, the most beautiful woman I have ever seen. Agustín Pimentel placed her in a cabin along with Chaplain Nistal and a four-man escort, threatening with death anyone who bothered her. We queued up at the door to admire her, for she was lavishly dressed and accompanied by two handsome Croat slave girls, and it was very strange to have such a woman among coarse men like us, when the blood was still not dry on the deck. We did not even touch the booty she brought with her, for two days later, she was sent to Naples in the galleass, with the liberated captives and the *Virgen del Rosario* as escort—the Turkish galley had been holed and sunk—and was ransomed there some time later in exchange for three hundred thousand gold coins of which we never caught so much as a glimpse, despite all our efforts and the dangers we had faced. Later, we learned that the pasha grew quite mad with rage when he was told what had happened and that he swore revenge. Our poor pilot Braco paid the price in full when, a year and a half later, he was captured on board one of our ships on the sandbanks off Lemnos. He was identified as one of the men involved in the capture of the Cypriot galleass, and the Turks flayed him alive, very slowly, and then stuffed his skin with straw and hung it from the topsail of a galley and paraded it from island to island.

That is what the Mediterranean is like. Between its narrow shores, everyone knows everyone else and there is always some unfinished business; and such, too, is piracy and war: as you sow, so shall you reap. On that day, off the island of Fournoi, the people doing the reaping were the one hundred and fifty dead and wounded Turks, give or take a few, whom we threw into the sea, for they all duly drowned. Then the overseers chained fifty or so of the uninjured Turks to the benches, despite the protests of the Basques from the *Caridad Negra*, who wanted to cut off their heads and slit their throats for good measure. In the end, they were so up in arms about it, refusing even to obey their captain, that don Agustín Pimentel had to allow them to cut off the ears and noses of the five or six renegades found among the captured Turks. As for private booty, when the order came to stop the plundering, I had filled my pockets with a few handfuls of silver, five good strands of pearls, and whole fistfuls of Turkish, Venetian, and Hungarian gold coins. It is no exaggeration to say that what we felt as we fell upon all that wealth was sheer joy. It was quite something to watch grown men, bearded soldiers clothed in leather and clanking with metal, laughing like children over their full purses. After all, that is why we Spaniards left the safety of our own country, left hearth and home, prepared to suffer vicissitudes, hard work and danger, rough weather, the fury of the seas, and the devastation of war. As Bartolomé de Torres Naharro wrote in the previous century:

> *We soldiers only prosper*
> *If there's a war to fight;*
> *Like the poor in darkest winter*
> *Who long to see the light.*

Better dead or rich, we thought, but gentlemen at least, rather than poor and wretched, bowing the knee to the latest bishop or marquis. This was a concept defended by Cervantes in the character of Don Quixote, who placed the honor of the sword above the glory of the pen. If poverty is good because Christ loved it, I say, may those who preach poverty enjoy it. Disapproving of a soldier stealing gold for which he paid with his blood, be it in Tenochtitlán or from under the nose of the Great Turk, as we were doing, shows a complete ignorance of the harshness of a soldier's life, and of the suffering he must endure to win that booty in battle, where he is exposed to bullets and injury, to cold steel and to fire, and all to earn a reputation, a living, or both things at once, for it comes to the same thing:

> *Here we do not die in bed*
> *Sipping from a sweetened cup,*

Cosseted before we're dead;
No—bullets or a thrusting sword
Will cut our lifeblood's precious cord.

Anyone who quibbles over a soldier's booty or pay is forgetting that rewards and honor are what drive us all on: sailors set to sea in search of them, farmers plough the fields, monks pray, and soldiers fight. But honor, even if won through danger and wounds, never lasts long if it does not come with the reward that sustains it. The fine image of the hero covered in wounds on a battlefield soon turns sour when people turn away in horror at the sight of his mutilated limbs and face while he begs for alms outside a church. Besides, Spain has always been rather forgetful when it comes to handing out rewards. If you want to eat, they tell you, go and attack that castle. If you want to be paid, board that galley. And may God help you and reward you. Then they watch from behind the safety of a barricade and applaud your feats, because applause costs nothing, and rush to profit from them, bestowing on that booty far more perfumed names than we do and wrapping themselves in the colors of a flag torn to shreds by the same shards of metal that tore our flesh. For in our unfortunate nation, there are few generals and still fewer kings like the general Caius Marius, who was so grateful for the help given by barbarian mercenaries in the wars with Gaul that he made them citizens of Rome, in contravention of the local laws. When he was criticized for this, he replied: "The law speaks in too quiet a voice to be heard above the clash of war." Not to mention Christ himself, who honored and, above all, fed his twelve soldiers.

10. THE ESCANDERLU CHANNEL

In the previous chapter, I used the expression "As you sow, so shall you reap," and it's very true. It's also true, as the Moor Gurriato said, that God blinds those who want to lose, to which I would add, don't count your chickens before they hatch. Five days after capturing the galleass, we fell into a trap, or perhaps it would be truer to say that we entered it of our own accord by pushing our luck too far. Emboldened by that large prize, don Agustín Pimentel decided to travel north, following the coast, to sack a small town inhabited by Ottomans, Foyavequia, which is in Anatolia, on the narrow Escanderlu channel. And so, after burying our dead—Sergeant Zugastieta, Corporal Conesa, and other good comrades—in Turkish soil on the island of Fournoi, we sailed north, past Chios, and from there to the east of Cape Nero and the entrance to Smyrna. We entered the aforementioned channel, where we hove to far from the coast, waiting for night to fall. We did so confidently, despite one disquieting sign, for having sent the Maltese galley the *San Juan Bautista* ahead as scout, we had heard no more from her; indeed, no one has seen or heard of her since, and so we will never know if she sank or was captured, if there were survivors or not, because not even the Turks gave any explanation. Like so many mysteries that sleep beneath the waves, the galley was swallowed up by the sea and by history, along with her three hundred and forty men on board—knights, soldiers, sailors, and oarsmen.

Misfortunes rarely come singly. Even though the *San Juan Bautista* had not rejoined us as planned, don Agustín Pimentel was confident that she had simply been delayed and would join us later, and that, besides, three galleys were quite sufficient to attack the rather insignificant fortress of Foyavequia, which had already been sacked by the Knights of Malta in sixteen hundred and sixteen. Darkness fell. We filled our stomachs with cold boiled beans—we weren't allowed to light a fire—a handful of olives, and one onion between four. Then, at the Angelus hour, with an overcast sky and not a breath of wind and with our lanterns extinguished, we began rowing across the calm sea toward land.

It was a dark night, and we were about a mile from the town, the three galleys very close together, when the lookout thought he saw something behind us, out at sea: the shapes of ships and sails, he said, although he couldn't be sure because there were no lights to betray their presence. We stopped rowing. The galleys moved closer together, where a meeting took place around the flagship. It might be that the shapes were low clouds lit by the last light of evening, or some vessel far out to sea; but they could also be enemy ships—one or several—in which case, having our escape route cut off by them was very worrying indeed, as was the possibility of our galleys being attacked while they were anchored off the beach and our men were fighting on shore. Greatly put out, our general dispatched the skiff to reconnoiter while we waited anxiously. The reconnaissance party returned at the start of the middle watch and reported that there were five or more shadows, galleys to judge by their shape, which apparently dared not approach for fear of being either discovered or captured. This disturbing information persuaded don Agustín Pimentel not to proceed. They might be Turks from Chios or Mytilene, merchants traveling in convoy, or perhaps a flotilla of corsairs preparing to travel west. We discussed each possibility and wondered if we could simply disappear into the dark, but it was unlikely that we could do so without being seen or heard, and it was dangerous too, given that we did not yet know who we were dealing with. And so, holding firm to the order not to light fires on board, with the guard doubled to warn us of any nighttime attack, we were told to rest in turns, but to be ready for action. And so we waited, our weapons beside us, with one eye open and unease in our hearts, for the light of day to decide our fate.

"We're in for a rough time, gentlemen," said Captain Urdemalas.

He had just climbed from the skiff up the ladder at the stern, after a meeting in the captain's cabin on board the *Caridad Negra*. The three galleys were all facing out to sea, their oars motionless in the leaden water. The sky remained overcast, and there was still not a breath of wind.

"It's quite simple: tonight, we'll either be dining with Christ or in Constantinople."

Diego Alatriste turned toward the Turkish galleys, studying them for the hundredth time since the dawn first began to define their shapes against the dark horizon, where a distant storm was threatening. There were seven ordinary galleys with one lantern apiece and a larger one with three, possibly their flagship. There must have been a thousand or so soldiers on board, not including the crew. There were twenty-four pieces of artillery on the eight prows, as well as swivel guns and sakers on the sides. There was no way of knowing whether they had sought us out or whether they had just happened to be sailing those waters at the right moment. Whatever the truth of the matter, they were now less than a mile away, formed up in battle order, and very astutely covering any escape route out to the open sea. They had waited patiently and cautiously all night, knowing that they had their prey trapped. Whoever was in charge knew what they were doing.

"The Maltese galley will go first," Urdemalas told us. "Muntaner insisted, saying that the statutes of his order oblige him to do so."

"Well, rather them than us," said the galley master, relieved.

"It makes no difference. None of us is going to get off lightly."

The officers and subalterns on the *Mulata* exchanged glances. No one needed to say a word, their thoughts were written on their faces. Captain Urdemalas was merely confirming what Diego Alatriste and the others knew already: there were two enemy galleys for every Christian galley, and two more besides, and there was no point in taking refuge on land because we were in Turkish territory. There was nothing for it but to risk life and liberty. We were certain to end up either dead or captured, unless a miracle occurred—and it was up to us to make that miracle happen.

"We'll have to be under oars at all times," Urdemalas

went on, "unless those black clouds to the west bring us some wind, in which case, we'll have more of a chance. But we can't count on that."

"What's the plan, then?" asked Ensign Labajos.

"Very simple, because there is no other option. The Maltese galley will go first, the *Caridad Negra* second, and we'll bring up the rear."

"I don't like the idea of being last," said Labajos.

"It comes to the same thing. I doubt any of us will get through because as soon as they see us move, the bastards will close in. Anyway, Muntaner is going first, leaving a space for us to try our luck. We'll make as if we are heading straight at the enemy, then try to cut away and escape along their left flank, which seems to be their weaker point."

"Do we help each other?" asked Sergeant Quemado.

Urdemalas shook his head and, as he did so, raised a hand to his cheek, quietly cursing God and all his saints because the toothache was still tormenting him and had only been made worse by too many hours without sleep. Diego Alatriste knew what he was thinking. For Urdemalas, and for all of them, it had been a very long night, but a good one in comparison with what might lie ahead: either at the bottom of the sea or at the oars of some Turkish galley. Soon, that toothache would be the least of Captain Urdemalas' problems.

"No one helps anyone else," Urdemalas replied. "It's every man for himself, and the Devil take the hindmost."

"Unfortunately, we're the hindmost," Sergeant Quemado remarked.

Urdemalas shot him a scathing glance.

"It was just a manner of speaking, damn it. If we don't help each other and row hard, there's just a chance that one of our ships might escape."

"Then the Maltese galley is done for," commented Labajos coldly. "If they're the first in line, the Turks will fall on them at once."

Urdemalas pulled a face, as if to say that this was not his affair.

"That's why they call themselves knights and take their vows, and when they die, they go to Heaven. Those of us who have things less cut and dried must tread more carefully."

"That's what it says in the Gospels, sir," said Quemado. "I once saw a Flemish painting of Hell, very lifelike it was too, and I swear on the king of spades that I, for one, am in no hurry to weigh anchor."

This was the usual tone to take, thought Alatriste, what was expected of them. Everything was happening according to the rules, including that light, nonchalant air, even at the mouth of Hell itself. Any fears you had, you kept to yourself. Eight centuries of war against the Moors and one

hundred and fifty years of making the rest of the world
tremble had refined both language and manners: a Spanish soldier, like it or not, could not allow himself to be
killed in just any way, but in accordance with the expecta-
tions of enemies and friends. Those gathered at the stern
of the *Mulata* knew this, as did the other men. This was
what they were paid for, even if they never received that
pay, and it was with these thoughts in mind that Alatriste
was studying the other soldiers. At that moment, any one
of them would have preferred to be in bed with a fever
rather than fit and healthy on board that ship. Standing
in groups, in the embrasures, in the corridors, and in the
central gangway, soldiers and sailors were watching their
officers in mortal silence, knowing how the cards would
fall. Among the oarsmen, though, some were fearful and
others joyful, imagining themselves already free, because
for the captive chained to the bench by the enemy religion, every sail on the horizon was a hope.

"How are we going to deploy the men?" asked Labajos.

Urdemalas made a sawing motion with the edge of one
hand on the palm of the other.

"Our aim is to cut through their lines and repel all
would-be boarders. And if we get through, I'll need two fal-
conets, the two-pounders, at the stern. The chase might be
a long one."

"Shall we give the men some food, just in case?"

"Yes, but I want no ovens lit. Give them some raw garlic and wine to warm their stomachs."

"The galley men will need something too," said the galley master.

Urdemalas leaned back against the stern, underneath the lantern. He had dark circles under his eyes and looked grimy, greasy, and exhausted. A combination of toothache and uncertainty had drained the color from his face. Alatriste didn't even bother to wonder if he himself looked like that; even without the toothache, he knew that he did.

"Check the shackles on all the forced men, and the manacles on the Turks and Moors. Then give them a little of that arrack liquor we got from the galleass, a measure per bench. That will be the best encouragement we can give them today. But no concessions, eh? If anyone's caught slacking, we cut off his head, even if I'm the one who has to pay the king. Do I make myself clear, galley master?"

"As clear as day. I'll tell the overseer."

"If you give a forced man drink," commented Sergeant Quemado, with a mocking grin on his face, "he's either fucked or about to be."

Unusually, no one laughed. Urdemalas fixed the sergeant with a mirthless stare.

"For the other men," he said curtly, "give them a sip of arrack as well as the garlic and wine. Then make some ordinary wine available, very weak, mind." At this point, he turned to the German gunner. "As for you, sir, you will fire using langridge shot and tinplate, from close to and at my orders. Otherwise, Ensign Labajos will be at the prow, Sergeant Quemado on the starboard side, and Señor Alatriste on the port side."

"It would be a good idea to give the oarsmen as much protection as possible," said Alatriste.

Urdemalas gave him a surly look and held it for just a moment longer than necessary.

"You're right," he said at last. "Pad the pavisades with whatever we have, sails included. If they kill a lot of our oarsmen, we're done for. Pilot, make sure the compass and all the instruments are well secured in the binnacle. And I'll need the two best helmsmen, the pilot, and eight good musketeers by my side. Any questions?"

"None, sir," said Labajos, after a silence.

"Needless to say, there's to be no attempt to board their ships. We concentrate on bombarding them with langridge, stone shot, and harquebus and musket fire. And that's that. If we hang around, we're lost. And if we get through, then we have to row like madmen."

There were a few tense smiles.

"God willing," murmured someone.

Urdemalas shrugged.

"And if He's not willing, then at least He'll know where to find us come Judgment Day."

"And let's just hope He puts the right pieces back together," added Sergeant Quemado.

"Amen," muttered the galley master, crossing himself.

And rather shiftily, everyone followed suit, including Alatriste.

Anyone who claims never to have felt fear is a liar, because you never know what might happen. And on that morning, facing the eight Turkish galleys blocking our exit to the open sea, just before a confrontation that is now described in reports and in history books as the naval battle of Escanderlu or Cap Nero, I recognized the feeling, which I had known on other occasions: my stomach tightening to the point of nausea and creating an unpleasant tingling sensation in the groin. I had grown up a lot since my first experiences at Captain Alatriste's side, and for all my smugness and youthful arrogance, the two years that had passed since the Ruyter Mill, Breda, and Terheyden had made me more sensible and more conscious of danger. What was about to happen was not an adventure to be undertaken with the flippancy of a boy; it was a grave event whose outcome was unknown and that could end in death—not, after all, the worst of endings—but also in captivity or in mutilation. I was sufficiently mature to understand that in a few hours' time I might find myself chained to the oars of a

Turkish galley for the rest of my life—no one in Constantinople would be prepared to ransom a poor soldier from Oñate—or biting into a piece of leather as they amputated an arm or a leg. It was the fear of mutilation that most frightened me, for there is nothing worse than having an eye missing or a wooden leg and finding oneself turned into some kind of waxen image, disfigured and broken, condemned to endure other people's pity, condemned to poverty and to begging for alms, especially when one is still in the full flower of strength and youth. This, among other things, would not be the image Angélica de Alquézar would want to find if we were ever to see each other again. And I have to say that the latter prospect made my legs quake.

These were my rather grim thoughts as I, along with my comrades, finished preparing the pavisade along the sides and prow of the *Mulata* with rolled-up sailcloth, palliasses, blankets, packs, rigging, and whatever other obstacles we could put between us and the Turkish bullets and arrows that were about to fall on us like hail. Each man would be thinking his own thoughts, but the truth is that we all put on a brave face. There were, at most, depending on the individual, a few tremulous hands, incoherent words, absorbed stares, mumbled prayers, or macabre jokes that met with uneasy laughter. Our three galleys were almost oar to oar, our prows facing the Turks, which

were now about a cannon shot away, although no one
fired a cannon to check this, for they and we knew that
there would be ample opportunity to fire—and to better
purpose—when we were nearer. When the moment came,
everyone would try to fire first, but only when they were
as close as possible to the enemy. The silence on the enemy
galleys was absolute, as it was on ours. The sea was as
smooth as a sheet of lead, reflecting the sky, while black
storm clouds moved southward over the coast of Anatolia,
which lay behind and to each side. We were armed and
ready, the match-cords were lit, and all that was lacking
was the order to row toward our fate. I had been assigned
to the port side of the boat where, duly provided with half-
pikes, spears, and pikes, we would have to repel any attempt by the Turks to board when we crossed the enemy
line. The Moor Gurriato was beside me—I suspect on Captain Alatriste's orders. He seemed utterly calm, apparently
oblivious to everything that was happening. Although he
was as prepared to fight and to die as everyone else, it was
as though he were merely passing through, an indifferent
witness to his own fate, despite the fact that, as a Moor, this
would be a far from enviable one if he fell into Turkish
hands. It would not be long before he was betrayed by some
galley slave or even by his own comrades; for the energy
that makes men throw themselves into battle can turn to
something quite contemptible when it's a matter of sur-

viving defeat. Even more so in captivity, where so many strong spirits wavered, reneged, or submitted in exchange for liberty, life, or even a miserable piece of bread. We are, after all, only human, and not everyone is capable of facing difficulties with the same courage.

"We will fight together," the Moor Gurriato said to me. "All the time."

That consoled me a little, although I knew perfectly well that when you are fighting on the threshold of the next life, each man is fighting for himself, and there is no greater solitude than that. But he had said the right thing, and I was grateful for the friendly look that accompanied those words.

"You're very far from your country," I said.

He smiled and shrugged. He was dressed in Spanish fashion, in breeches and espadrilles, but his chest was bare; he carried a curved dagger tucked in his belt, a half-sword at his waist, and a boarding ax in his hand. He had never seemed to me so serene or so fierce.

"You and the captain are my country," he said.

His words touched me, but I disguised my feelings as best I could, and said the first thing that came into my head:

"Still, there are better places to die."

He bowed his head, as if thinking.

"There are as many deaths as there are people," he

replied. "No one ever really expects his death, although he may think he does. He merely acccompanies his own death and remains at its disposal."

He stood for a moment, staring at the tar-smeared deck between his feet, then looked at me again:

"Your death is always with you, and mine is always with me. We each carry our own death on our backs."

I looked around for Captain Alatriste and finally spotted him at the prow end of the corridor, giving orders to the harquebusiers on the fighting platform there. He had been put in command of the port side of the galley and had appointed Sebastián Copons as his adjutant. He looked as cool and calm as ever, his hat down over his eyes, his thumbs hooked in the belt from which hung sword and dagger. He was wearing his old buffcoat, which bore the marks of former battles, and he was clearly ready once more to confront whatever fate might bring him, with no fuss, no bravado, no pointless gestures, but with the aplomb one would expect of such a man or of the man he was trying to be. There are as many deaths as there are people, the Moor Gurriato had said. I envied the Captain's death, when it came. I heard the Moor's soft voice beside me.

"One day, you might regret not having said good-bye to him."

I turned and came face to face with his intense, dark eyes, with those long, almost feminine, eyelashes.

"God," he says, "gives us a very brief light in between two very long dark nights."

I studied him for an instant: his shaven head, the silver earrings, the pointed beard, the cross tattooed on one cheekbone. I did so for as long as his smile lasted. Then, giving in to the impulse his words had placed in my heart, I walked down the corridor, avoiding the many comrades crowding it, and went over to the captain. I said not a word, because I didn't know what I could say. I merely leaned against the fighting platform, looking across at the Turkish galleys. I was thinking about Angélica de Alquézar, about my mother and my little sisters sewing by the fire. I was thinking, too, about myself, when I first arrived in Madrid, sitting, one sunny winter's morning, at the door of Caridad la Lebrijana's inn. I was thinking of the many men I could become, and who would perhaps stay there forever, cut short, food for the fishes, without me ever becoming any of them.

Then I felt Captain Alatriste's hand on my shoulder.

"Don't let them take you alive, son."

"I won't, I swear it," I answered.

I felt like crying, but not out of sorrow or fear. I felt, rather, a strange, quiet melancholy. Far off, above the absolute silence and stillness of the sea, a flash of lightning flared, so far off that we couldn't even hear the accompanying thunder. Then, as if that zigzagging light had been a signal, the drum sounded. At the stern of the *Caridad Negra*, next to the lantern and with a crucifix held up high, Brother Francisco Nistal raised his other hand and blessed us all. We bared our heads, knelt down, and prayed. The chaplain's words came to us in short bursts: *In nomine . . . et filii . . . Amen*. As we knelt, the royal pennant was raised on the stern of the flagship, while on the galley of the Knights of Malta, the silver eight-pointed cross appeared and on ours the white flag bearing the Saint Andrew's cross, each flag being greeted with a blast on the bugle.

"Shirts off!" ordered the galley master.

Then, in a terrible silence, we took our places and the galley began to row toward the Turks.

The silent storm continued to rage in the distance. The glow of the lightning broke up the gray horizon and glittered on the still, leaden water. The galley was equally silent, apart from the sound of the oars in the water—the rhythm as yet quite relaxed—the breathing of the oarsmen and the clink of the chains in time with their rowing. They were taking it in turns to row, quite slowly, so as to conserve their energy for the final stretch, and even the galley master refrained from using his whistle. We were silent, too, our eyes fixed on the Turkish ships that bristled with weapons ready for battle. And halfway there, while we veered slightly off to the left, the Maltese galley began to overtake us on our right. We watched her forge ahead, sails furled, muskets, harquebuses, and pikes sticking up above the pavisade, oars keeping to a precise rhythm, in and out of the water; and at the stern, where the awning had been taken down, stood its captain, Brother Fulco Muntaner, clearly visible with his long gray beard, white corselet, and red overtunic with white cross. Bareheaded and sword in hand, he was surrounded by his trusted comrades: Brother Juan de Mañas from Aragon, son of the Count of Bolea; Brother Luciano Canfora from Italy; and the novice knight Ghislain Barrois from Provence. As they passed us, almost brushing our oars with theirs, Captain Urdemalas took off his hat to them. "Good luck!" he cried. Muntaner, as calmly as if he were sailing into port, made a dismissive gesture in the direction of the eight Turkish galleys, shrugged, and said in his strong Mallorcan accent: "Very small fry."

When the *Cruz de Rodas* had passed us, taking the lead, the *Caridad Negra* followed at the same easy pace, the flag bearing the royal arms fluttering feebly at the stern, for the only breeze was that created by the galley as it moved. Thus we watched the Basques preceding us in the attack, and we waved to them with hands, hats, and helmets. There went Captain Machín de Gorostiola and his surly, silent men, the match-cords of their muskets and harquebuses burning from prow to stern. There was don Agustín Pimentel with his page holding his helmet. He looked very erect and elegant in his expensive Milanese armor, one hand on the hilt of his sword, and showed all the aplomb befitting his rank, his country, his king, and the God in whose name we were about to be torn to pieces.

"May Our Lady help them," someone murmured.

"May she help us all," said another.

The three galleys were now rowing along in single file, keeping very close together, nose to tail, while the silent lightning continued to flicker over the still, gray sea. I was at my post, between the Moor Gurriato and the man in charge of one of the *pedreros*, who was holding a smoking linstock in one hand while fingering a rosary with the other and murmuring a prayer. I wanted to swallow, but my mouth was too dry. The sip of arrack and watered wine had left my throat dry.

"Row harder!" ordered Captain Urdemalas.

The order, the galley master's whistle, and the crack of the whip on the backs of the slaves were all one. Trying to conceal my nervous fingers, I tied my scarf around my head and put on my steel helmet, securing it with a chin-strap. I checked that I could easily unfasten the chains on my breastplate if I were to fall into the sea. My espadrilles with their rope soles were tied on tightly at the ankles; in my hands I held the shaft of a half-pike with a razor-sharp blade and the upper third of the shaft carefully greased. At my waist were my sword and dagger. I took several deep breaths. I had all I needed, but there was a hollow in my stomach. I unfastened my breeches and peed into the scupper—even though I didn't much feel like it—in between the rhythmically moving oars; no one paid any attention, indeed most of my fellows were doing the same. We were all of us battle-hardened men.

"Everyone to the oars! Now—row hard!"

We heard the sound of cannon shot at the prow and stood on tiptoe to get a better view. The Turkish galleys, which we were fast approaching and which until then had not stirred, were beginning to move. The decks swarmed with turbans, red hats, the tall toques worn by janissaries, djellabas, Moorish cloaks, and colorful haiks. A puff of white smoke appeared at the prow of the Turkish galley nearest to us. The silence following the explosion was broken by a shrill clamor of whistles, flutes, and trumpets, and from the Ottoman ships came the usual battle cries and shouts. The *Cruz de Rodas* responded with three short blasts on the bugle, followed by a roll on the drums and cries of "Saint John! Saint John!" and "Remember Saint Elmo!"

"That's the Maltese galley," said an old soldier.

A series of explosions and arrows rose up from the Turkish galleys; cannons and moyens began to fire on the *Cruz de Rodas*, with some loose bullets reaching us and whistling over our heads. The galley master, his assistant, and the overseer raced up and down the gangway, lashing the backs of the slaves.

"Full ahead now!" howled Captain Urdemalas. "Row for your lives, my boys!"

The smoke was growing denser by the minute, and the harquebus fire increased along with the Turkish arrows whistling through the air in all directions. The enemy ships were closing in on our lead galley, now that it was clear she was making a rash attempt to escape. We saw the *Cruz de Rodas* plunge impassively into the smoke, in between the two nearest galleys, and so determinedly that we heard the crunch of planking and oars as they broke. Our flagship followed, heading off to the left. We could hear Machín de Gorostiola and his fellow Basques shouting: "Santiago! *Ekin! Ekin!* Spain and Santiago!" and the *Mulata* went behind, into the roar of combat and the cries of men fighting for their lives.

The galley master's whistle shrilled in our ears while his whip flayed the backs of the oarsmen and the galley flew over the waves; for that fast, intermittent whistling marked the space that separated us from death or captivity. Still unable to believe our momentary good luck, we were looking back at the galleys now pursuing us. We had crossed the Turkish lines, although the distance between us and our pursuers was minimal. The sea was as smooth as oil, and the silent lightning flashes still lingered in the west. There would be no saving wind. The *Caridad Negra*, which had gone on ahead of us, was to the right of the *Mulata* now, rowing desperately in a bid to escape the five Turkish galleys at our rear. Behind us, still only a cannon shot away, the Maltese ship, surrounded by three enemy vessels, was fighting furiously, swathed in smoke and flames, and we could still hear cries of "Saint John! Saint John!" amid the din of its hopeless struggle.

It had been a miracle, although of limited scope. Once the *Cruz de Rodas* had penetrated the Turkish line, where it immediately came under fierce attack, the *Caridad Negra* took advantage of the space left by that maneuver to pass through, not without attracting enough cannon fire to smash her trinquet mast and not without breaking some of her oars when she slipped between the Maltese galley and the nearest enemy ship. This gave us an advantage, fast behind her as we were, because we reached them when the enemy cannons had just been fired and before they could be reloaded; thus we met only with harquebus fire and a rain of arrows. Our starboard oars touched those of the *Cruz de Rodas*, which, caught helplessly among the Turk-ish galleys, with more approaching at full speed, was boarded from three sides simultaneously, twice on one side and once at the prow. With all our five senses focused on avoiding a Turkish galley approaching from the left, we were too preoccupied to appreciate her sacrifice at the time—although we saw at the stern, by then overwhelmed by Turks, how Captain Muntaner and his knights were fighting for their lives. There ensued a pandemonium of shouts and curses; arrows flew past, impaling themselves in the pavisade, in masts, and in flesh. Our helmsman, with Captain Urdemalas screaming orders into his ear—like one of those devils you get in plays put on at Corpus Christi—flung the tiller to one side in order not to collide with the *Caridad Negra*, which, with its felled mast dragging through the water, was lurching off course. As he did this, the enemy galley rammed us in the stern. Three or four oars splintered and broke, there came a babble of Turkish voices, the moans of galley slaves, and the battle cries of those of us who rushed to repel the boarders. The contact lasted only an instant, but it was enough for a group of bold, vociferous janissaries to leap across. Our half-pikes, harquebuses, muskets, and *pedreros* soon dealt with them, while from the topmasts, the cabin boys emptied firepots and bottles of tar onto them, drenching their foredeck and forcing them to retreat, while we continued on our way without further damage.

"Come on, lads!" roared Captain Urdemalas. "We're nearly there! Come on!"

Our captain was perhaps too optimistic, but then, given

the circumstances, he had a duty to be, urging on the frantically rowing slaves, whose backs were raw and bleeding.

"Overseer! Give them another drink of arrack! Now row, damn it! Row!"

Not even the strong Turkish liquor could work miracles however. The oarsmen, almost mad with exhaustion, their backs covered in sweat, bruises, and blood, were almost at their limit. The galley was flying along, as I said, but so were the five Turkish galleys in hot pursuit, and whose cannons occasionally scored a hit—with a subsequent crunch of broken planks and cries of pain—or else cut through the air as if through a length of cloth and fell into the sea, sending up a column of spray at our prow.

"The *Caridad* is getting left behind!"

We all rushed to the starboard side to see what was happening, and a woeful clamor filled the ship. Badly battered as she crossed the Turkish line, with many oars broken and too many oarsmen dead, wounded, or exhausted, our flagship was losing impetus and we were gradually overtaking her. In a matter of moments, she had gone from being a pistol shot away from our prow to being almost abeam. We could see don Agustín Pimentel, Machín de Gorostiola, and the other officers looking anxiously behind at the Turkish galleys that were fast catching them up. The *Caridad*'s oars were out of rhythm, sometimes clashing with each other, and several were utterly still, dragging through the water. We also noticed that a few dead galley slaves had been thrown, unmanacled, into the sea.

"That's them done for," said one soldier.

"Better them than us," commented another.

"There'll be plenty more of that to go around."

The *Caridad Negra* was slipping further and further behind. Some of us shouted encouraging words, but it was no use. Crowded along the edges of the boat, leaning over the pavisades, we saw that she was hopelessly lost, her oars all awry, with the Turks almost upon her and the crew powerless to do anything but watch as we moved away. Some Basques called out to us from the fighting platforms, but we could no longer hear what they said. Then they raised their hands in farewell and rushed to the stern, harquebuses and muskets smoking and at the ready. At least the Turks would pay a high price for their booty.

"Officers to the stern!" came the cry, as the order was passed on down the ship.

A deathly silence filled the galley. As the saying goes, shepherds only gather when a sheep has died. We saw Sergeant Quemado, the galley master, and Ensign Labajos heading, grave-faced, toward the back of the ship, while the other men made way for them. Captain Alatriste joined them. He passed by without seeing me, or so it seemed. His eyes were cold and inexpressive, absent, as if they were contemplating something beyond the sea and beyond everything. I knew that look. That was when I realized the Basques on the other galley were only preceding us into disaster.

"The oarsmen can't go on," said Captain Urdemalas.

Diego Alatriste glanced at the rowers. They were clearly exhausted, indifferent now to the lashes of the assistant galley master and the overseer, and incapable of keeping up the necessary rhythm. Like the *Caridad Negra*, the *Mulata* was flagging, and the Turks, meanwhile, were gaining fast.

"They'll be on us in no time."

"Perhaps the soldiers, or at least some of them, could row," said the galley master.

Ensign Labajos retorted indignantly that this was out of the question. He had discussed the matter with some of the men, he said, and no one was prepared to take up the oars, not even in the present situation. God will provide, they said. Since it looked like they were going to end their lives there, no one wanted to die a galley slave.

"Besides, it would be a waste of time with five ships on our tail. My men are soldiers, and they need all their energy to do their job, which is fighting, not rowing."

"If they catch us, a lot of us are going to end up rowing in chains anyway," said the galley master grimly.

"Well, that's for each man to decide."

Diego Alatriste studied the men crowding the corridors and the fighting platforms. Labajos was right. As they waited for a sentence to be handed down against which there could be no appeal, and despite their anxieties, those men still looked as fierce and dangerous and formidable as ever. They were the best infantry in the world, and Alatriste knew why. Soldiers like them—or *señores soldados,* as they demanded to be called—had been soldiering for almost a century and a half and would continue to do so until the word "reputation" was erased from their limited military vocabulary. They might suffer misfortunes and exposure to fire and steel, they might find themselves mutilated or dead, unpaid and inglorious, but they would never cease to fight as long as there was a comrade living before whom they must maintain faith and decorum. Of course they wouldn't row, not even to save themselves. They would, of course, as individuals, be prepared to row for their lives and liberty, but only if they could be sure that no one would ever hear about it. Alatriste himself was capable, if it came to it, of taking his seat at a bench and placing his hands on an oar, indeed, he would be the first, but neither he nor the biggest rogue on board would do such a thing if he lost face in the eyes of the world—for this was what Spain was like—the one thing that neither kings nor favorites nor priests nor enemies, nor even illness and death, could ever take from him: the image he had forged of himself, the chimera of someone who proclaimed himself to be a gentleman rather than anyone's slave. For a Spanish soldier, his profession was his honor. All this went entirely against the words spoken by a Berber corsair in a play Diego Alatriste had seen, words that came unbidden to his lips:

The Christian takes his stubborn honor
To such absurd extremes,
That even to touch the end of an oar
Is a great dishonor, it seems.
And while their foolish, childish ways
Cause them to preen and smirk,
Our ships come home stuffed full of these jays,
But for us it's simply work.

He said nothing however. This was not the moment for poetry, nor was it in his nature to quote lines of verse. He merely concluded to himself that this attitude would doubtless seal the fate of the *Mulata*, just as it would, in time, bring about the ruin of Spain and of them all, although by then it would no longer be any business of his. At least, in men like him, such desperate arrogance offered a certain degree of consolation. There was no other rule to cling to once you knew of what stuff flags were made.

"Bloody honor," said Sergeant Quemado.

They all looked at each other, grave and solemn, as if there were nothing more to be said. They would have given anything to be able to find some alternative words, but there were none. They were professional soldiers, rough men-at-arms, and rhetoric was not their strong point. They could allow themselves few luxuries, but choosing where and how to end their lives was one of them. And that was what they were doing.

"We have to turn round and fight," said Ensign Labajos. "Better that than just running away like cowards."

"As the captain said," put in Sergeant Quemado, "it's a choice between dining with Christ or in Constantinople."

"With Christ it is, then," said Labajos sternly.

Everyone turned to Captain Urdemalas, who was still stroking his sore cheek. He shrugged, as if leaving the decision to them. Then he glanced over the stern. In the distance, far behind, the Maltese ship was still embroiled with the three Turkish galleys, still battling away amid much smoke and harquebus fire. Between them and the *Mulata* lay the *Caridad Negra*, about to be caught by her pursuers—the enemy ships seethed with people ready to board. He turned back to face his men, resigned to the inevitable.

"There are five galleys," the pilot Braco reminded them glumly, "plus the others who will arrive once they've finished off the Maltese crew."

Labajos removed his hat and threw it down on the deck.

"There could be fifty of them for all I care!"

Captain Urdemalas was studying Diego Alatriste, who was clearly keeping his opinions to himself, for he was the only one who had not yet spoken. Alatriste nodded soberly, without opening his mouth to speak. Words were not what were expected of him.

"Right," said Urdemalas, "let's go to the aid of those Basques. They'll be glad to know they're not going to die alone."

11. THE LAST GALLEY

What Lepanto was like I do not know, but I will never forget the battle of Escanderlu: the deck shifting beneath your feet, the sea always ready to swallow you up if you fell, the shouts of men killing or dying, the blood pouring down the sides of the galleys, the thick smoke and the fire. There was still no wind, and the water remained as smooth and gray as a sheet of tin, while, in the distance, the strange silent storm continued unleashing its lightning, a remote imitation of what men are capable of doing with their will alone.

Once the officers had reached a decision, and we men had screwed up our courage for what lay ahead, the helmsman turned the galley around so that we could go to the aid of the *Caridad Negra*, which was now locked in battle with the first of the Turkish galleys, her deck filled with furiously fighting men, with shouts, screams, and the sound of shots being fired. On the basis that it would be better to fight together than separately, Captain Urdemalas performed a brilliant maneuver—with the help of some skillful rowing elicited from the exhausted oarsmen by more lashes from the galley master and his assistants—and placed our prow right at the stern of the flagship, so that the galleys were virtually touching, allowing us to pass from one to the other if necessary. You can imagine the relief and the shouts—*Ekin! Ekin!*—that greeted our arrival, because by the time our prow touched their stern, Captain Machín de Gorostiola and his men, although still stoutly fending off the boarding parties from the two enemy galleys, were basically fighting with no hope of winning. Another two galleys were heading toward us, while the fifth was approaching from the rear, hoping to batter us with its artillery before its men attempted to board. The Spanish galleys—we had tied ropes and hawsers around the masts to keep the two vessels together—formed a kind of fortress besieged on all sides, with the difference that we were in the middle of the sea, and the only "walls" we had to protect us from the enemy assault were the pavisades that were growing ever more tattered and holed by the hail of bullets and arrows and by our own fire, pikes, and swords.

"*Bir mum kafir! . . . Baxá kes! . . . Allautallah!*"

The janissaries were extraordinarily valiant. They came

PIRATES OF THE LEVANT

on board in waves, urging themselves on in the name of God and the Great Turk to cut off the heads of the infidel dogs. And such was their scorn for death, you would have thought the houris of Mohammed's paradise were right at our backs. They clambered aboard along the rams of their galleys, even running along the yards of their own ships or across the oars, which they leaned against the sides of our galley. Their battle cries and guttural shouts were terrifying, as was their appearance—brilliant caftans, shaven heads, tall hats, and large mustaches—and the scimitars, which they wielded with deadly precision in their attempts to break our resistance. God and king were nevertheless well served, for the Spanish infantry, faced by the enemy's valor and scorn for death, still had a few cards up its sleeve. Each wave of Turks crashed into the wall of our harquebuses and muskets, which unleashed volley upon volley, and it was remarkable how, in the midst of all that madness, our old soldiers remained as serene as ever, calmly performing their work of firing, reloading, and firing, and occasionally asking pages and cabin boys to fetch them more ammunition. And us younger folk, lither and more agile, infantrymen and sailors, attacked in good order, first with pikes and half-pikes and then, in close combat, with swords, daggers, and axes. This combination of lead, steel, and sheer courage kept the enemy reasonably at bay, biting and nipping at them more often than a dog's fleas; and the fragile redoubt of the *Caridad Negra* and the *Mulata* continued to spit fire at the five Turkish galleys surrounding them. Some drew nearer while others retreated so that their people could rest, attack with more artillery fire, and then try to board again, and after a long period of intense fighting, it became clear to the enemy that victory was going to cost a great deal of their blood and ours.

"Forward for Spain and Santiago! Attack! Attack!"

The show, as they say, had only just begun, and we were already hoarse with shouting and sick of the smell of smoke and blood. Others, less constrained, hurled insults at the Turks, as they did at us, in whatever language came most naturally—Castilian, Basque, Greek, Turkish, or Frankish—calling them dogs and sons of whores, and *bardağ*, which in Arabic means "sodomite," not forgetting the pig that impregnated some Muslim mother and other pleasantries about the perverse sect of Mohammed. To which the Ottomans responded with imaginative variants in their own tongue—the Mediterranean has always been particularly fertile in insults—on the debatable virginity of Our Lady or the dubious manhood of Jesus Christ, as well as acerbic comments on the chastity of the mothers who had borne us. It was, in short, all very much in accord with the place and the situation.

Bravado apart, we all knew that for the Turks it was

merely a question of patience and keeping up the attack. They had at least three times as many men as we did and could cope with any losses and withdraw now and then to rest and regroup, meanwhile never giving us a moment's respite. Moreover, whenever we managed to fight off one of the enemy galleys, she would take advantage of the greater distance to fire on us—to devastating and bloody effect—with a fifty-pound cannon and other similar weapons. As well as the cannonball itself there were the splinters and fragments that flew in all directions and de-molished the pavisades, which we would crouch behind as our only protection when they fired on us. There were bod-ies blown to pieces, guts and blood and debris everywhere, and in the water, between the ships, floated dozens of corpses, either men who had fallen in while boarding or who had been thrown in to clear the decks. Many galley slaves—ours and theirs—had been killed or wounded too, and still in their chains, unable to seek protection, they clung together among the benches and beneath their bro-ken oars, shrieking in terror at the furious attacks from both sides and begging for mercy.

"Allautallah! Allautallah!"

We must have been fighting for at least two long hours when one of the Turkish galleys, in a skillful maneuver,

managed to position its ram right by the prow of the *Mulata,* and another great horde of janissaries and Turkish soldiers poured on board, determined to overwhelm us. Our
men fought like tigers, defending every inch of deck with
remarkable courage, but the Turks were stronger than we
were, and, with great losses, we gradually had to relin-
quish control over the benches and the fighting platforms
at that end of the ship. I knew that Captain Alatriste and
Sebastián Copons were there somewhere, but in the smoke,
the musket fire, and the confusion I couldn't see them. An
order came to cover the breach, and as many of us as were
able rushed to do just that, filling the gangway and the
corridors on both sides. I was among the first, for I was not
prepared to stand by while they made mincemeat of Captain Alatriste. We closed on the Turks just beyond the
mainmast, the yard of which lay on the deck. I jumped
over it as best I could, shield and sword before me, trampling over the wretched oarsmen who were crouched between the benches and the shattered oars. One, in his
agony, even grabbed my leg. He looked like a Turk, so I
dealt him a blow with my sword that almost severed his
manacled hand. In situations of such pressing danger, reason has no place.

"Forward for Spain and Santiago! Attack!"

We finally fell upon the enemy, and I was among the
first, caring little for my own safety, so caught up was I in

the fury of the fighting. A swarthy Turk came at me, as hairy as a wild boar. He was wearing a leather helmet and carried shield and sword. Before he even had time to make a move, I closed on him, shield to shield, and grabbing him around the neck—my fingers slipping on his sweat-slick skin—I managed to trip him up and deal him a couple of thrusts with my sword before we both fell to the deck. I tried to get his sword off him, but it was tied to his wrist, and then he grabbed the edge of my helmet, intending to push my head back so that he could slit my throat, meanwhile uttering the most fearful of screams. Still clasped to him, I silently felt behind me, took out my dagger, and stuck it in him two or three times, inflicting only minor wounds, which seemed to hurt him nonetheless, because his screams took on another quality. He stopped screaming altogether when a hand pulled back his head and a curved dagger sliced open his throat. I scrambled to my feet, feeling bruised and wiping the blood from my eyes, but before I could say thank you, the Moor Gurriato was already furiously stabbing another Turk. And so I put away my dagger, picked up my sword and my shield, and returned to the fight.

"*Sentabajo, cane!*" yelled the Turks, as they attacked. "*Allautallah! Allautallah!*"

That was when I saw Sergeant Quemado die. In the ebb and flow of combat, I had ended up at his side. He was

gathering together a group of men to attack the janissaries on the fighting platforms. We leaped onto the galley benches—where there was scarcely an oarsman left
alive—and fought our way down along the corridors, gradually retaking what they had taken from us, until we
reached our trinquet mast and the ram of their galley. It
was then that Sergeant Quemado, who had been urging
on any laggards, was hit by an arrow that pierced both
cheeks from side to side. While he struggled to remove it,
he was killed stone-dead by a shot from a harquebus. This
caused some of our men to hold back, and we nearly lost
what we had gained with so much courage and blood,
but we raised our faces to Heaven—although not to pray
exactly—and attacked like wild beasts, determined to
avenge Quemado or to die there on the ram of that Turkish galley. What happened subsequently beggars description, and I will not say here what I did—only God and I
know that. Suffice it to say that we regained the prow of
the *Mulata*, and that when the battered Turkish galley
turned and retreated, not one of the Turks who had
boarded our ship went with it.

And so we spent the rest of the day, as stubborn as any
Aragonese, withstanding volleys of artillery and repelling
successive boarding parties from not just five galleys now, but
seven. The three-lanterned flagship and the other Turkish
galley had joined the fight in the afternoon, bearing, impaled

on their yardarms, the heads of Brother Fulco Muntaner and his knights. And by way of a trophy, for it would bring them little in the way of booty, the Turks were also towing the shattered, bloodied *Cruz de Rodas*, which was now as flat as a pontoon. It had been no small feat to take it either, for the knights fought so ferociously that, as we learned later on, not one was taken alive. Luckily for us, neither the flagship nor its escort was in any state to fight again that day, merely approaching now and then to relieve the others or to fire on us from a distance. The third Turkish galley, badly damaged in the battle, had sunk without a trace.

By late that evening, both the Ottomans and we Spaniards were utterly exhausted, but while we were comforted that we had been able to resist so great a number of enemies, they were enraged because they had been unable to break our spirit. The sky was still stormy and the sea still leaden, which only accentuated the grim nature of the scene. As the light faded, a slight westerly breeze got up, but being a shoreward wind, it was of no use to us. Not that even a favorable wind would have changed anything, for our ships were in a terrible state. The rigging was peppered with bullets, the yards had been toppled and the sails reduced to tatters; the *Caridad Negra* had lost its mainmast, which floated beside us along with corpses, ropes, planks, and broken oars. The cries of the wounded and the stertorous breathing of the dying rose up like a monotonous chorus from the two galleys, which remained tied to each other, motionless on the water. The Turks had retreated a little toward land, until they were about a cannon shot away, and there they threw their dead overboard, repaired rigging and other damage, while their captains met in council. We Spaniards could do nothing but lick our wounds and wait. We were a pathetic sight, lying, along with the galley slaves, among the broken benches or in the gangway, in the corridors or on the fighting platforms, exhausted, maimed, broken or badly wounded, smeared with smoke from the gunpowder, and with our hair, clothes, and weapons caked with blood—our own and other people's. To cheer us up, Captain Urdemalas ordered what little remained of the arrack to be shared out among us, while to eat—the oven had been destroyed and the cook was dead— there was dried shark's meat, watered wine, a little oil, and some hardtack. The same was done on the other galley, and men even came and went on the two ships, talking over the events of the day and enquiring about such and such a comrade, regretting those who had died and celebrating the living. This did cheer people a little, and some even began to think that the Turks would go away or that we could repel further attacks, of which according to others, there were sure to be more the following day, if they didn't try to board us during the night. But we had seen that the Turks, too, were in very bad way, and that gave us hope, for in such desperate plights, the doomed man clings to any illusion. The fact is that our gallant defense emboldened the most hopeful among us, and some even thought up a funny trick to play on the Turks. Two live chickens were kept in cages in the storeroom; their meat and eggs—although they did not lay much while on board—were used to prepare stews and broths for the sick. The jokers made a raft with a little sail on it, and after tying the two creatures onto the raft, they took advantage of the occasional gentle breeze to send the creatures off to the enemy galleys, amid much laughter and shouts of defiance. We all laughed too, especially when the Turks, although stung by the insult, picked the birds up and took them on board. This raised our spirits, which we certainly needed; indeed, some men began to sing, so that our enemies could hear us, the old shanty that the sailors used when they hauled the yard. In the end, the men formed a large chorus of voices, broken but not quelled, as they stood facing the Turks and sang:

Heave ho, the pagans,
Heave ho, the Saracens,
Heave ho, Turks and Moors,
They all bow down to Abram's sons.

Soon we were all leaning over the sides, shouting at the dogs at the tops of our voices and, amid great jubilation, telling them to come a little closer, that we'd be delighted to have a couple more boarding parties to finish off before we went to bed, and if they weren't men enough to do that, then they should go back to Constantinople to fetch their brothers and their fathers (if they knew them), and their whorish mothers and sisters, for whom, of course, we were reserving some very special treatment. And even the wounded, swathed in bloody bandages, raised themselves up on their elbows and joined us in howling out all the rage and fear we carried within us, finding comfort in that boasting, so much so that not even don Agustín Pimentel or the captains made any attempt to stop that outpouring. On the contrary, they urged us on and even joined in, aware that, condemned to death as we were, we needed something that would encourage us to put a still higher price on our heads. If the Turks wanted to hang *them* on their yardarms too, they would first have to come and cut them off.

In a further act of defiance, our commanders ordered the lanterns on the poop rail to be lit, so that the Turks would know where to find us. We reinforced the ropes keeping the two galleys together and let go the anchors—we were in shallow water—so that no unforeseen wind would carry us toward the enemy. The men were also allowed to rest, although with their weapons at the ready and taking turns on watch, just in case the enemy should decide to attack in the dark. But the night passed calmly and windlessly, with the sky clearing slightly to reveal a few stars. I was relieved from my watch just as I was about to fall asleep through sheer exhaustion; then, feeling my way past the men lying in the darkness on the deck—both galleys were filled with a chorus of moans and cries worthy of a troupe of French beggars—I reached the embrasure where, in a kind of bastion made of torn blankets and remnants of rigging and sailcloth, Captain Alatriste, the Moor Gurriato, and Sebastián Copons had taken shelter. The latter was snoring loudly, as if he were putting his very life into it. They, like me, had all been lucky enough to escape unscathed from that terrible day, apart from the Moor Gurriato, who had suffered a slight scimitar wound in one side, which Captain Alatriste had bathed with wine and then sewn up—an old soldier's skills—with a thick needle and thread, leaving one stitch loose so that any bad humors could drain out.

I lay down without saying a word, too tired even to open my mouth, but I couldn't sleep, my body too bruised and aching. That encounter with the hairy Turk and with all the others who came after had left me stiff in every limb. I was thinking, as I imagine everyone else was, about what the next day would bring. I couldn't imagine myself at the oars of a Turkish galley or in a prison on the shores of the Black Sea, and so, since victory on our part seemed most improbable, my future looked set to be distinctly brief. I wondered what my head would look like hung from a yardarm, and what Angélica de Alquézar would think if, possessed of some mysterious clairvoyant powers, she were to see it. You might imagine that such thoughts would have plunged me into bitter despair, and there was something of that, but the horse does not think the same thoughts as its rider. Viewed from the warmth of a good fire and a well-provided table, things look very different than when viewed from a trench or from the fragile deck of a galley, where placing life and liberty at risk is one's daily bread. We were certainly desperate, but we were like young bulls bred only to fight, and so that lack of hope seemed natural. As Spaniards, our familiarity with death allowed us to stand and wait patiently for it; we had no alternative. Unlike other nations, we judged each other according to how we bore ourselves in the face of danger. That was why our character was such a curious blend of cruelty, honor, and reputation. As Jorge Manrique said, centuries of fighting Islam had made us free men, proud and certain of our rights and privileges.

They're earned by monks and pious nuns
Through prayers and supplications;

*By valorous knights through waging wars
'Gainst Spain's old enemies—the Moors.*

This explains why, accustomed as we were to harsh fortune, with Christ's name always on our lips and our soul on a knife-edge, we accepted our fate on that sad day, if it was indeed to be our final day, as we had on so many similar days, which had all been rehearsals for this one. We did so with the resignation of the peasant watching the hail flatten his crops, of the fisherman finding his nets empty, of the mother certain that her child will be born dead or will be carried off by a fever without ever leaving its cradle. Only the pampered and the comfortable and the cowardly, who live with their backs turned on the realities of life, rebel against the inevitable price that sooner or later we all have to pay.

There was the sound of a harquebus shot, and we all half sat up, uneasy. Even the wounded stopped moaning. Then there was silence, and we relaxed.

"False alarm," muttered Copons.

"Fate," said the Moor Gurriato stoically.

I lay down again next to the captain, with nothing to cover me but my steel breastplate and my tattered doublet. The night dew was already soaking us and the planks we were lying on. I felt cold and moved closer to the captain in search of warmth. After the rigors of the day, he

smelled, as ever, of leather and metal and dried sweat. I
knew he would not mistake my shivering for fear. I sensed
that he was awake, although he did not stir for a long time.
Then, very carefully, he removed the scrap of torn sail from
his own body and placed it over me. I was no longer a child,
as I had been in Flanders, and that gesture did not so much
warm my body as my heart—a sail, after all, gives very little protection.

At dawn, we shared out more wine and hardtack, and while
we were eating that sparse breakfast, the order came to
unchain any of the slaves who were prepared to fight. We
looked at each other; we must be in very bad straits if we
had to resort to such extremes. Turks, Moors, and natives
of enemy countries, such as the English and the Dutch,
were excluded from the measure, but for the others this
offered a chance, if they fought well and survived, of having their sentence or part of it redeemed on the recommendation of our general. This was not a bad opportunity
for the slaves from Spain and from other Catholic nations,
for if they stayed at the oars, they were doomed to go down
with the ship if it sank—because almost no one would
bother to unchain them in the event of shipwreck—or else
remain as slaves, but rowing for the Turks, which they
could only avoid if they renounced their religion in
exchange for their freedom. (In Spain, a slave baptized a

Christian was always a slave.) And some did choose that route, especially the younger men, for reasons that are easy to understand. This, however, was less frequent than you might think, for even among galley slaves, religion is a serious, deep-rooted matter, and despite the misery of captivity, most Spaniards taken by the Berbers or the Turks remained true to the one faith so that the words of Cervantes—a captive who never renounced his faith— would not be applied to them.

> Perhaps they are simply cruelly bored
> By the harshness of a captive's life,
> And so, in the jaws of that bitter vice,
> They embrace Mohammed's faith as lord:
> A way that's easy, a way that's broad.

And so it was that we unshackled as many Spanish, Italian, and Portuguese slaves as offered their services, and they were duly issued spears and half-pikes. The two galleys, which had lost a third of their soldiers and sailors, thus found themselves with sixty or seventy new recruits, determined to die fighting rather than be drowned or cut to pieces in the fury of battle. Among them—one of the first to ask to be unchained and given a weapon—was a rower at the stern called Joaquín Ronquillo, a Gypsy and a jewel of Málaga's ruffianry, as well as an acquaintance of ours; he was a very dangerous man and much feared on board, so much so that for some time we had kept our savings under his bench, where they were safer than in the house of a Genoese banker. This Ronquillo fellow—shaven head, black doublet edged in red, a treacherous gleam in his eye— joined our group, bringing with him a small band of like-minded men, who looked about as honest as he did. Shortly afterward, we were given orders by Ensign Labajos, who appointed Captain Alatriste as our commander—he and Labajos were the only officers of any rank left among the soldiers on the *Mulata*—to head a fighting squad to provide reinforcements wherever the Turks proved most of a threat, especially the area around the skiff and the ladders on either side of the stern, which would give the enemy access to the corridors leading to the fighting platforms. We were all urged to defend the galley plank by plank; Father Nistal again blessed us from the deck of the *Caridad Negra*, and we and Machín de Gorostiola's Basques—to whom we were still bound for good or ill—wished each other luck. Just as we took up our positions, and when the sun had barely risen in a clear sky over the same dead calm sea, the seven Turkish galleys, with shouts and the noise of cymbals, flutes, and trumpets, began to row toward us.

Ensign Labajos had died in the midst of the battle, overwhelmed by Turks, as he repelled yet another boarding party at the stern of the *Mulata*, where Captain Urdemalas had also been wounded. Diego Alatriste was leaning against the awning supports, washing the blood from face and hands with seawater, which made any scratches and surface wounds sting like mad. His whole body hurt. He was watching the men throwing overboard any dead bodies cluttering the devastated deck, which was a chaos of broken planks, shattered rigging, blood, and exhausted men. The fighting had lasted four hours, and when the Turks withdrew to recover and to disentangle and replace the broken oars on their galleys, both masts on the *Mulata* had been brought down, the yards and torn sails lying either in the water or on top of the *Caridad Negra*, whose trinquet mast had been lost and her mainmast cut in two. Both galleys were still together and afloat, although the losses on both ships had been appalling. On the *Mulata* the galley master and his assistant were dead, and the German gunner had been killed when a cannon he was firing exploded, killing him and his helpers. As for Captain Urdemalas, Alatriste had just left him, or what remained of him, lying facedown on the floor of his cabin at the stern, where the barber and the pilot were using their fingers to scoop out gobbets of blood from the huge gash—from kidney to kidney—inflicted by a Turkish scimitar.

"You're in command," Urdemalas had managed to say between groans, cursing the man who had wounded him.

In command. There was a grim irony to those words, thought Alatriste as he surveyed the bloody, splintered thing that had once been the *Mulata*. All the storage compartments, including the one set aside for gunpowder, were full of wounded men, piled body on body, begging for a sip of water or something to cover their wounds. But neither water nor bandages were to be had. Above, in what had been the rowing chamber, and which was now a confusion of blood and debris, lay galley slaves alive and dead, the survivors moaning amid what remained of their benches and the shattered fragments of mast, rigging, and oars. And in the corridors and on the fighting platforms, beneath a searing sun that made the steel of breastplates and weapons burn, the surviving soldiers, sailors, and freed slaves were bandaging their wounds or those of their comrades, handing round whetstones to repair the battered blades of swords and knives, and gathering together what they could find of gunpowder and bullets for the few muskets and harquebuses that were still working.

· To drive all of this from his head for a few moments, Alatriste sat down with his back against the side of the ship, unfastened his buffcoat, and, with a mechanical gesture, took out his copy of don Francisco de Quevedo's book *Dreams*. He used to leaf through it in quiet moments, but now, however hard he tried, he couldn't read a single line;

the words danced in front of his eyes, his ears still rang
with the recent sounds of battle.

"You've been called to a meeting on the flagship, sir."

Alatriste looked at the young page delivering this order,
uncomprehending at first. Then, reluctantly, he put the
book back in his pocket and very slowly stood up. He walked
down the corridor on the starboard side past the people
lying there, and putting one leg over the side and then the
other, grabbed hold of a loose rope to swing himself across
to the *Caridad Negra*. As he did so, he glanced over at the
Ottoman galleys. They had retreated to the same distance
as on the previous night while they prepared for their next
assault. One of them, badly damaged during the last attack, was dangerously low in the water, almost sinking, and
there were a lot of comings and goings on deck; and the
flagship with the three lanterns had lost its trinquet mast.
The Turks were also paying a high price.

He discovered that the situation on board the *Caridad
Negra* was not much better than on the *Mulata*. The galley slaves had suffered terrible losses, and Captain Machín
de Gorostiola's Basques, vacant-eyed and faces black with
gunpowder, were taking advantage of that breathing space
to rest and recover as best they could. No one broke their
grim silence or looked up when Alatriste walked past on his
way to the general's cabin, the floor of which was covered
with trampled pieces of paper and dirty clothes. Standing

around a table, with a pitcher of wine that they were passing one to the other, were don Agustín Pimentel, with a wound to his head and his arm in a sling, Captain Machín de Gorostiola, the *Caridad Negra*'s galley master, and a corporal named Zenarruzabeitia. The pilot Gorgos and Father Francisco Nistal had both died during the last assault. Gorgos had been slit open, and the chaplain had been felled by a musket shot as he was walking up and down the gangway in the name of Christ, oblivious to everything, brandishing crucifix and sword and promising eternal glory for all, a glory he would now be enjoying himself.

"How's Captain Urdemalas?" asked Pimentel.

Alatriste shrugged. He was no surgeon. But the fact that he was there alone made it clear that no one else of any higher rank on board the *Mulata* was still standing, Captain Urdemalas included.

"The general thinks we should surrender," said Machín de Gorostiola bluntly. Many thought he adopted this blunt manner deliberately to be like his men, who adored him.

Alatriste looked at him rather than at don Agustín Pimentel. The Basque was a short man with a black beard, very white skin, a large nose, bushy eyebrows that met in the middle, and the rough hands of a soldier. He was a sturdy Basque, a peasant with little education but a great deal of courage. He was the very opposite of the elegant general who, pale from loss of blood, grew still paler when he heard the Basque's words.

"It's not that simple a matter," he protested.

This time, Alatriste did turn to look at the general. He suddenly felt tired, very tired.

"Simple matter or not," said Gorostiola in a neutral tone, "after the way we've fought, would it be honorable now to strike the flag?"

"Honorable," repeated Alatriste.

"Or whatever word you choose."

"In the eyes of the Turks."

"Yes."

Alatriste shrugged again. Gauging whether or not it would be honorable to surrender after the sacrifice of so many lives was not his business either. Gorostiola was observing him with great interest. They had never been friends, but they knew and respected one another, each in his own sphere. Then Alatriste looked at the galley master and at the corporal. Their faces were set hard; in fact, they looked somewhat embarrassed.

"Are your men on the *Mulata* going to surrender?" asked Gorostiola, handing him the pitcher of wine.

Alatriste drank—he had the devil of a thirst on him—then wiped his mustache with his hand.

"I imagine they would agree to anything, either surrendering or fighting on. They're beyond reason now."

"They've already done more than could be expected of them," said Pimentel.

Alatriste put the pitcher down on the table and looked hard at the general, whom he had never seen from such close quarters before. He reminded him slightly of the Count of Guadalmedina, the same style: the fine figure beneath the splendid Milanese steel breastplate, the trim mustache and goatee, the white hands, the gold chain around the neck, the sword with a ruby in the hilt. He was from the same caste of Spanish aristocrats, although this highly inelegant situation had tempered his arrogance— it's always best to talk to noblemen, Alatriste thought, when they've just been punched in the face. Nevertheless, the general retained his noble appearance, despite his pallor, the bandages, and the blood staining his clothes. Yes, he definitely reminded him of Guadalmedina, except that Álvaro de la Marca would never have considered surrendering to the Turks. Then again, the general had held up fairly well so far, far better than many others of his class and character. But courage can be dented too, as Alatriste knew from experience, especially in a man who has been wounded and who bears a heavy burden of responsibility. He decided that he was in no position to judge someone who had been fighting for two days, sword in hand, alongside everyone else. Every man has his limits.

"I see you have a book with you."

Alatriste patted the book distractedly, then took it out of his pocket and handed it to the general, who leafed through its pages with some curiosity.

"Hmm, Quevedo," said the General, returning it to him. "What's the point of a book like that on a galley?"

"It makes days like these slightly more bearable."

He put the book back in his pocket. Gorostiola and the others were staring at him in bewilderment. They could understand having some kind of religious book, but not a book like that, although needless to say, none of them had ever heard of Quevedo. The general picked up the pitcher again and said:

"I'm sure I could obtain satisfactory conditions."

Those last two words prompted Alatriste and Gorostiola to exchange glances. There was neither surprise nor scorn in those glances, only the weary impartiality of two veterans. Everyone knew what conditions the general was referring to: a reasonable ransom for himself, who would be well treated in Constantinople until the money arrived from Spain, and a ransom perhaps for another officer. The others, the soldiers and sailors, would remain on the galleys and in captivity for the rest of their lives, while Pimentel would return to Naples or to Madrid, where he would be admired by the ladies and congratulated by the gentlemen as he recounted the details of his Homeric battle. It would have made more sense, Alatriste thought, to have surrendered before the slaughter began. The dead would still be alive, and the maimed and wounded would not be piled up on the galleys, howling in agony.

Machín de Gorostiola interrupted his thoughts.

"We need to know your opinion, Señor Alatriste, as the only officer left on the *Mulata*."

"I'm not an officer."

"You're all we have. So don't play with words."

Alatriste looked at the trampled papers and clothes beneath his tattered, blood-stained espadrilles. His opinion was one thing, being asked to give it was another, as was giving it.

"My opinion . . ." he murmured.

He had known what his opinion was the moment he walked into the cabin and saw those faces. Everyone, apart from the general, knew as well.

"No," he said.

"I beg your pardon," said Pimentel.

Alatriste wasn't looking at him, but at Machín de Gorostiola. This wasn't a matter for the likes of Pimentel, it was a matter for soldiers.

"I said that the men on the *Mulata* do not agree to surrender."

There was a long silence, during which the only sound came from behind the bulkhead, the moans of the wounded where they lay in the hold.

"Surely you need to ask them," said Pimentel at last.

Alatriste coolly shook his head. His eyes, still colder, fixed on the general's.

"You have just done so, Your Excellency."

A faint smile flickered across Gorostiola's bearded face, while the general made a grimace of displeasure.

"What does that mean?" he asked curtly.

Alatriste continued to hold his gaze impassively.

"The other days were for killing, perhaps today is a day to die."

Out of the corner of his eye, he saw that the galley master and the corporal were nodding approvingly. Machín de Gorostiola had turned to Pimentel. He seemed pleased, as if a heavy weight had been removed from his shoulders.

"As you can see, Your Excellency, we are all in agreement. We're Basques, Devil take it."

Pimentel raised the pitcher of wine to his lips with his good hand, but when it reached his lips, it trembled slightly. Finally, half angry and half resigned, he replaced the pitcher on the table with a look on his face as if he had drunk vinegar. No general, however respected at court, could surrender without the agreement of his officers. That could cost you your reputation or, sometimes, your head.

"Half of our men are dead," he said.

"Fine," replied Alatriste, "let's avenge them with the other half."

. . .

The attack that afternoon was by far the fiercest. One of the Turkish galleys had sunk, but the other six came rowing toward us against the westerly breeze, their flagship first, intending to board us all at once. That would mean six or seven hundred men—more than a third of them janissaries—against just over one hundred Spaniards, those of us who could still fight. Battering us with their artillery as they approached, they plowed straight into both galleys, crushing our already broken oars as they did so and trying to hole the sides with their rams, hoping to sink us if they could. We were able to repel some boarders with our swords and muskets, but other galleys attached themselves to us with grappling irons. And such was the impetus of their attack that, whereas, on the *Caridad Negra*, the Basques were so mixed up with the Turks that it was impossible to fire a musket with any certainty that you would hit one and not the other, on the *Mulata*, they had seized the port-side fighting platform and the trinquet mast and got as far as the mainmast and the skiff, taking over half the ship. Somehow, though, we held firm and fought back, largely because of a piece of good luck. Leading the Turks on this attack was a janissary of massive build, who shouted and yelled and dealt fierce two-handed blows with his scimitar. We found out later that he was a famous captain, Uluch

Cimarra by name, highly esteemed by the Great Turk. Now, it happened that, just as this mighty beast reached the skiff from which our men were retreating, leaving it unprotected, he met the group of freed galley slaves led by the Gypsy Ronquillo and his gang, armed with spears, half-pikes, scimitars, and swords taken from the dead. They fell on the giant janissary with such ferocity that Ronquillo managed to stick a spear through the giant's eye with his first blow. The janissary let out a howl, pressed his hands to his face, and dropped to the deck, whereupon the other men, producing from somewhere or other yellow-handled slaughterer's knives, finished him off in a trice, like dogs on a boar. Astonished to see their paladin slain in this fashion, the Turks stopped in their tracks. And they were still standing there, hesitating, when Captain Alatriste decided to take advantage of the situation by roughly rounding up all the men who were there, some twenty of us. We rushed forward, certain in the knowledge that we either had to fight hard or be killed. And since killing or dying were all one to us, we charged shoulder to shoulder, Captain Alatriste, Sebastián Copons, the Moor Gurriato, and I, along with Ronquillo and his gang, as well as others, who, seeing us forming an orderly group, joined forces with us. And since there is nothing more consoling during a disaster than the sight of a group behaving in a disciplined manner, standing firm and attacking, all the other men who had become scattered or were fighting alone attached themselves to us as well, like men rushing to fall in with the last infantry squad on the parade ground. And so, growing in numbers as we went, we advanced down the galley, and the Turks stopped killing and even turned tail and ran, trampling on the galley slaves lying between the shattered benches, either dead or laid low by wounds or pain, until we reached the ram of the Turkish galley, still laying about the enemy with our swords and knives. When many of them dived into the water, some of us ventured onto the galley itself, and you can imagine the brio with which our handful of men boarded the ship, shouting "Spain and Santiago!"—all except me; I was shouting "Angélica! Angélica!" Seeing us there, black with gunpowder and red with blood, as fierce and pitiless as Satan himself, the Turks started hurling themselves into the sea in ever larger numbers or running to the captain's cabin at the stern to take refuge there. Thus we seized the trinquet mast with no effort at all and could have seized the mainmast too if we had dared.

Captain Alatriste had stayed behind on the *Mulata*, urging people to attack the other ships surrounding us, but I, hothead that I was, boarded the Turkish vessel along with the boldest of our men. However, as I was fighting a group of Turks, one of them, dealing me a swinging two-handed blow, broke the blade of my sword. With what remained of my blade I attacked the nearest man to me and wounded him badly in the neck. Another man struck me with his scimitar—fortunately with the flat of the sword—but he could not strike a second time because the Moor Gurriato sliced open his head, from his turban to his throat, with an ax. Another man, lying on the deck, tried to grab my legs. I fell on top of him, and he stabbed at me with a dagger and would have killed me if he could. Three times he raised his arm, and three times his strength failed him, and so when I started knifing him in the face with my broken sword, he finally let go and leaped over the side into the sea.

It was quite some prize, a whole galley to ourselves, but more men are killed by overconfidence than by adversity, and so, dragging two of our wounded by the clothes, we beat a cautious retreat, while the Turks in the cabin pelted us with arrows and musket fire. Then, seeing the quantities of gunpowder and lit match-cords available at our end of the ship, someone had the idea of setting fire to it—which was imprudent to say the least, given that it was attached to ours and could have brought disaster on us all. The Christian galley slaves, many of them Spaniards, still chained to the benches, cried and pleaded with us, for with our arrival, they had thought their freedom was assured. Now, though, seeing us about to set fire to the ship, they begged us desperately not to leave them there, but to unchain them, otherwise, they would be burned alive. But we could not delay or do anything for those poor unfortunates and so, with heavy heart, we ignored their pleas. When the flames grew, we returned to the *Mulata*, cut the boarding ropes that bound us to the Turkish galley and pushed it away as best we could with pikes and bits of broken oar, taking advantage of the favorable breeze. It moved off gradually, filled by black smoke and ever higher flames that devoured the trinquet mast. The screams of the galley slaves as they were roasted alive were terrible to hear.

Halfway through the afternoon, the *Caridad Negra*, holed in one side and slowly sinking, suffered such a fierce attack from the Turks that the survivors, with the prow in Turkish control, along with most of the rowing chamber, had to seek refuge in the captain's cabin, even though we were helping them from our side. General Pimentel had been wounded again, this time by arrows, and he was carried—like a Saint Sebastian—onto the *Mulata*, where he would be safer. Then it was the turn of Captain Machín de Gorostiola to be laid low by musket fire, which blew off one hand, leaving only a limp remnant hanging from his wrist. He wanted to cut it off so that he could continue fighting, but his strength failed him and his knees buckled. He fell to the floor where he was finished off by the Turks before his soldiers could save him. This might have discouraged other men, but it had the opposite effect on the

Basques, who, beside themselves with rage, bawled out their desire for revenge, crying *"Mendekua!* Forward for Spain! *Ekin! Ekin!"* and urging one another on in Basque and cursing in Castilian, and they fought to the last man with unimaginable fury. Not only did they clear their decks of Turks, they boarded the enemy ship as well, and whether because that galley had been so badly damaged or been holed by cannon shot below the water, it began to list, still attached by grappling irons to the *Caridad Negra,* which continued to sink. The Basques returned to their own ship, and seeing that it was about to go under and that nothing could be done, started climbing onto the *Mulata,* bringing with them as many of their wounded as they could and, of course, their flag. Shortly afterward, we had to cut the ropes and hawsers and leave the vessel to sink, which it did, along with the Turkish galley, which turned up its keel before going down. It was a terrible sight: the sea full of debris and struggling Turks, the galley slaves screaming and drowning while they struggled in vain to remove their chains. Faced by such a tragic scene, we stopped fighting, while the Turks went about rescuing their men from the water. In the end, the five surviving Turkish galleys retreated to their usual distance; every one of them was badly damaged, with blood running into the scuppers and between the oars, many of which were broken or not moving at all because the oarsmen had died.

. . .

There were no more attacks that day. As the sun set, the *Mulata* lay motionless and alone on the sea, surrounded by enemy galleys and corpses floating in the still water, with one hundred and thirty wounded men crammed together belowdecks and sixty-two uninjured men scanning the darkness. As a defiant act, the *Mulata* again lit her lantern. But there was no singing that night.

EPILOGUE

The following morning, at sunrise, the Turks were not there. The men on watch woke us at first light, pointing at the empty sea where all that remained was the debris of combat. The enemy galleys had slipped away in the dark, in the middle of the night, having decided that it wasn't worth capturing a miserable, ruined galley at such a high cost in lives. Still incredulous, looking in all directions and seeing not a trace of the Ottomans, we embraced each other, weeping with happiness and giving thanks to Heaven for such grace. We would have called it a miracle but for the suffering and blood it had taken to preserve life and liberty.

More than two hundred and fifty comrades, including the Knights of Malta, had lost their lives in combat, and of the four hundred galley slaves of all races and religions who made up the crews of the *Caridad Negra* and the *Mulata*, only about fifty remained. Of the captains and officers, the only survivors were don Agustín Pimentel and Captain Urdemalas, who somehow managed to recover from his wound. Among the soldiers and sailors, the only subaltern officers who survived were Captain Alatriste, the pilot Braco, and Corporal Zenarruzabeitia, who had taken refuge on our galley along with General Pimentel and twenty or so Basques. Another survivor was the galley slave Joaquín Ronquillo, who, on the recommendation of our general—once informed of his action against the janissary—had his six remaining years at the oars reduced to one. As for me, I emerged in reasonably good health, apart from a wound inflicted in the latter stages of the battle by an arrow from a Turkish crossbow which pierced my right thigh; it didn't do too much damage, but left me with a limp for two months. The *Mulata* remained afloat, although in need of innumerable repairs. We spliced together bits of rope to make cables, and while some men worked at bailing her out, we patched up the broken deck, and after improvising a mast and sail from what remnants we could find and recovering several oars, we managed to make it to dry land, part under sail power and part under oars. Then we set up a watchtower in case of any surprise attacks, but, fortunately, the place proved to be rocky and uninhabited, and in only two days we had made the galley seaworthy again. During that time, many of our wounded died. We put them with the other Spaniards who had died on board and those whose bodies we had rescued from the sea and from the beaches. And before weighing anchor again, we buried them all at Cape Nero—a melancholy business. Since we had no chaplain or anyone to provide a funeral service, and since both General Pimentel and Captain Urdemalas were incapacitated on the galley, it fell to Captain Alatriste to provide a graveside prayer. We gathered around, bare heads bowed, and said a Paternoster together. Then the captain, for lack of anything more appropriate to say, and after swallowing hard and scratching his head, recited a few short lines which, despite coming from a soldierly comedy or some such thing, struck everyone as perfectly suited to the occasion:

Free they are of all their guilt,
To eternal glory they have risen,
There to taste far greater joys
Than exist in this our earthly prison.

All these events happened in the month of September sixteen hundred and twenty-seven, at Cap Nero, which is on the coast of Anatolia, facing onto the Escanderlu channel. And while Captain Alatriste pronounced that unusual prayer for the dead, the setting sun lit up our motionless figures as we stood around the graves of all those good comrades, each one with its own cross made of Turkish wood—a last defiant act in their memory. There they stayed, accompanied by the murmur of the waves and the cries of the seabirds, waiting for the resurrection of the flesh, when they will perhaps rise up from the earth fully armed, with the pride and glory that befits all faithful soldiers. And until that distant day, they will stay where they are, sleeping the long, honorable sleep enjoyed by all valiant men, next to the sea on which they sold their lives at such a high price, fighting over gold and booty, but fighting, too, for those far from trifling things, country, God, and king.

EXTRACTS FROM A FLORILEGIUM OF

POEMS

BY VARIOUS SPANISH WITS

Printed in the seventeenth century with no place of
publication or date, and preserved in the "Count
of Guadalmedina" section of the Archive and Library
of the Dukes of Nuevo Extremo in Seville.

BY DON MIGUEL DE CERVANTES SAAVEDRA
TO THE MEMORY OF THE SPANISH SOLDIERS WHO PERISHED

WHEN LA GOLETA WAS LOST

From this battered, sterile land,
From these clods of earth brought low
Three thousand soldiers' holy souls
Rose, still living, to a better home,
Having, first, expended all
The strength and effort of their arms,
Until, at last, so few, so weary,
T' the enemy's blade they gave their life.
This land has been eternally,
Down the centuries, till now,
Full of doleful memories.
Yet no better souls from that hard breast
Will ever rise to Heaven's light,
Nor Heaven receive such valiant hearts.

BY LICENCIATE DON MIGUEL SERRANO
FROM SANTA FE DE BOGOTÁ, TO THE YOUNG SOLDIER
ÍÑIGO BALBOA

By destiny, a son of Flanders field,
And now the faithful shadow of your leader.
You're young—apprentice still—and keenest reader
Of the Don and Lope—no men to yield!

You're faithful, loyal, and marked out by fate,
To suffer at the hands of treach'rous love
Put in your path by destiny above—
Revenge for that and Alquézar must wait.

A good companion in the darkest night,
With dagger drawn, you were the bravest soul
—I speak unvarnished truth, entire and whole.

And that is why my words ring true and right,
That though you were a boy, a lovesick foal,
Nor you nor Alatriste lost a fight.

BY THE SAME

TO CAPTAIN DON DIEGO ALATRISTE Y TENORIO, VETERAN OF

FLANDERS, ITALY, BARBARY, AND THE LEVANT

Through old Madrid, where once he used to live,
Wanders a ghost, the erstwhile valiant captain.
Be careful what you call him—he'll not forgive;
Wound him, and the price could be your skin.

As vassal to his king, he used his sword
To save a sovereign and a favorite.
His footsteps pace the spot where once his lord
Ignored him quite and never gave him credit.

He finds no rest, when easeful rest is sought;
His sword is up for hire, but not his honor,
For, shorn of honor, life for man is naught.

He came from glory, to glory goes, ready
To face dread destiny—his bella donna—
And though his heart may tremble, sword stays
    steady.

BY DON FRANCISCO DE QUEVEDO
TO THE MEMORY OF THE DUKE OF OSUNA, VICEROY
OF NAPLES, WHO DIED IN PRISON

Although his country has denied him praise,
His deeds will always be his best defense;
Imprison'd by Spain, he died—poor recompense
For one who conquer'd Fortune all his days.

They wept in envious mourning, one by one,
Those other grateful nations not his own,
His fitting epitaph, the blood-red moon,
His tomb, the Flanders battles that were won.

Vesuvius, at his funeral, made roar,
And Naples, Sicily, and Etna shook;
His soldiers' flood of tears grew more and more.

I' the Heaven of Mars, a favor'd place he took;
The Danube, Tagus, Meuse, and Rhine forsook
Their calm and moaned and murmured, weeping
    sore.

BY SISTER AMAYA ELEZCANO, ABBESS OF THE CONVENT OF THE BLESSED ADORATRICES, TO THE PERSON OF CAPTAIN DON DIEGO ALATRISTE

O my gallant and venturesome captain,
My gentleman, faithful and true,
You reap, with the blade of your sword,
Still more laurels to add to your fame,
Yet, woe to the man who finds fault
With the cut and the dash of your life,
For the man who knows how to keep quiet
Is the same man who knows how to fight.

Don't miss the rest of
the Captain Alatriste series by

Arturo Pérez-Reverte